4/24 SZAKOWSKI 4/24

K

BETTER TO BE LUCKY

A ROY BALLARD MYSTERY

©2020 by Ben Rehder.

Cover art and interior design © 2020 by Bijou Graphics & Design.

All rights reserved.

This novel is a work of fiction. Names, characters, places, and incidents are either the product of the author's imagination, or, if real, used fictitiously. No part of this book may be reproduced or transmitted in any form or by any electronic or mechanical means, including photocopying, recording, or by any information storage and retrieval system, without the express written permission of the author or publisher, except where permitted by law.

To John Kelly, my favorite blag merchant.

ACKNOWLEDGMENTS

DON'T KNOW WHAT I'D DO without this amazing team of advisors, editors, and early readers: Tommy Blackwell, Donny Gray, Becky Rehder, Helen Haught Fanick, Mary Summerall, Marsha Moyer, Jo Virgil, Joe Hammer, Stacia Miller, Linda Biel, Leo Bricker, Naomi West, Richie West, and Karen Ortosky. Any errors are my own.

1

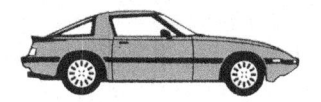

BRETT GOT RELEASED ON A Tuesday afternoon, and Paul was there to pick him up in the rusty Chevy truck. Beautiful spring day in central Texas. Clouds here and there, all kinds of wildflowers lining the highway median.

Brett was wearing the same blue jeans and denim shirt he'd been wearing on the way in, sixteen months earlier. Now they were a little loose. You had to watch yourself inside or you'd go soft. Thicken up. Or you could do sit-ups, push-ups, fucking leg lifts all day, which is what Brett had been doing, because you might as well improve yourself, right? Come out hard and ready.

Your mind, on the other hand—wasn't much you could do for that. Read a little, if you had any interest, but there wasn't much fiction in the library. Nothing with violence in it, or sex, because they didn't want the inmates getting ideas. Plenty of nonfiction aimed at teaching you a trade. Plumbing. Electrical. HVAC. Some of the guys took correspondence courses to get their GED, but Brett didn't see the point. You get an equivalency or not, somebody wanting to hire you, when they read farther down and see your record, the interview is pretty much over. Waste of time for everybody. So, instead of reading or studying, you lie around daydreaming, or talking with your cellmate, and what good could come of that? Brett figured, like a lot of things, it depended on your perspective.

"Slow it down a little," he said.

Paul glanced over at him, but eased off the gas. They had the windows open, fresh air streaming in, Brett wanting to whoop and holler just from the sheer thrill of freedom. It was a fine thing. Fragile.

"Don't need you getting pulled over," Brett said.

Brett knew there was pot in the car somewhere. He could smell it. Probably a roach in the ashtray. Not a big deal for Paul, but for Brett, he'd be fucked before he even got back on his feet. Parole violation. Set a record for the shortest release ever.

A few miles down the road, passing under the interstate, Brett said, "You talk to any of the guys? Franco?"

"Not in a while."

That was okay. Brett would make contact. Brett was tight with Franco, but Paul not so much.

"Find a liquor store," Brett said. "I want to celebrate."

Wednesday and Thursday night it rained, and then, on Friday night, Brett decided it was time to visit Little Manny, the Mexican kid who'd earned probation by turning snitch. Make sense of that. Didn't matter that they were equally guilty, that they'd broken into the building together. They offered the deal to Manny and he took it. So Brett waited until Paul was in bed, after midnight, before grabbing the keys and slipping away.

Took the Chevy east on Riverside. Turned north and cruised past the little joint where Tejano music was blaring, and sure enough, there was Little Manny's blue Cutlass parked behind the building. Brett wondered what it took to get fired from a job like that. Being on probation obviously wasn't enough. Gotta whip your pecker out and piss on the dance floor?

He went to the end of the block, hung a U, then came back and found a spot on the street, half a block down, where he could see the Cutlass. Killed the ignition, the lights, and sat in the dark. He'd brought along a bottle of Wild Turkey, because he knew there'd be a wait. No big deal. He was used to waiting. He'd been waiting for sixteen months.

Manny finally came out at a quarter past three, and by then the parking lot was nearly empty. Fewer cars on the street, too, so Brett let Manny get a block ahead before following in the Chevy.

When they got on the interstate heading south, Brett had to keep an eye on his speed, but it wasn't a problem, because Manny stayed well under the limit. Exited at Stassney and turned west, which meant he was probably still living in the same duplex as before, with the same girl, and their boy would be about four now.

Five minutes later, Manny pulled into the driveway behind a dark Toyota and Brett parked at the curb like he belonged there. The neighborhood was quiet. Brett climbed out, and he could see Manny beside the Cutlass, outlined in the glow from the yellow porch light, looking this way, wondering who'd followed him home at this hour.

Brett began walking up the driveway, no rush, saying, "Manejas como una vieja." *Teasing him. Setting the mood. Telling him he drives like an old woman.*

"Quién es?" *Manny said.*

"Quién piensas?"

Took Manny a second to place the voice, then, "Brett? Aw, shit, man. That you?" *Nervous.*

Brett spread his arms out, presenting himself, like ta-da. "Live, and in person."

"Fuckin' A," *Manny said. Trying to sound enthusiastic, but look at him stealing a glance at his front door. Wondering if maybe he should run for it, but Brett was too close now.*

"You can relax, pendejo," *Brett said.* "Everything's cool."

Six feet away, Brett could smell the beer and cigarettes wafting off Manny like a stale funk. That barroom stench trapped in the old T-shirt he was wearing, and his white painter's pants, even his scuffed work boots. Little Manny, short and thin and weak.

"I never came to see you," *Manny said, getting right to it.* "Shit, man, I meant to, but I never did."

Brett laughed. "There's a whole list of people never came to see me."

"Wanted to say I was sorry. Tell you why I did it."

"Man, I know why. Ain't no big deal. You got a kid to support. And your old lady."

"Yeah, Sonia," Manny said.

As far as Brett could tell, there wasn't another soul awake for blocks. No cars passing, no dogs barking, no music, no voices. A dull light showing through the front window of Manny's place, enough to guide him to bed after a long night. Climbing in with Sonia, maybe kissing her on the forehead, letting her know he was home.

"Shit, I'da done the same thing if they'd come to me first," Brett said. "You get a deal, you take it." That seemed to make Manny feel better. Settle him down. Brett had no idea what he would've done, but turning snitch wasn't on the list.

"No sense in us both goin' in," Manny said.

Brett was leaning against the Cutlass, careful not to touch it with his hands. "And I had less to lose," he said.

Manny looked at the front door again, just a quick peek, but Brett knew he wasn't going anywhere. He wanted to, but he wouldn't.

"How long you been out?"

"Three days," Brett said.

"Where you stayin'?"

"With my brother, for the time bein'. 'Til I can get something else."

"How's he doin'?"

"As dumb as he always was."

Manny nodded, then said, "Shit, man, it was good to see you." Trying to wrap it up.

"I been lookin' for work, but nothin' yet," Brett said.

"Yeah? Still doin' carpentry?"

"If I can find it."

"You will, man. Market's real busy."

"For now"—Brett jerked his head toward the Chevy—"I got a pound of primo weed on my hands. Interested?"

Look at Little Manny grinning now. "I wish, man. I gotta stay clean, you know? Stay outta trouble."

"Shit," Brett said, drawing it out. "Where's the fun in that?"

Manny shrugged. "You know how it is."

"Yeah, I guess. Know anyone who might take it off my hands?"

"Naw, man. I don't hang around those guys no more."

"Bein' a good family man."

"Tryin'."

"I can respect that. Hey, at least burn one with me. My way of sayin' no hard feelings. A quick one, then I'll hit the road."

"Yeah, okay."

At the Chevy, Brett popped open the toolbox mounted in the back, saying, "Got me a hidey-hole in here," then saying, "Grab that bottle off the passenger seat, will ya?"

Paul's tools were in the toolbox, and Brett came around the truck with the framing hammer, waiting there in the dark for Manny to emerge, and when he did, Brett swung down fast and hard. Manny was turning, and the steel head of the hammer caught him just above the left temple. Brett could feel it sink in, like busting a hole in drywall.

Manny grunted and fell straight down, between the open door and the truck itself. Brett could see Manny's legs twitching, his jaw moving back and forth. Moaning soft and low.

Brett leaned down and swung the hammer again.

2

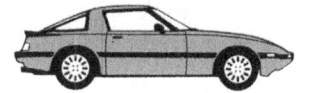

NORMAN CONLEE HAD AMASSED A fortune in the pharmaceutical industry—a level of wealth some people would call obscene for anyone operating in healthcare. I wasn't going to let my opinion on that topic sway me one way or the other, but for the purposes of the case I'd just started, that information might be relevant. Or it might not be.

I waited in his living room, seated on a sofa that probably cost as much as many lower-market automobiles. The leather was downright creamy. In front of me was an enormous wall of plate-glass windows that looked onto a gorgeous rectangular swimming pool surrounded by a flagstone patio. On the right side of the pool was a terraced waterfall. To the left of the pool was a custom-designed kitchen area built around a large stainless-steel barbecue grill.

Beyond the pool, past a wide, gentle, downward slope of perfectly manicured St. Augustine grass, was Lake Austin. A matching flagstone sidewalk bisected the lawn and ended at an elaborate double-decker dock, with a speedboat resting on a hydraulic lift. Boat traffic was light, because it was early in the season yet—late April—and it was a weekday.

Everything, indoors and out, was immaculate. Clean. Organized.

No clutter. Squared off. Plumped. Vacuumed or swept. Polished. The same had been true out front. No evidence of any recent damage. Conlee had had it all fixed quickly—long before he'd received the insurance reimbursement.

I waited patiently. Our meeting was scheduled for 2:00. It was now 2:17.

The house itself was large enough that any sounds were faint. I heard people talking, but I couldn't make out the words. A man and a woman. Or a man and two women. Hard to tell.

I waited some more. The talking stopped.

Three minutes later, Norman Conlee—tall, handsome, gray-haired—entered the room from my right and came straight to me. He appeared to be in his late sixties.

"Mr. Ballard?"

We shook hands.

"Mr. Conlee," I said. "How are you doing?"

He took a seat in a matching leather chair facing me and said, "I'm afraid I don't have a lot of time. I have a teleconference soon."

"How soon?"

"It starts when I join it. People are waiting."

"No problem. I'll do my best to—"

"If we could keep this to five minutes, that would be ideal."

"Five minutes?"

"That's what I have available."

"No problem. Truth is, I'm in a rush, too. Pilates at three o'clock."

He stared at me.

I said, "In case they didn't tell you, I'm a legal videographer and—"

"I don't know what that is."

"We record depositions, crime scenes, courtroom cases—things like that. But mostly I focus on insurance fraud. If someone claims to have an injury, I'm the guy who follows him around with a camera until he plays rugby or dances the Charleston. In this case, your insurance company hired me to determine who vandalized your fountain and your Jaguar."

"So you're basically a private investigator."

"Well, I'm not licensed to be a PI, but sort of."

"I'm not crazy about this situation at all."

"Which situation?"

"Of you hanging around my house, trying to figure this out."

"But I'm not planning to—"

"I don't really have the time or inclination to have a person in or around my home for days on end. Honestly, the hassle factor involved—modifying my habits and schedule—would outweigh any possible benefit. And my assistant—Carmen Romero—I think you met her earlier—"

"Yes, she let me in and brought me to this room."

"She doesn't have the time, either. She has a full list of items I need her to do every day, which includes taking care of my wife. She has some health issues."

"Busy crew around here," I said. "But I won't be—"

"It's just a fact of life," Conlee said. "I work seventy hours a week and I still can't get it all done. I figure the vandalism was neighborhood kids, and they'll get bored and move on to something else. They probably already have."

Behind him, through the windows, a young woman in a blue-and-white striped T-shirt dress and sandals appeared on the patio and sauntered toward the pool with a towel draped over her shoulder. She was tall, with reddish-blonde hair pulled into a ponytail. Reminded me of someone I knew.

I said, "The thing is, I won't be hanging around, and my plan won't really impact you or Carmen or your wife. You won't have to do a thing or give it a moment's thought after this meeting."

He let out an impatient sigh. "What exactly is your plan?"

My client had warned me that Conlee was going to be difficult—and possibly obnoxious. Correct on both counts.

"For starters, I'll install a couple of security cameras. I notice there aren't any, or at least none that I could see."

"I don't need security cameras. I have a Smith and Wesson."

I couldn't tell if he was joking or not.

"I don't really think that's the best way to—"

"If I catch them, it will be. Besides, I'm getting bids to install a six-foot iron fence along the front of the property. In the meantime, I don't want security cameras in my home. I forbid it."

He *forbid* it. Or would it be *forbade*? *Forbidded*?

"No cameras inside. Just outside. Discreetly placed." He opened his mouth again to object, but I continued. "It's the best course of action right now, before the losses get any higher. The damage so far totals nearly eighty thousand dollars."

The fountain itself was $57,300. I'd wondered if that was a typo when I first read the case file. Maybe somebody had typed an extra zero. But, no. It was a hand-carved stone fountain with three tiers. Imported from Italy. It had horses and angels and stood about nine feet tall. It had fallen over and sustained enough damage to be a total loss.

The Conlees at first thought the fountain incident was just bad luck—perhaps shifting soil— but nine days later, somebody flattened the tires on Norman's Jaguar and poured brake fluid over every panel, destroying the paint job. The Conlees had a two-car garage, in which they parked a couple of his-and-hers Mercedes, but Norman's Jaguar was routinely parked in the circular drive in front of the house. Unfortunate.

"I'm aware of the numbers," Conlee said.

"I mean, that doesn't sound like teenage hijinks."

"I don't know what else to tell you," Conlee said.

The young woman outside dropped the towel on a lounge chair and lifted her T-shirt dress over her head, revealing a fuchsia bikini. She began to take selfies with the pool and the lake behind her. She snapped a few, looked at them, then moved ten feet to the right.

"So you're okay with the cameras?" I asked.

"That's not what I said."

I'd had enough of this guy. Life was too short. What was this resistance all about?

"You want me to take off?" I asked. "I can if you want. Your insurance company can't force anything on you."

"Exactly. And ultimately, the financial losses are their problem, not mine. It's why people have insurance."

"Okay, but just so you know—my understanding is that if you don't cooperate, they probably won't renew your policy, and you'll have a hard time finding new coverage under the circumstances. So if somebody comes back with a gas can and decides to—"

"Okay, enough," said Conlee, shaking his head in disgust. "I get it. I'm being extorted into doing whatever they want. So put a couple of cameras outside and let's move on."

The young woman reclined in the lounger and took more selfies. The lounger was parallel to the wall of windows, so I had a clear view.

Not that I was ogling or anything. She turned her head toward the windows, and for a moment, it appeared she was looking right at me. She smiled. I looked at Conlee.

"I have a few questions," I said.

He checked his watch, then looked at me, waiting.

I said, "Can you think of anybody with a grudge against you? Any enemies or people you've pissed off?"

"I've already told the police all of this stuff. I guess that was a waste of time."

"I saw the reports," I said, "but sometimes fresh details can come to mind when you go over it again."

He spoke fast, obviously hoping to get this out of the way as quickly as possible. "If I had any enemies, I would've told the police and perhaps we wouldn't be sitting here right now."

"Does anybody else live here?"

"Just my wife and me, and Carmen."

"May I ask who that is?" I nodded toward the woman at the pool.

He turned around and looked, then faced me again. "That's my wife's niece," he said.

"Also known as *your* niece," I said.

"Not by blood," he said. "She's staying here temporarily."

"Mind if I get her name?"

He gave me a pointed look. "For what reason?"

By now, it was apparent that Conlee probably pissed people off on a regular basis. That kind of personality could create a long list of people who might decide to get back at you.

"I'm putting together a swimsuit catalog and she looks like she'd fit right in," I said.

He glared at me. "That's way out of line."

I said, "I tend to make jokes when I encounter a difficult person. It's not very productive, so I consider it a bad habit. But if you'd just answer my questions, we can both get on with our day. Or boot me out and start over later with someone new, because this problem isn't going away. Your choice."

I could tell he was startled I'd spoken to him that way.

"Fine. Her name is Olivia."

"Last name?"

"Reed."

"How long has she lived with you?"

"She's been here several months. Maybe five or six."

"Does she have friends over to the house?"

"I don't allow it. Just her boyfriend."

"What's his name?"

"Franco."

"Last name?"

"I couldn't even tell you."

"What does he look like?"

"Big guy. Maybe six-three. In good shape. Short brown hair."

"What does he do for a living?"

"He manages a restaurant. I couldn't tell you which one."

"Is he here now?"

"At the house? Not as far as I know. His car would be out front."

"Is your wife here?"

"She's napping right now."

"Does anybody else come and go on a regular basis?"

"Our yard guy comes once a week."

"What's his name?"

"Clancy."

"Is that his first or last name?"

"I couldn't tell you. Carmen hired him."

"How long ago?"

"I'd say at least a year."

"Any issues with him?"

"None at all. He's very reliable and does a good job. He would have no reason for vandalizing our property, if that's what you're thinking."

"Any other service people come and go?"

"We have a maid service once a week. And a landscaping crew. And a pool cleaner."

"Had any problems with any of those people?"

"None at all. None of them could possibly be involved."

I tended to agree with him.

"I need to make one more request," I said. "You're not going to like it, but there's not much I can do about that."

"What is it?"

"I want to come back tomorrow and talk to everybody—your niece, your wife, Carmen, and even Franco."

He said, "Three minutes ago, you said this meeting would be the last of it."

"I meant with you. You don't have to join us tomorrow."

"Nobody here has any idea who's been committing the vandalism, and none of them are any more interested in wasting their time than I am."

I'd anticipated this response. Planned for it, actually.

"Okay, then how about a compromise? You give me their phone numbers and I'll call them. That way I can ask questions with a minimum of inconvenience. Surely that's reasonable."

Conlee made some noises of dissatisfaction, but ultimately he agreed to text their numbers to me. Then he said, "Are we done?"

"Just one more question. Does your company get much hate mail?"

I already knew the answer to that question, of course, and I could see Conlee's face getting red. I couldn't help but enjoy it a little.

He spoke slowly. "Anybody who would send us hate mail doesn't understand the nature of the pharmaceutical industry. Developing any drug requires years of research, clinical study, painstaking steps toward FDA approval, and then massive marketing campaigns, which can cost a fortune. It's the profit motive that drives all of that. You take profit out of the picture and why would anybody try to create a new drug?"

Oh, I don't know. For the good of humanity? To save lives? To end suffering?

"But some people can't afford it, so they die," I said.

"Are we supposed to give it away and let our company go bankrupt?" he asked. "Besides, we have special programs for those people."

Those people.

"We're getting sidetracked," I said. "Can you think of anybody who sent your company a nasty email or a letter or anything like that? Any threatening phone calls? Anything on social media?"

"No, and I can't imagine the vandal would be stupid enough to send a message first."

"Last month I followed a guy who supposedly had a neck injury," I said. "I got some great video of him playing in a rugby match. Some people are dumber than dirt."

"In that case, you should catch the vandal in no time and we can all get on with our lives," he said.

Norman Conlee was obviously never wrong about anything. I decided it was time to let him join his conference call.

3

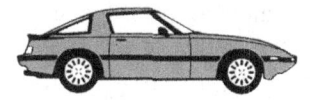

THE CONLEE HOME WAS NOT far from an Austin landmark called Ski Shores Café, a lakeside hamburger joint that has been in operation since 1954, just as the sign proclaimed. It had never been one of my regular stops when I was a teenager because it was on the other side of the lake from me, but every now and then, when a buddy of mine invited me out on his boat, we'd swing by for a burger and a cold one.

After I got a couple of cameras set up outside the Conlee place, I stopped at Ski Shores and grabbed a picnic table on the lower deck, right beside the water. Only one other table was occupied—by a couple of guys in their early twenties wearing ball caps backward. Dudes. Or bros. Or possibly the rare dude-bro hybrid.

The temperature hovered in the seventies and turtles were floating nearby, waiting for crumbs to be dropped into the sun-speckled water.

After the waitress took my order—a Border Burger and a whiskey ginger—I sat quietly and pondered what I knew. And what I didn't know.

With the bulk of my cases, I knew the identity of my subject and where he lived and worked. I knew what make and model of car he drove. I knew what injury he claimed to have, and what activities and physical limitations the alleged injury would prohibit. Then I'd put the subject under surveillance until I had video evidence indicating he was faking. Or, occasionally, I'd reach the conclusion that the injury was legit and he wasn't faking.

The Conlee case was obviously different. I had no idea who'd been committing the vandalism, or if there was more than one person, or why they were doing it, or whether they would return to attempt more damage.

The waitress brought my drink and went to check on the guys at the other end of the deck. I took a big sip, then removed a small metal flask from my front pocket and discreetly added another ounce of Jameson's to adjust the whiskey-to-beer ratio more to my liking. Couldn't have been more than an ounce or two in there to start with.

"I saw that," a voice above and behind me said. "Pretty sneaky."

I turned and saw a woman standing on the upper deck, leaning against a post. She had a drink in her hand.

"Not sneaky enough, apparently," I said.

"Isn't it illegal to bring alcohol into a place that serves it?"

She was petite, with sandy medium-length hair. Maybe forty years old. She was wearing khaki shorts and a dark-green off-the-shoulder blouse.

"Well, if you take it literally, then yes. But I see it as more of a guideline."

"That's terrible," she said. "Such blatant disregard for the law."

"I know. It really is. You want some?"

She hesitated, and I didn't blame her. She didn't know me.

"I'm not a weirdo," I said. "I promise."

"Well, that's disappointing," she said.

I laughed, then I made a gesture to the other side of my picnic table—an invitation—and she made her way down the steps and joined me. She placed her cup on the table. I noticed she had half a dozen bangle bracelets on her left wrist. No rings on that hand, though.

I took my flask out again and deftly poured an ounce or so into my new companion's cup.

"I need to get me one of those," she said. She stirred the drink with a straw and took a sip. "Much better. Thanks."

"I'm Roy Ballard," I said.

"Scarlett Bishop."

"Nice to meet you."

"Same here. If Tammy catches us with this, she's going to be royally pissed."

"Tammy is the waitress?"

"And the manager."

"Then let's not get caught."

"Deal."

"I take it you're a regular?"

She nodded. "I live just down the street. Half a mile. Walking distance."

Right then, Tammy arrived with my burger and fries, and she chatted with Scarlett for a few minutes.

After Tammy left, I said, "I'd be happy to cut this burger in half."

"Thanks, but I'm okay. I might steal a fry, though."

"Help yourself."

She took one and bit it in half. Her eyes were as green and bright as Lake Austin.

I picked up the burger. "Pardon me if this gets sloppy."

"I've heard that before," she said.

I left out a loud guffaw. "Did you really just say that?"

"Couldn't help myself. You set me up."

I took a bite.

"Border Burger?" she asked.

My mouth was full, so I nodded.

"That's my favorite," she said.

I finished chewing and said, "I believe these are Sierra Fuego jalapeños, probably grown in the southern portion of New Mexico, if I'm not mistaken. Harvested in late February."

"You have an amazing palate," she said.

"It's true, but I don't like to brag."

"Just so you know, I don't usually do this sort of thing—just sit down with a stranger and accept free whiskey."

"If we talk long enough, I won't be a stranger."

"True," she said. "Besides, I think you know my neighbors. I saw your car parked at the Conlees' house. I live a couple doors down from them."

"Interesting," I said. "You're very observant."

"I don't know about that. I haven't seen a car like yours in a long time. What kind is it?"

"Mazda RX-7," I said.

"That's right. With the weird engine."

"Rotary, designed by a guy named Wankel."

"I'd forgotten about those."

"Nineteen eighty-two model," I said. "I haven't owned it long."

It was an indulgence to help me get through a tough time. You didn't see many of them around anymore, so obviously I didn't use it for surveillance. I still had my Caravan and my Camry for that.

"Midlife crisis?" Scarlett asked.

I started to make a glib reply, but instead I said, "Maybe."

"At least you're honest," she said. "All you need now is a hot twenty-year-old to ride around with you."

"I thought I had to get a toupee first, then the hottie. I'll have to check the regulations."

She laughed and took another fry. I took another bite of my burger. We both drank from our spiked beverages. The lake was smooth and calm.

"Do you know the Conlees well?" I asked.

"Not really. Norman was on the HOA board for a few years, and I see Evelyn's post on Nextdoor occasionally, but that's about it. I walk past their house on the way here."

"How long have you lived on Mañana Street?" I asked.

"About six years. I bought the house after my divorce. It's a quiet street, which is nice, because I work from home."

"What do you do?"

"I'm a graphic artist."

"Oh, yeah? What kind of art?"

"All kinds of stuff, but I design a lot of logos."

"Any I've seen?"

She began to name a few large corporations and several other clients throughout the state and country. I ate while she talked.

When she was done, I said, "That's an impressive list. I've seen your work. Good stuff."

"Thanks. How about you?"

"It's been years since I designed a logo," I said.

"You're just a natural-born smart-ass, aren't you?"

"It's the booze talking. I'm a legal videographer."

"As opposed to an illegal one?"

"I've been one of those on occasion, too."

I shoved the basket of fries in her direction and she looked at me like, *What are you trying to do to me?* But she ate a few more.

"What exactly is a legal videographer?" she asked.

So I gave her the one-minute description. When she asked me what I was doing at the Conlee house, I fudged a bit. "I was documenting some of the repairs at the house," I said. "Insurance companies like to make sure things are fixed to a certain standard. I'm guessing you've heard about the problems there."

"The vandalism? Everybody on the street knows about it. A cop stopped at my house to ask if I'd seen anything or if I have security cameras. I do, but I didn't have any video that would help."

"That's too bad."

"Whoever did it probably never passed my house," she said. "Not if they knew where they were going. The road dead-ends south of me. That's what makes the street so quiet. What did you think of Norman?"

I sensed I could speak freely.

"He felt like a long-lost brother. We're thinking of backpacking Europe together."

"Ha. So it's not just me. Did you meet Evelyn?"

"I did not, or anybody else. He wanted me in and out of there as fast as possible."

"She's okay, honestly," Scarlett said. "A lot nicer than Norman, for sure, although I haven't seen her in several months."

"Do you know Carmen, the assistant?"

"Yeah, I like her. Sometimes I see her out walking and we chat. I don't know how she puts up with him, though. He's just such a jerk."

Tammy came by again and I ordered us two more whiskey gingers. Scarlett did not object.

"And the niece?" I said. "Olivia?"

"I've talked to her a couple of times. She moved here from Sacramento about six months ago. She's an influencer."

"Like, social media?"

"Right. I don't know how well she does at it, but she had like a million followers the last time I checked."

"What does she, uh, influence about?"

"Clothes, makeup, jewelry."

"That explains the selfies she was taking by the pool. I saw her through the windows."

"She's got the looks for it," Scarlett said. "Imagine being able to lounge by the pool all day, take some photos, and make money from it. Does that sound snarky? Maybe it's harder than I think."

Our second round arrived and I noticed that Tammy gave Scarlett a quick, coy glance—*Girl, what are you getting into?*—before she left us alone. My first sip of this fresh drink told me it was stronger than the first one, so I decided I'd better keep my flask in my pocket this time.

"Where does Olivia post? Instagram?"

"That's the biggest site for that kind of thing."

"You ever meet her boyfriend Franco?" I asked.

"Impressive that you know all these names. Did Norman actually share all this willingly with you?"

"Reluctantly."

"I haven't met Franco, but I've seen him coming and going. Tall guy. Likes to walk around shirtless most of the time, showing off his abs. Drives a Porsche Taycan."

"What color?"

"Dark blue. I'd say royal blue."

"My understanding is that he manages a restaurant," I said.

"If you say so."

"Managing a restaurant must pay more than I thought if he can afford a Porsche."

"Maybe Olivia bought it for him with all that sweet influencer cash."

The two guys at the other end of the deck got up and left. We were the only customers.

"Any neighborhood gossip about the vandalism?" I said.

"Sure, but nobody knows who's doing it. I can't imagine it would be anybody on our street."

I asked her some additional questions about the Conlees and life on Mañana Street, but she didn't have any information that would break the case open for me. That was okay. It was a beautiful day and she was good company, with a nice smile and an infectious laugh.

We drank and talked and before long, the sun was dipping low.

"I should head home," she said.

"I need to hang out and let my head clear a little bit. Or maybe I'll grab an Uber. That might be better."

She looked at me and smiled.

I smiled back.

"Or you could walk with me to my place," she said. "Leave your car here."

"And come back for it later?" I asked.

"Yeah," she said. "Tammy won't mind. She won't tow it or anything. It'll be safe and sound."

I can only imagine what my expression said. I wanted to go with her, of course—whether she was simply inviting me to visit with her until I'd sobered up enough to drive, or if she was offering something more. And I'm sure she could see that.

But I think she could see the hesitation, too. If I accepted—if I went with her—I'd be starting a new chapter in my life. As difficult as it was, I felt that the time had come. I'd waited long enough.

I took out my wallet and removed enough cash to cover the tab, plus a generous tip.

4

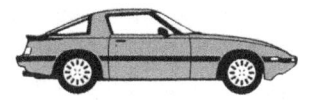

WE MADE NO ATTEMPT TO sober up. Instead, we sat in her backyard on a cobblestone patio beneath an enormous cypress tree and drank more Irish whiskey. I'd Uber later. No big deal. Come back for my car tomorrow.

There was still just enough light to see the lake running flat and dark to the northeast. Right around the next bend, it would pass under the iconic Pennybacker Bridge.

"This is a beautiful home," I said.

"Thank you."

Earlier, we'd entered through the front door, stopped in the kitchen to make drinks, and then proceeded out the back door. Her place was more modest than the Conlees' but every bit as nice.

"I'm gonna tell you something," she said, and even though I still didn't know her well, I could hear the slight slur in her words. "Some people assume I must've gotten the better end of the deal from my ex when we divorced, but it was the other way around. I earned a hell of a lot more than he did. I took a pretty big hit when we split, but it was worth it. Not that there was anything wrong with him. We just weren't right together. He's actually a good guy." After a pause, she added, "I don't know why I'm telling you all of this."

"No reason not to," I said.

"But you don't need to hear all that."

"I honestly don't mind."

"Really?"

"Really."

"There was just no spark there," she said.

"That's the way it goes sometimes," I said.

"What about you?" she asked.

"I had no spark with him, either," I said.

She found that incredibly funny, and I figured the whiskey was making her a more appreciative audience.

When she was done laughing, she said, "No, but what's your story? Are you divorced or what?"

"Mostly what," I said.

"Am I going to have to torture it out of you?" she asked.

I let that one go and said, "I had a first marriage that ended many years ago. More recently, I had a partner who became more than just a partner. We were engaged, in fact. But then..."

I stopped for a moment. How much did I want to share—not just about Mia, but about my work? Did it really matter?

"But then what?" she asked.

"What I do for a living can be dangerous sometimes. I won't bore you with a bunch of details, but sometimes part of my job is catching people who are committing fraud, which means following them around, and as you might guess, they don't like getting caught."

"Actually, that sounds like fun."

"Occasionally, not often, there's an incident. One of those got out of hand, and my partner had to shoot a guy."

"Jesus," Scarlett said softly. "She shot him?"

"She did."

"What happened?"

"He died."

"Wow. That's terrible. For her, I mean. Well, maybe for him, too, unless he had it coming."

"Oh, it was justified, but it tore her up anyway. She saw a therapist, which helped, but she didn't want to do the job anymore, which is understandable. Then she realized she didn't want me to do it anymore, either."

One solitary boat moved slowly upstream with its running lights on. Packing it in for the night.

I said, "I didn't make the choice, she did. So I didn't have to decide if I would give it up or not."

"Would you have?"

"I've thought about that a lot, but I just don't know. It would've been hard. I can't imagine giving it up."

"How long ago was all this?" Scarlett asked.

"Three months."

"Still pretty fresh."

"Yeah."

"So it hurts."

"It does. Quite a bit."

"Was there a spark there?"

"A forest fire," I said. "Not gonna lie."

"Do you talk to her?"

"Not for about six or seven weeks now."

"Do you think you'll ever get back together?"

"At this point, no."

"No chance?"

"No chance."

"Would you if you could?"

"That's a tough one," I said. "The selfish part of me says yes, but I wouldn't want her to be riddled with anxiety every day because of my work."

A moment passed. I couldn't see Scarlett's face well at this point.

"When you think of her, does it make you wish you weren't here right now?" she asked.

"It does not," I said. "Life goes on. I'm glad I'm here."

She rose from her chair and stood in front of me, then leaned down and placed one hand on either armrest of my chair.

"Me, too," she said.

She placed her mouth over mine. I kissed her back, gently at first, and then we both became more insistent. More into it. Then Scarlett stood up, took me by the hand, and led me inside.

My new chapter had begun.

5

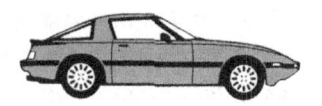

"HOW HAVE YOU BEEN FEELING *since our last visit?*"

Mia was almost reluctant to admit that the past week had been even better than the week before that, but there was no denying she'd been experiencing much less anxiety lately. Sleeping better. Laughing more often. Getting out and doing things. Visiting with friends. Shopping. Exercising.

"Good," she said from her usual chair in Beth's office. It was a peaceful space in a home that had been converted into an office on San Antonio Street. It was in the heart of Austin, but the towering oak and pecan trees surrounding the home dampened sounds and gave it an isolated feel.

"You want to expand on that a little?" Beth asked with a grin.

"I do, but I'm afraid to jinx it. I know that's silly—I don't really believe in that stuff—but I don't want to have a setback."

"Nothing wrong with being practical like that. But give yourself credit for making real progress, and remember there's no harm in enjoying it. If it slows down or you take a few steps backward, you're acquiring all the tools you need to deal with it. And you know you can gain it back."

Mia nodded.

"So do you feel as good as last week?" Beth asked.

"Actually, even a little better. It's like something is lifting. That's the best way to describe it."

"Something lifting?"

"Right."

"That's interesting. Do you feel pretty good all day, or does it come and go?"

"It's fairly consistent."

"Any idea what might explain the improvement?"

"I'm not sure."

"Could it be your new business? You're a licensed private investigator now. That's pretty exciting."

"It is, and I've already closed a case, but I don't think that's why I'm feeling good."

"What was the case?"

"Skip trace on a bail jumper. The guy posted enough stuff on social media that I figured out where he was. Pretty simple."

"That had to have been rewarding, though."

"Yeah, I guess it was."

"Have there been any other recent changes you haven't told me about?"

"Like what?"

"Have you met anyone new?"

"No, it's nothing like that. There isn't anyone. There hasn't been. You know that."

"I had to ask."

"I know."

"When do you leave to see your brother?"

"Monday morning. So I'll miss my next session."

"I have it noted in my calendar. How are you feeling about the trip?"

"I find that I'm looking forward to it, rather than stressing out or dreading it, which is what I would've done just a month ago."

"It's his birthday, you said?"

"Right. And I haven't seen him since early last year, before he moved. We talk and FaceTime and all that, but it's not the same as being in the same room."

"I'm sure you'll have a great time. What else is going on?"

Mia blurted it out before she lost her nerve. "I've been thinking about Roy a lot."

Beth didn't show any great surprise. "We haven't talked about him in a while. You know it's okay to think about him, right? You shouldn't try to avoid it."

"I know."

"What sort of thoughts are you having?"

"Mostly I wonder how he's doing."

"How do you think he's doing?"

"That sounds like such a therapist question," Mia said.

"That works out perfectly, since I'm a therapist. So what's the answer?"

"I think he's probably doing great. In things like this, he's very pragmatic."

"How so?"

"I'm sure at some point he decided it was time to move on—that I wasn't coming back—so he would've done that. He would've moved on."

"A lot of people would."

"Yeah, I know."

"Do you blame him if he did?"

"Absolutely not."

Beth didn't say anything. Mia had become familiar with that tactic. Beth would remain silent when she suspected that Mia had more to say. And she was usually right.

Mia said, "But now I'm not so sure I've moved on. Or that I can. I can't tell you what a relief it is to say that out loud."

"You can always open up in here. You have to, in fact. That's the only way to make progress."

"I know, but it's hard sometimes."

"How long have you been wondering if you've moved on?"

"A couple of weeks."

"That's kind of interesting—that you've felt better in the past few weeks, and you've also been wondering if you can move on from Roy."

"Oh, God," Mia said. "That's kind of obvious, huh? I didn't pick up on that. Are you saying I'm feeling better because I'm considering the possibility that Roy and I might not be done?"

"I think it's something you need to think about."

Mia took a sip from the mug of tea on the table in front of her. "I will."

"Do you think you're done?"

"Meaning Roy and me?"

"Right."

She said, "All I know is I miss him so badly it literally hurts. Not in the same way it did, but more like you'd expect. Does that make sense?"

"Elaborate a little bit."

Mia was beginning to feel tense, so she took a deep breath. "When we broke up, and a few weeks before that, I couldn't distinguish between the feelings I had about him and the shooting and the guilt and everything else. It was all wrapped up together. But now, it feels the same as when I've broken up with other people in the past. Somehow it feels more...normal. Those feelings—about the breakup—aren't tied to the shooting as much as they used to be."

"So if you can separate your feelings about the shooting from your feelings about Roy, where does that lead?"

6

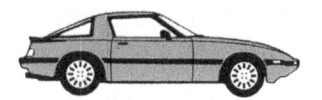

WE WERE UP SO LATE that I slept until nine-thirty the next morning. I woke up in Scarlett's king-sized bed alone. I could hear music somewhere in the distance. Sunlight was leaking through the blinds of the two windows opposite the bed.

I stretched and assessed the situation for a moment.

Only a minor hangover. That was fortunate.

Any feelings of guilt or remorse? No. None at all. That part thrilled me.

I rolled out of bed and found my clothes stacked neatly on a chair in the corner. That was definitely not my doing. I pulled them on, then went to one of the windows and peeked through the blinds. Another gorgeous view of the lake. This house and the land it sat on had to be worth a fortune. Good for Scarlett.

I left the bedroom and made my way toward the music. I hadn't seen the whole house last night, so some of this was new to me as I wandered down a long hallway, passed two more bedrooms, and found the doorway to a large den in the easternmost corner of the house.

Scarlett was sitting at a desk, behind a large Macintosh computer. She had arranged her office to allow her to face the windows, toward the lake, as one would expect.

She'd heard me coming and swiveled forty-five degrees in her chair.

"Good morning," she said.

I leaned against the doorway and said, "Just so you know, I don't usually do this sort of thing—sleep this late."

"That's not the rumor on the street," she said. "I hear you're sort of a sleep whore."

"It felt good."

"There's coffee in the kitchen," she said.

"Thanks. How long have you been up?"

"Since seven-thirty."

"Seriously?"

"I had a project due by noon," she said. "I'll nap later. Another great benefit of working from home."

A Johnny McGowan song was playing from twin speakers mounted in diagonal corners of the room. Scarlett had a large Danish-style desk, with two matching chairs and a massive bookshelf that occupied an entire wall of the room. Some of the shelves held books, while others had framed photos, interesting curios, and other knickknacks. The remaining two walls were adorned with several large abstract paintings featuring vibrant colors and unique shapes. Contemporary art, I guess, but I liked them okay.

"I should get out of here and let you work," I said.

"No need to rush, because I just finished the project and sent it off to the client," she said. "I can walk you down to your car. Unless you're in a hurry."

"Not at all," I said.

I felt something pushing against my ankle and looked down to see a large orange tabby cat. He was rubbing hard against my legs and purring loudly.

"That's Hank," she said.

I leaned down and rubbed his head. "Cool cat."

"He used to hang around Ski Shores—obviously a stray—so I took him in."

Kind of like me, I thought.

"I bet he's grateful," I said.

Hank abandoned my legs and wandered to some other part of the house. I walked over and sat in one of the chairs near Scarlett's desk.

"Except for the neutering part," Scarlett said, laughing.

"That's a tough trade—food and shelter for, uh, your cathood."

I'd had one-night stands before—if that's what this turned out to be—but this didn't have that morning-after awkwardness some of them had. It felt comfortable.

"He mostly just sleeps in the sun all day," Scarlett said. "And eats. And stares out the window at birds."

"Life's rough."

I realized just then that I hadn't checked my phone since waking up. For the past three months, I'd checked my phone first thing every morning, just to see if Mia had called or sent a text. It always ended in disappointment. I'm sure that feeling wasn't going to magically vanish, but I considered it progress that it hadn't been the first thing on my mind.

Scarlett said, "I'm mildly hung over. How about you?"

"Just a little. Not bad."

The Johnny McGowan song ended and next came the Waylon Jennings version of "Only Daddy That'll Walk the Line."

Scarlett said, "I'm going to get some more coffee. Want me to bring you a mug?"

"You don't have to do that."

"I don't mind. How do you like it?"

"Just a little bit of cream and sugar would be great."

"Be right back."

She rose from her desk and exited the den. I stood and walked over to the bookcase. She appeared to enjoy a wide range of fiction and nonfiction. I saw several titles from Austin residents Helen Haught Fanick and Marsha Moyer.

Then I looked at some of the photos. The first one showed Scarlett and a couple of other young women about her age—probably nineteen or twenty at the time. They were at the Pier, a popular lakeside restaurant and beer joint not unlike Ski Shores, but with a stage for live music. It had been one of my favorite places until it had closed several years back.

"Wish I could still fit into that bikini," Scarlett said as she came back into the room. She joined me and handed me a mug.

"Thanks," I said. I nodded at the photo. "We might've been there at the same time. If we were, I probably checked you out."

"Or one of my friends. They were a little showier than I was."

"Who are your friends?"

"Glenda and Ashley. We're just as tight as we always were."

"You make quite a trio. Bet you turned a lot of heads."

"We had a lot of fun, that's for sure. Still do."

"Where did you go to high school?"

"Austin High. You?"

"Westlake. A year behind Drew Brees."

"I know that name, but he…isn't he an athlete?"

"That's right. He won this thing called the Super Bowl. You might have heard of it."

"I don't really watch sports very much."

We chatted for several more minutes, and then she said, "How about I change real quick, and we walk you to your car?"

"Sounds great."

She started to leave, but she turned around and gave me a quick, soft kiss. I still had my mug in one hand, so I wrapped the other arm around her and pulled her closer. There's something about the kisses in the early days of a relationship that can never be duplicated. The passion. The promise. It's new and fresh.

"I'm glad you stayed the night," she said.

"I'm sure it will wear off soon."

We kissed some more, and the plan to walk to my car got derailed. We went to her bedroom and stayed there for more than an hour.

Afterward, at just past eleven o'clock, while Scarlett was in the shower, I checked my phone. There was a text waiting from early that morning. It was from my client, Daniel Ivy.

Seen the news? Norman Conlee was shot last night. Currently in critical condition.

7

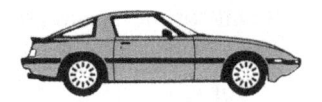

I TEXTED HIM BACK IMMEDIATELY, of course, and he called, but he had no details beyond what was reported in the media.

"In case you're wondering, we also carry his life insurance policy," Daniel said.

"How much?"

"Five million."

"Ouch."

"And it's double indemnity."

"Whoa. So ten million total."

"What're you, some kind of math whiz?"

Daniel knew me well enough to rib me like that.

"I minored in math in college," I said.

"Wait for it," Daniel said.

"But I majored in Miller Lite."

"There we go."

"Happy to oblige."

"Anyway, with ten million on the line, you can probably gather that we'd like for him to survive."

"You corporate types are so big-hearted. Was the shooting at his house?"

"It was."

"Indoors or out?" I asked.

"The article didn't say."

"On his property, or out on the street?"

"Don't know that either."

"The good news is, I set up a couple of cameras in front of the house yesterday, so if we're lucky…"

"That would be awesome."

I was sitting on the patio in Scarlett's backyard again, under the enormous cypress tree.

"He was against it—me installing the cameras—so I had to twist his arm pretty hard," I said. "You were right about him being—"

"An ass?"

"Pretty much. I had to be a bit of an ass right back, which isn't difficult for me, fortunately."

"You learn anything good?"

"Not really. He was possibly the most reluctant person I've ever interviewed, which is being charitable."

"But why? I don't understand why he wouldn't want all the help he can get."

"I think he simply doesn't want to deal with it, and he won't listen to opinions from anybody, because he always knows best, which is one of the things you warned me about."

"My phone calls with him were not pleasant. I can't imagine dealing with him face to face."

"That's what you pay me for," I said.

Daniel said, "Can we conclude that the person who committed the vandalism also did the shooting?"

"It'd be a hell of a coincidence if they aren't connected," I said. "Except one thing seems weird: If you wanted to shoot Conlee, why start with vandalism? Why not just shoot him right off the bat? Why risk getting caught trashing his Jag or his house when you really want to kill him?"

"Maybe Conlee caught them in another act of vandalism, and the person shot him just to get away," Daniel said.

Scarlett came out the back door, and when she saw that I was on the phone, she started to go back inside to give me privacy, but I gestured her over. She sat across from me.

"Good point," I said to Daniel. "Want to come work for me?"

"It's tempting, but I'm still hoping your old partner will come back."

It was the kind of remark a person just blurts out without thinking, but it caught me like a punch to the gut. That's the way the days went sometimes—I'd be rolling along just fine, and then I'd hear a song or catch a scent in the air that reminded me of Mia. I'd think about the conversations we'd be having right now, or the way we'd approach a case if we were still partners.

Daniel quickly added, "Sorry, I didn't mean to bring you down. I shouldn't have said that."

"Don't worry about it."

"That was dumb."

"Seriously, not a big deal. As for Conlee, he wondered if it was just neighbor kids being punks. Honestly, at first I considered that a possibility. I can picture him being the 'get off my lawn' type. In fact, with a personality like his, there's no telling how many people might want to get back at him for one thing or another."

"Okay, well, check your cameras and let me know if you got anything."

We disconnected and I faced Scarlett. "My client, Daniel. He had some unexpected news for me."

"What is it?"

"Norman Conlee was shot last night. He's in critical condition."

"That's nuts," Scarlett said, her eyes wide. "Where? At his house?"

"Yep."

"How did we not hear that?"

"Well, it's a pretty good distance, and we were inside, and we were kind of preoccupied. Also, we might've been asleep by then. I don't know what time it happened."

"But still, wouldn't there have been sirens?"

"Maybe, but not necessarily. And even if there were, we had the fan on, and some music, so…"

"Do they know who did it?"

"Not yet." At this point, I'd known her long enough to feel more comfortable sharing details, so I said, "Remember when I said I was sent to the Conlees' to record the repairs? There's more to it than that. My client hired me to see if I could catch the vandal in the act, so yesterday I was setting up cameras outside the house, and also trying to learn whatever I could from Norman, which wasn't much."

"Why didn't you tell me all that yesterday?"

She didn't seem irritated, just curious.

"With you being one of their neighbors, I just wanted to be cautious."

"Oh, I get it. For all you knew, I could be the vandal," she said, laughing. "Right?"

"Believe me, I've run into weirder stuff than that. I always have to consider the possibilities—like, say, maybe you and Norman had a fling that ended badly."

"Because I'm a cheap harlot."

"More of a strumpet, but that's splitting hairs. Let's settle on 'a woman of ill repute.'"

"All I can say about that is…eww. Not with Norman. Also, why aren't you checking your cameras this very minute?"

"Because I'm enjoying this conversation. The company. The lake. This coffee."

"But I think you should look. Can we look?"

She seemed excited.

"*We*? You want to see it?" I asked.

"Sure. You might have gotten the shooting on video. That would be amazing. Creepy, too, but amazing. You could solve the case."

"Yep," I said, and sipped some coffee, just casual as hell.

She knew I was playing with her.

"Your client pays you to lollygag?"

"I'm the best in the business. They're fortunate to have me. So I work at my own pace. They accept that. The results speak for themselves. Shall I go on?"

"I'm sure you could, but I want to see the video."

I pulled my phone from my pocket and Scarlett leaned closer. I was glad at that point that I was no longer using a photo of Mia as wallpaper.

I opened the app for the security cameras and noticed very quickly that I'd received no notifications of recorded events since 5:47 yesterday afternoon, which was about the time Scarlett and I were enjoying our second whiskey ginger.

"Huh," I said.

"What?" Scarlett asked.

"Either I didn't capture anything on the cameras, which seems odd, or…"

"Or what?"

I clicked the latest event on one of the cameras. What I saw was a tall, muscular, shirtless guy walking past the camera slowly, possibly looking for something. Or maybe not.

"That's Franco," Scarlett said.

I checked the other camera, but the only events recorded on that one were triggered by squirrels running up and down a tree.

I tried to open one of the cameras with a live view—and got nothing. Same with the other one.

I said, "The cameras have to be connected to Wi-Fi, and I didn't want to use Conlee's internet service, so I used an extra cell phone as a hotspot. I hid it under a fake rock not much bigger than the phone itself. But neither of the cameras are online now."

She was looking at me. "You're like some kind of spy, aren't you? Hidden cameras and fake rocks?"

"Not much of a spy, apparently, if my cameras don't work."

I scrolled backward and looked at some earlier recorded events, but the only one of interest showed Franco parking his blue Porsche Taycan not long after I left. Nobody else came or went from the premises.

"I don't understand how both cameras could be offline."

"Any idea why?"

"I guess the phone battery could've died, but it seemed plenty strong to me. Normally it would've lasted for quite a few days."

I tried the find-my-phone feature, but the extra phone was offline. Either the battery had died or someone had turned it off. Or destroyed it.

"So what's your plan now?" Scarlett asked.

"Why don't we take a little stroll down to the Conlee manor and see what's going on?"

Her expression told me she was intrigued. "You mean like surveillance?"

"Well, what we in the videography game call a look-see."

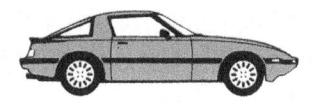

AS WE WALKED, SCARLETT ASKED, "What if the cops are still at the house? Like the crime-scene team or whatever?"

"There's a chance of that, but I doubt it. They've had plenty of time to process the scene. Right now I'm just hoping he was shot on his property and not in the street."

"Why's that?"

"If it was in the street, the sheriff's office would handle it. I think."

Back in the 1980s, the city of Austin had annexed various stretches of land along and around the lakefront—for taxation purposes, obviously—but it had been done in patchwork fashion, and some of the jurisdiction maps looked like octopus tentacles. Most of the lakeside houses on Mañana were in Austin Police Department jurisdiction, whereas the houses on the other side of the street were covered by the sheriff's office.

"And you prefer APD?"

"For this case, yes."

"Why?"

"Because they're already on top of it because of the vandalism. Better to keep it in one agency."

I didn't get into the fact that there was a sheriff's detective named

Ruelas who disliked me almost as much as I disliked him.

"Makes sense," Scarlett said.

Some of the homes we were passing were actually fairly modest, but the location on the banks of Lake Austin made them worth several million dollars. Many of them were built decades ago as weekend retreats, not for full-time residence. Other homes had obviously been built within the past few years and were much larger and more impressive. I saw a couple that had to be seven or eight thousand square feet. All of the lots had plenty of trees, so you could only catch glimpses of the lake.

We crossed a small bridge above a creek that fed into the lake. The railings on either side of the bridge were metal between short stone columns, and in those columns were small ceramic tiles with various names and messages and personalized designs on them—obviously from people who lived along the street.

"Hell of a neighborhood you live in," I said. "Could it be any more idyllic?"

"I like it a lot. As long as work keeps coming in."

"Any reason it wouldn't?"

"Nope. It's all going great. Sometimes I forget how fortunate I am."

We were almost to the Conlee house, and from here, I didn't see any police units or other city vehicles out front. They had already processed the scene and moved on.

A minute later, we stopped at the end of the driveway. The gate was closed. I saw Norman's Jaguar, eighty feet away, parked in the circular drive in front of the house. But there was no activity. Nobody outside. No sign that a shooting had taken place.

Scarlett said, "I expected—well, I don't know what I expected, but it wasn't this."

I called the one person I thought might give me some accurate information, and she answered on the third ring.

"This is Carmen."

"Carmen, it's Roy Ballard. I'm sorry to disturb you right now, but—"

"We're at the hospital. This has been so terrible. He's in intensive care."

"Who are you with?"

"Evelyn. She's in the waiting room while I came down to get us some coffee."

"What about Olivia and Franco?" I asked.

"They left about thirty minutes ago. We've all been here since about two in the morning."

"Can you tell me what happened?"

"I can tell you what I know, but it isn't much. For some reason, Norman went outside—I think maybe he heard something or saw something, or he was just checking on things. He was a lot more irritated by the vandalism than he let on. Anyway, he got shot in the chest. That's all anybody knows. Olivia and I found him, and he tried to talk, but he couldn't. I tried to stop the bleeding while Olivia called 9-1-1."

"Where was he exactly?"

"About halfway to the street. I noticed his gun on the ground beside him."

"Was Franco around?"

"No, he wasn't here."

"Did you see or hear anybody running or driving away?"

"No, nothing like that. I'm sorry, but I need to get back upstairs to Evelyn."

I thanked her, but she'd already disconnected. I told Scarlett what Carmen Romero had just told me.

"That's terrible," she said. "Norman is not my favorite person, but he didn't deserve that."

I nodded and said, "I'd better go check my cameras."

"But the gate is closed," she said.

"I'll climb over."

"Isn't that trespassing?"

"Norman understood that I might need to come back every few days," I said. "Besides, I have a right to retrieve my property."

She looked at me skeptically. "Okay, but I'll wait here."

"Wise lady."

I vaulted the gate—gracefully, I might add—and walked up the driveway. I went straight to the artificial rock that concealed the cell phone. I lifted it and saw nothing but grass.

"Roy," Scarlett called from the street.

Right then, a blue Porsche turned into the driveway and the gate slowly swung open. I waited where I was. The Porsche came up the driveway and parked behind the Jaguar. Franco and Olivia climbed out.

"Good morning," I called out.

Franco came straight toward me, saying, "What are you doing here?"

"I'm Roy Ballard, from the—"

"I know who you are, but what are you doing here?"

Now he was five feet away. He was taller than I'd expected—maybe six-four. And more muscular. An imposing guy, and he knew it.

I said, "The Conlees' insurance company hired me to—"

"I *know* all that, but why are you *here*, right *now*?" Franco said, and he edged even closer to me. He was completely in my space now. Trying to intimidate me.

"How about you step back a little bit?" I said.

"Why?"

"Franco," Olivia said.

"Good manners would dictate it," I said. "You know—social etiquette."

"Fuck etiquette," Franco said.

"That's one point of view," I said. "Or you could just step back."

"Why don't *you* step back?" Franco said.

"Okay, sure," I said. "I'll do that."

I moved back about two feet. And Franco immediately stepped forward, crowding me again. He grinned at me. Smug. Daring me to do something.

I said, "Franco, what's the point of all this?"

Olivia said, "Aren't you the guy that met with Norman yesterday?"

"Yeah, that's him," Franco said, keeping his eyes on me.

I looked at Olivia. "You were eyeballing me through the window. It was a tender moment. I'd wondered if we'd ever meet."

She smiled a little bit.

"The fuck're you talking about?" Franco said.

"You should probably just leave," Olivia said.

"I'm not going anywhere," Franco said.

I laughed. "I believe she was talking to me," I said.

"Norman got shot last night, and now I find you snooping around," Franco said. "That ain't cool, man."

"I had cameras on the property, so I was checking to—"

"Norman didn't want you here in the first place, or the cameras,"

Franco said.

"Maybe not, but we reached an agreement."

"He wasn't happy about it," Franco said. "He told me that after you left. So what you need to do is hit the road and don't come back."

"Jack," I said.

"What?"

"It's from a song. Hit the road, Jack. Catchy little number."

"What the fuck does that—"

"Hey, here's a question for you. Did you steal my phone?"

"What are you talking about?"

He was lying. I could tell by the way his eyes darted toward the fake rock for just an instant.

"So that means yes." I looked at Olivia again. "Can you confirm that?"

"Confirm what?"

"That Franco stole my phone."

"Did you leave it in the house yesterday?" she asked.

"No, it was out here, under a fake rock."

"I don't even know what that means."

"That's good to hear," I said. "Don't let him drag you into his mess. Hey, did you see or hear anyone running away last night?"

"Don't answer him," Franco said.

"I just want to ask her a few questions."

"You're not a cop," Franco said.

"True. I'm also not an astronaut or a cowboy."

Franco poked me in the chest with two fingers. "You need to get out of here. Right now."

"Stop it, Franco," Olivia said. "It's not worth it."

"Technically, you just committed assault," I said to Franco.

"What, this?" he said, and he poked me again. Harder.

"Yes, that," I said.

"Does that mean you're gonna tattle on me?" he asked.

"No, but I wanted to make sure you understood the situation."

"The situation? What does that mean?"

"It means you shouldn't touch me again."

Of course, a meathead like Franco couldn't resist that sort of invitation. He poked me a third time, hard enough to make me sway backward a bit.

I said, "Franco, you need to see this text from Evelyn and you'll understand everything."

I raised my phone in my left hand, but it was just a distraction, and it worked. He looked at it.

At that point, I could have hit him in the face, and that would've been satisfying, but some guys can take a punch like that and come after you even harder. I didn't know if Franco was that type or not, but I didn't want to chance it, so I popped him in his throat with my right fist. Not hard enough to collapse his trachea, which could be deadly, but firm enough to create a world of panic in his little brain. He grasped his throat with both hands and drew a raspy breath. Then he doubled over.

"Jesus," Olivia said. "That was mean."

I leaned down and put my mouth near his ear. "Next time you're gonna need dental work. You hear me?"

He nodded slightly.

I looked at Olivia. "Norman gave me your number. I'm going to call you later with some questions."

"It's cute that you expect me to answer," she said.

9

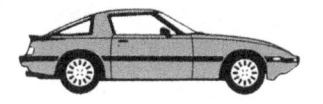

"THAT WAS CRAZY," SCARLETT SAID. "And scary. My heart is pounding. Isn't yours?"

"A little bit," I said.

We were walking back toward her house.

"Weren't you scared?" she asked. "He's huge."

I started to tell her that size has nothing to do with it, and that small guys can be just as dangerous as big guys, but I simply said, "Yeah, he's a big guy."

"Pretty gutsy of you."

Was it? I said, "Nobody wants to get beat up, including me, but what else was I gonna do?"

"Maybe you could've talked your way out of it."

We were crossing the little bridge again.

"It's good to remind a guy like Franco that acting like an ass can have consequences. Maybe he won't do it next time."

"So you're basically performing a public service," Scarlett said.

"Exactly."

"This is all so weird," she said. "How often does something like that happen to you?"

"Now and then," I said. "I didn't see that one coming, to be honest."

"You think he shot Norman? I mean, why else would he act like that?"

"Oh, there could be a lot of other reasons," I said.

"Like what?"

"Maybe Norman really did tell him he didn't want me around, so Franco figured that gave him permission to order me off the place. Or maybe he was just showing off for Olivia. Or maybe he's just an all-around douchebag who likes to act tough. Those types are very common. Hell, it could've been 'roid rage, or maybe he has some kind of personality disorder."

"You think he took your phone?"

"I think he probably did. He glanced toward the rock when I asked about it."

"But how would he have found it? Isn't that the point of the fake rock—so people can't find it?"

"Yeah, but Norman could've watched through a window as I set the cameras up. Regardless, it was sloppy work on my part."

"How so?"

We turned into her driveway.

"I should've put the fake rock in a spot covered by one of the cameras," I said. "That way I probably would've gotten video of the person taking the phone."

"Smart," she said. "You know, your life is kind of like a detective show."

"Ah, yes, it's a thrill ride. Nothing like waiting around for ten or twelve hours with a video camera, only to have the subject never leave the house. That's how it usually goes."

"But occasionally you get into a street fight. Or a driveway fight."

"Not often, but it happens. Now I'm just hoping the cops don't show up at your house."

"You think he'll call them?"

"I don't know. Maybe. If he does, it'll be his word, and Olivia's, against ours. By now his throat is probably bruised, so they might be inclined to give me a hard time."

"Maybe so, but the good news is, I recorded the whole thing."

We had just reached the front door, so I turned to face her.

"Did you really?"

"Absolutely."

"You might've saved my butt."

"It's a butt worth saving," she said.

"Thank you. You mind texting me that video?"

"I will. You know what else I need to do?"

"What?"

"Give you a ride to get your car. We forgot all about it."

When we passed the Conlee house a few minutes later, the Porsche was still in the driveway, but Franco and Olivia were nowhere to be seen.

"Hope I didn't drag you into a mess," I said as she turned into the parking lot for Ski Shores. "If the cops show up, just give them my number."

"No worries," she said. "It was entertaining as hell."

"We should do it again," I said.

"Get drunk and get into a brawl the next day with a possible gunman?"

"Exactly."

"Just say when."

An hour later, I was seated in front of my computer in my rental home in Austin Lake Estates. Even though this house was roughly two miles from Scarlett's place, it was on the other side of the lake, so it had taken me thirty minutes to drive home.

I'd rented this place after Mia and I had split, and so far, I was happy with it. I'd converted one of the three bedrooms into an office, which consisted of a desk, a set of bookshelves, and a couch for the occasional nap.

I spent a few hours doing what I should've been doing yesterday afternoon—research on the various people close to Norman Conlee.

I started with Franco, for obvious reasons. I was able to pull his license plate number from the video clip of him parking his Porsche at the Conlee home yesterday, and when I ran the plate, I learned that his last name was Keller. That information allowed me to access his criminal history. He'd been arrested for driving while intoxicated two years ago, but other than that, he was clean.

I poked around on social media and found his parents' names, and learned that they occupied the same social strata as Norman and Evelyn Conlee, meaning they were wealthy as hell. That probably explained Franco's Porsche, as opposed to his managing a restaurant, which was actually a bar-and-grill type of place on Highway 71, near Spicewood.

I searched for any other direct link between the Conlees and the Kellers and found none. Norman and Evelyn did not appear to know Franco's parents or belong to any of the same organizations or clubs.

Next I did some research on Olivia Reed. Her Instagram page was wide open, as you'd expect from a social media influencer. She marketed herself as a fashion and lifestyle model, and she had nearly a million and a half followers. That was impressive, but I quickly ascertained that was nowhere near the highest levels. Kylie Jenner, for instance, had well over 100 million followers. Cristiano Ronaldo, the soccer star, had 150 million.

Olivia Reed's Instagram page was filled with tasteful photos of her in various high-end clothing and occasionally a swimsuit. The page had a girl-next-door vibe to it. Many of the photos were selfies, but some were not. The photos didn't appear to be painstakingly staged or over-edited, and maybe that was the trend now. In most of the posts, she'd tagged or mentioned a brand of clothing, jewelry, cosmetics, hair-care product, or the like. I noticed several of the photos had been taken around the Conlee pool, but I didn't see her in the fuchsia bikini from yesterday. Maybe that was a trial run, or maybe she hadn't been satisfied with how the photos had turned out. She frequently used Franco's Porsche as a prop in the photos, and a Suzuki motorcycle that probably also belonged to him.

I searched for more information about her on other sites. If Olivia Reed had ever been actively employed, I couldn't find any record of it. She had no criminal record in Texas, was not registered to vote, and owned no real estate in Travis County.

A ding from my phone interrupted me. Scarlett had just texted her video to me, as I'd requested. If the cops should show up at my door, which I figured was unlikely at this point, I'd be able to show them what had really happened. Of course the video didn't capture the conversation between Franco and me—not at that distance—but it clearly showed him poking me three times before I retaliated. Any decent cop would look at that video and realize Franco and Olivia had left out a few pertinent details.

That camera work is terrible! I replied. *You'll never get a job in Hollywood.*

She sent a laughing emoji, and I went back to my research on Olivia. Why had she left Sacramento and come to stay with her aunt in Texas? That seemed like a strange move to make for a woman of her age.

So I focused my attention on some California-based websites, and I found my answer fairly quickly.

A newspaper article from less than two years earlier, when Olivia Reed was twenty-two years old, revealed that she'd been involved in an auto accident, and although she'd escaped with minor injuries, the driver had broken both legs. That person was a state senator. Olivia had been the only passenger in his Cadillac, and the subtext of the article clearly implied that she and the married senator occasionally engaged in a little late-night polling, so to speak.

10

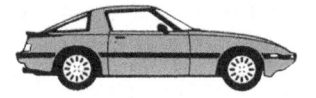

I read that article, plus several others published in the following days, but there were few additional details, other than the fact that the senator slowly recovered from his injuries, and that he claimed repeatedly that Olivia was nothing more than an enthusiastic campaign volunteer with whom he had developed a friendship. His wife stuck by him and said it was a personal matter. The senator and his aides refused to comment further.

Interesting.

Now that I knew about the incident, so what? Olivia Reed had possibly been sleeping with a married man, but was it relevant to the vandalism and the shooting? If the car crash had happened a month ago and it had taken place here in Austin, I might be able to envision an angry wife seeking revenge on Olivia. But two years ago, halfway across the country? I couldn't see any possible connection.

Still, I decided to share it with Scarlett. I texted a link and a short message: *Here's something fun.*

Then I got up and went into the kitchen to scrounge up some lunch. I'd forgotten I had some leftovers from Austin's Pizza on Cuernavaca, not far from my house. Perfect. I didn't even heat it up, because cold pepperoni pizza is a gift from the gods, and anyone who disagrees has terrible taste and poor judgment.

By the time I'd returned to my computer with several slices on a plate, Scarlett had texted me back.

That's crazy. I realize now that I lead a quiet, boring life. How do I spice things up like this?

Start slow, I said. *Maybe hook up with a county commissioner. Then work your way up.*

She sent a laughing face, then said, *What are you going to do now?*

Take a nap, I said. *Master pinochle. Rebuild my blender.*

I mean with the case. What will you do next, if you don't mind telling me?

I thought about it for a moment. *I have no idea, but when all else fails, ask questions. That's an old saying I just coined.*

I wanted to speak to Evelyn Conlee—I hadn't even met her yet—but I didn't have her number. Norman had never sent it. So I called Carmen Romero instead.

After she answered and I identified myself, she said, "I'm sorry I was such a mess on the phone this morning. We were all pretty flustered."

"No problem," I said. "It's not easy to think straight in a situation like that. How is Norman doing?"

"About the same," she said.

"And Evelyn?" I asked.

"She's doing okay."

I told her what I wanted, and she said I could come over that afternoon.

There was no sign of Franco or Olivia as I pulled into the Conlee driveway at four o'clock. No Porsche parked out front. The Jaguar was there, though. I parked the RX-7 behind the Jaguar and went to the front door. Carmen answered my knock.

When I'd met her briefly yesterday, I'd been thinking she was in her early forties, but now I realized she was probably closer to fifty. Her short brown hair had a scattering of gray in it, and it suited her. She was about five-eight, with a slim, athletic build.

I asked about Evelyn again, and Carmen said, "She was pretty upset last night, but she's doing better today, I think. The doctors told us they expect Norman to be stable for several days, so that's a good sign, I hope."

I said, "Is she available for a few questions?"

"I know that's why you drove over, but she just fell asleep a few minutes ago and I'd hate to wake her. If you have questions about last night, I'd be happy to answer them."

"That would be great."

"Let's go in here."

She led the way into a nearby library, where we sat in two matching upholstered chairs.

"What time did it all happen?" I asked.

Carmen took a deep breath. "It was just after midnight. I'm a fairly heavy sleeper, but it woke me up immediately."

"The shot did?"

The house was overwhelmingly quiet. No conversations. Nobody cooking or cleaning. No television or radio playing.

"Yes, but it took me a moment to realize what it was. It was just a loud noise, but after a few seconds, I began to realize it was a shot. Or I assumed it was. I didn't know what else it might be."

"Just one shot?"

"That's all I remember."

"What happened immediately after you heard the shot?"

"I was leaving my bedroom just as Olivia was coming out of hers, so we went outside together, and we found Norman."

"You weren't worried about running into someone with a gun?"

"Honestly, I figured Norman had fired the shot. In hindsight, that was a foolish assumption to make, but I wasn't particularly scared at the time. I could picture Norman firing a shot into the air to scare someone away, or even if he saw a shadow."

"What happened after you found him?" I asked.

"I immediately put pressure on the wound and Olivia called 911."

"Was Norman conscious and talking?" I asked.

"He was moaning, but he didn't answer any questions. And then he lost consciousness."

"So you didn't hear or see the shooter, or anybody running or driving away? Nothing like that?"

"Nothing at all. Everything was quiet. This is all about the life insurance, right? All these questions? In case Norman…"

She didn't finish the thought.

I said, "Yes, my client carries that policy for the Conlees, too. It would be helpful for us to know who committed the vandalism and now the shooting, assuming it's the same person or persons."

She shook her head. "I tried to convince Norman to install some security cameras after the first incident, but he wasn't interested."

"Did he give a reason?"

She gave me a pained grin. "He doesn't usually give reasons. He just gives orders. And edicts."

It was apparent she didn't know I'd placed cameras on the premises yesterday—surely she would've asked about that by now—but it didn't surprise me that Norman Conlee hadn't mentioned it to her. Why would he tell her something she didn't need to know? That wasn't his style. He would consider that conversation a waste of time.

"I sort of got that sense myself yesterday," I said. "It must be wonderful not to be burdened with concerns about other people's opinions."

This comment was intended to feel her out. Would she push back to defend her boss?

I got the same grin from her again. "He's, uh, never uncertain. Sometimes I wish I had that quality."

"How long have you worked for him?" Then I added, "And Evelyn."

I knew the answer already, but I wanted to keep her talking.

"Seven years," she said. "I used to work in a clerical position at his corporate office, until one day he proposed that I become his personal assistant."

"Do you mind me asking what the position entails?"

"Just about everything to keep the household running. Shopping, errands, paying bills, arranging for any repairs or maintenance. They travel a lot, and I set all that up. Also, Evelyn has some challenges with her health, so I'm basically her home health aide."

"If I'm out of bounds, please let me know, but can you tell me what kind of health issue?"

"She has a nerve disorder that limits her mobility."

"I'm sorry to hear that."

"She doesn't let it bother her too much."

"Do you enjoy the job?"

"He pays me very well," she said.

"But there aren't any, like, problems?"

She looked at me. "No, not at all. You're asking all the same questions the detective asked me last night at the hospital."

"Do you remember the detective's name?" I asked.

"Her first name was Lynann. Her last name—I can't remember how to pronounce it."

"Chukwueze," I said.

"So you know her?"

"I do," I said. "She's sharp. The investigation is in good hands."

Lynann Chukwueze worked in the unit that handled crimes against persons, which could include anything from harassment or sexual assault to robbery or homicide. I was surprised she hadn't called me yet. Certainly my name must've come up during one of the interviews, and Lynann would wonder if I'd learned anything. She would also assume that I'd placed cameras on the property and might've gotten some valuable video.

I asked Carmen several more questions—both about the shooting and about life in the Conlee household—but I didn't learn much more of value.

So I branched into a different area.

"Did Franco or Olivia happen to mention anything about my visit earlier today?" I asked.

"I didn't know you were here," she said. "What time was that?"

"A little before noon," I said.

"I haven't seen them since we got back. They must've gone somewhere. They go out a lot."

Obviously, it had occurred to me by now that Carmen could be an excellent source of information going forward, if she trusted me and was willing to answer touchier questions than I'd asked so far. Her allegiance to the Conlees might be enough to keep her mouth shut—but I suspected otherwise. How hard should I push?

I hesitated for a moment, then went with my gut. "Franco and I had a little tiff," I said. "In fact, it got physical."

The comment threw her. "I'm sorry, what?"

"Yesterday, Norman and I agreed that I would set up a couple of security cameras outside—you know, to catch the vandal in the act.

Unfortunately, the cameras stopped working a little before six yesterday evening. So I came back to check on them earlier today. I was standing in the driveway when Franco and Olivia got back from the hospital, and Franco got upset that I was there. Then he started poking me in the chest and I made him stop."

Now Carmen appeared somewhat amused. "How did you do that?"

"I punched him in the throat," I said.

"Whoa. Seriously?"

"Just hard enough to get his attention."

"Did it work?"

"Like a charm. Usually does."

"Usually?" she said. "You've done that more than once?"

I told her the same thing I'd told Scarlett—that I occasionally encountered someone who doesn't want me investigating a case of purported fraud. "But Franco surprised me," I said. "Any idea why he'd react that way?"

"No idea," she said.

"He claimed Norman had changed his mind about the cameras," I said. "Would Norman have discussed that with Franco?"

"I suppose it's possible, or that Franco misinterpreted something Norman said."

"Even if Norman didn't want the cameras there, that was no reason for Franco to get aggressive," I said. "Does he behave that way a lot?"

"I'm afraid I don't know Franco well enough to answer that."

"The other problem was, somebody took the phone I was using as a hotspot."

"I'm not following."

"The cameras were using a cell phone for a signal. That phone was hidden under an artificial rock, but somebody took it."

"And you think it was Franco?"

"I have no idea. He denied it. I guess Olivia might've picked it up, even out of curiosity."

"Oh, I doubt it. She wouldn't concern herself with something like that." She lowered her voice. "She's kind of a narcissist. If it doesn't involve her, why would she care?"

"Well, maybe the phone will magically reappear," I said.

"If I see it around, I'll let you know."

"I would appreciate that. Hey, you mind checking to see if Evelyn might be awake now?"

"I'll check. Be right back."

She returned in two minutes. "Sorry. She's still asleep. May I have her call you?"

"That would be great," I said. "Also, can you give me permission to put more cameras out front?"

She hesitated. "I would be overstepping if I did that. You'd better wait and ask Evelyn."

"I'll do that," I said.

11

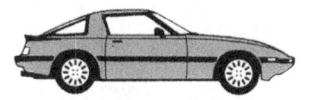

CARMEN HAD SPOKEN MORE FREELY than I had anticipated, and I'd learned quite a bit, but I wasn't necessarily any closer to solving the case, and I didn't have a lot of options at this point.

I came to the intersection of Mañana and Pearce and could've taken a left to exit the neighborhood quickly, but I took a right instead.

A minute later, I drove past Ski Shores and saw several vehicles in the parking lot, including Franco's Porsche, near the street. I passed by, but an idea popped into my head.

No. It was rash. Too spontaneous. It needed more planning.

I decided to do it anyway.

I turned around in a driveway, went back to Ski Shores, and pulled in. The parking lot slopes gently downhill toward the café, but the vehicles can't be seen from most of the tables outside the building. There was an empty spot next to Franco's Porsche, so I took it. I wish I'd been driving the Caravan or the Camry, but I was in the RX-7, so I'd make this quick and get out of there ASAP.

I always keep a couple of magnetic GPS trackers on hand, charged and ready to go. They've gotten cheaper, more reliable, and more accurate over the years, and the apps used to follow the tracker are slick and easy to use—all to the bane of cheating spouses and goldbricking delivery drivers everywhere. But I loved them, of course, despite the fact that it was illegal for me to place a tracker on a person's car without his or her consent.

I got out of my car with a tracker in hand and peered toward the café. Nobody coming. I bent down as if to tie my shoe, then quickly dropped onto my back and slid my arm under the driver's side of the Porsche, near the front fender. The car was too low to the ground for me to see what I was doing, but going by feel, I found a spot and attached it.

Then I pulled my arm back and stood up. Boom. Slick, fast, and easy. I got back into the RX-7 and drove away.

A mile down the road, I pulled to the shoulder and checked the tracker, just to make sure it was operating as it should. Everything looked good.

Then I made a call. Lynann Chukwueze answered on the third ring.

"The talented Roy Ballard," she said. "I was just about to call you."

"And I was just about to answer."

"You got something good for me?"

"Maybe. You want to grab some coffee?"

"What time is it?"

"Twenty 'til five."

"How quickly can you get downtown?"

"Thirty minutes max."

"Don't lie to me."

"Maybe forty."

"Okay, yeah. I can do that. I need to be somewhere at six-thirty."

"I'll tell you right now I don't have any video," I said.

"Ah, don't break my heart like that," she said.

"Sorry, but I do have some information you might like."

"Then come on down and bust this thing open for me," she said.

"Perhaps I should rein in your expectations a little," I said. "I'm headed your way."

Lynann Chukwueze is at least six feet tall, slender, and always dresses impeccably. She's quite striking, and she carries herself with a confidence that turns heads. Today, as she walked into the Hideout Coffee House on Congress Avenue, she was wearing a green knee-length V-neck dress with a modest slit on each side.

The coffee house—fairly quiet this time of day—occupies a long, narrow space with a cluster of small tables up front, near a plate-glass window, and then more tables against one wall, all the way to the back. I was waiting at a two-top with my coffee and hers. I had texted when I'd arrived and asked what she wanted.

Her heels clicked on the hardwood floor as she approached, and when she took her chair, I remained seated, because that's the kind of relationship we had. For me to stand and greet her would've been as unusual as one of her coworkers doing the same in their office.

"Thanks for meeting me," I said, and slid her coffee toward her.

She said, "You're a sweetheart, despite what everyone says. What do I owe you?"

"It's on me."

"You know I can't do that," she said. She took out a five and placed it on the table in front of me, where it remained. "How's that gorgeous fiancée of yours?"

I'd prepared myself for that kind of question. A lot of people still hadn't heard the news.

"Still gorgeous," I said, "but no longer my fiancée."

"No!" Lynann said, her eyes wide.

"Yep."

"What happened? What did you do?"

"I understand the inclination to put it on me, but she ran away to join the carnival. She's quite the weight guesser. It's a career move."

"Roy," she said.

Lynann knew that Mia had killed a man, and that I'd been involved in multiple violent incidents myself. "It was the work," I said. "She wanted me to stop, and I would've, but she also knew that..." I stopped and shook my head.

"Oh, I get it," Lynann said. "I wouldn't be able to quit this job for anything. Hell, I live for it. Anyway, I'm sorry to hear that. Y'all were perfect together, and I mean that."

"I appreciate it. You want to talk about Norman Conlee?"

"Absolutely. You got something good?"

"I don't know if it's good, or if you know it already—"

"Well, that sounds promising."

"Or if it has anything to do with the case—"

"This just gets better and better," she said.

Some detectives are fiercely protective of their cases and view involvement from an outsider like me as encroachment on their turf. Cooperation with those types is either difficult or impossible. Fortunately, Lynann Chukwueze was much more practical and realistic. I think the years had taught her—and me, come to think of it—that the facts are the facts and the truth is the truth, no matter how or where you learn it. But that didn't mean she didn't understand the power balance in the relationship, meaning she has it and I rarely do. So I needed to spill my information first and hope she would reciprocate.

I covered the most important point first. "My client hired me to catch the person trashing the Conlees' stuff, so I set up two cameras outside the house yesterday afternoon. Before you get all excited, the cameras both died a little before six o'clock last night, and I figured out this morning that the phone I was using as a hotspot was nabbed."

"Nabbed?"

"Heisted. Pilfered. Snatched. Misappropriated."

"But you didn't report it," she said. "I would've heard."

"I was holding off until I met with you," I said.

She gave me a skeptical look. "Holding off? More like holding out. This is the kind of thing we need to know."

"Well, I was considering the possibility that it might be some kind of misunderstanding with Norman Conlee, or someone else in the house—and in the process of trying to figure that out, I had a run-in with Franco Keller."

"What kind of run-in?" she asked.

"He got physical and I had to punch him in the throat."

She shook her head. "Why does that not surprise me? Just start from the beginning, okay?"

I talked for ten minutes, bringing her up to speed, including my initial conversation with a reluctant Norman Conlee, the missing hotspot, and my confrontation with Franco. Then I told her about my conversation with Carmen an hour earlier.

When I was done, Lynann said, "Franco didn't call it in, so I guess you're good there."

I hadn't mentioned that I had video of the altercation, because it would mean dragging Scarlett into this discussion, and I wasn't inclined to do that right now. What was the point? It's not like I was hiding anything. If I needed the video later, I'd use it.

"Which makes me think he took the phone," I said. "He didn't call about getting punched because he didn't want me telling you about the missing phone."

"What if Norman Conlee *did* tell him to remove it?" Lynann asked.

"It's still theft," I said.

"A weak case, especially if they give it back," Lynann said.

"Maybe so, but it also makes me wonder if there's another reason Franco doesn't want cameras around."

"Spit it out, Roy."

"Maybe Franco's the vandal, and he shot Norman Conlee. I know you've considered that, because you are a wise and seasoned investigator."

"Well, sure I have, and there's also the possibility he's just an asshole who likes to fight guys like you."

I grinned. "Guys like me?"

"You know—handsome, with pretty eyes and a smart mouth, but not exactly a visible threat. Kind of soft looking, really. Probably got a glass jaw."

"All I heard was handsome."

"Uh-huh. You got anything on Franco beyond your little squabble?"

"Uh, well…"

"I'll take that as a no, in which case, why are we here? I mean, it's lovely to see you, but—"

"Have you had a chance to dig up the dirt on Olivia Reed?"

Her expression didn't change. "What kind of dirt?"

I told her about the apparent affair with the married state senator in California, and the car accident that made it public knowledge.

When I was done, she said, "Hmmm."

"That's all? Hmmm?"

"Well, it's interesting, but how does it connect to the shooting?"

"I'm not saying it does, but at least I saved you the trouble of tracking it all down yourself, which you would've had to do eventually."

"Uh-huh."

"Think of the time savings," I said. "I did the legwork, so you can focus on the important stuff. I know your unit is short-staffed, so I wanted to help out."

"Right."

"Plus I value our relationship, and on top of that, you look particularly breathtaking today."

"You'll say anything, won't you?"

"Yes, but that compliment was sincere. You look hot."

"I got a date."

"What's her name?"

"Eleanor."

"She's going to be blown away. You're killing it."

"Thanks."

"And, yes, I would love to hear any details you might be willing to share. It'll stay with me—you know that."

She checked her wristwatch. "Gotta be quick. We found no brass and the wound was through and through, so unless we find that bullet, we won't know the caliber of the firearm or get any ballistics information. Several of the neighbors have security cameras, but they were set back too far from the road to give us anything useful."

"No vehicles driving by around the time of the shooting?" I asked.

"Nope."

"Maybe the shooter was on foot."

"Or maybe he turned his headlights off," Lynann said. "Didn't trigger the cameras."

"Or maybe he didn't have to walk or drive anywhere," I said.

"Franco wasn't there."

"As far as we know," I said.

"We found him on video at a convenience store six miles away, three minutes before Olivia Reed called 911. His alibi is solid."

"Why didn't you tell me that two minutes ago?"

"I was holding off on that," she said.

"Yeah, okay," I said. "Point taken. So Franco is in the clear. What about the three women of the house? Carmen and Olivia alibi each other, right?"

"They do. I talked to them right afterward, at the station, and Evelyn this morning at the hospital. I didn't learn much, and if anybody was lying, they fooled me. Carmen and Olivia don't have any apparent motive. None of them do, except Evelyn."

"The entire estate, plus the life insurance," I said.

"Right, but for the record, we have no reason to think she was involved. I've interviewed thousands of people, and she seemed legit shook up. Plus, she's in a wheelchair."

"Carmen said she had limited mobility, but I didn't know to what extent. I didn't see a ramp."

"There's one in the garage. That's how she comes and goes."

"What was her version of events?"

"She said she's a heavy sleeper and had no idea what had taken place until Carmen came and woke her up. That was right after the EMTs arrived."

She glanced at her watch again.

"This woman must be something special," I said.

"Second date," Lynann said. "I like her. Don't want to be late."

"What does she do?"

"She's a gynecologist," Lynann said, and then she quickly pointed at me. "No crude comments from you."

"But that's such a—"

"Nope. Don't do it," she said, getting up gracefully from the table. "I have to run. If you learn anything else, I'll expect to hear from you."

"You really do look great," I said. "Have fun."

She opened her mouth, hesitated, then said, "I'm sorry about you and Mia. That makes me sad."

I nodded, but didn't say anything else.

After she left, I sat quietly for a few minutes and finished my coffee, then shoved Lynann's five-dollar bill into the tip jar on my way out of the coffee shop.

12

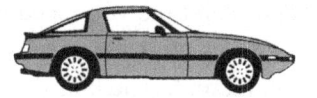

I STOPPED AT LAKEHILLS GROCERY on Cuernavaca for a six-pack, then drove along Mecca Road, through the heart of Austin Lake Estates, and continued past my rental house, down to the lake.

There was a nice little park down here with a swimming pool, clubhouse, basketball court, boat ramp and docks, and several picnic tables with barbecue grills. When I was a teenager, my friends and I could hang out at this park during the summer and have the place to ourselves. It was much busier nowadays because the population in the area had exploded.

Fortunately, right now, at nearly six o'clock, the park was not crowded, and I had a table to myself not far from the water. I sat on the top of the table, popped a Lone Star, and stared at the lake.

The sun was still above the treetops, the warmth washing over me, and bringing a memory to mind, unbidden. A moment in the sun three months earlier—Mia and me, sitting in the backyard of her Tarrytown home on an unusually balmy January day. I suspected then that she wouldn't be able to go on much longer.

I turned to look at her—to take her in—and the idea that she might not always be here, right beside me, was like a dagger piercing my heart.

She felt me looking and turned toward me.

"You okay?" she said.

"Do we need to talk?" I asked, my voice husky with emotion. I didn't want her to put it off just to spare me the pain.

"About what?"

"Anything," I said.

She smiled. A moment passed.

"No," she said. "Not right now."

She put her hand out, so I clasped it in mine, then turned my face toward the sun.

That memory weighed on my heart like an anchor. I knew it was pointless to make any attempt to change my train of thought. Experience told me it had to run its course. It was grief, plain and simple. You couldn't just hope it would go away. You had to process it, bit by bit, and each time you faced it head on, it became easier. Theoretically.

A speedboat passed with a skier in a wetsuit trailing. Having a ball out there. Music blaring.

I finished my beer and opened a second one. I was quite aware that I was drinking more lately than I used to. Carrying a flask now and then. When did I become the kind of guy who does that?

I wasn't sure where to go with this case.

Right now, I had more questions than answers, and this one was at the top of the list: Was all of it an inside job? Was I taking the easy and obvious path by assuming Franco was somehow involved? What would his motive be? As Lynann had told me, Franco had an alibi for the night of the shooting, so he would've had to recruit someone else to do it.

A crazy thought: Had something happened between Norman and Olivia? A forbidden relationship that had ended badly? Or Franco found out and got angry? Or maybe Franco had retaliated at Olivia's request. I had no evidence to support any of these possibilities.

On the other hand, yesterday Olivia had seemed sincere when she'd asked if I'd left the missing phone inside the Conlee house. She didn't seem to know anything about a phone under an artificial rock in front of the house. Had she suckered me? Wouldn't she have known about that? Or had Franco stolen the phone without telling her? Or were both of them perfectly innocent?

I could see a woman in the parking lot checking my car for a permit on the back window. The property owners' association was serious about enforcing the rules down here. I'm sure they encountered a lot of people trying to sneak in. On the weekends, they posted someone at the gate and wouldn't let vehicles in without a permit. That's how busy it got down here nowadays. I'm sure they had to deal with a lot of angry people offering various lame excuses.

I forgot to mail my annual dues. So sue me.

I didn't know my permit had expired. I can't believe you're being so picky.

What're you, the parking Nazi?

Wait a second. That reminded me...

Scarlett had said that Norman had been involved with the homeowners' association in their neighborhood for several years. As silly as it sounds, a lot of bad blood is created by neighborhood politics.

Maybe a resident needs approval to add a room or build a shed, but the HOA doesn't allow it. Or maybe the HOA cites that person for leaving his garbage cart at the curb for longer than allowed, or they tell him he can't shoot off fireworks, which he feels is his God-given right. Anger begins to build over something petty. It happens.

I pulled out my phone and found the website for the Mañana Street HOA. Found the list of three current board members. No phone numbers given, but I saw email addresses. I sent a short message addressed to all three.

Hi, folks.

My name is Roy Ballard and my client hired me to look into the recent vandalism in your neighborhood. Any chance I could sit down with one or all of you sometime soon and discuss it? I'm sure you would prefer for all the drama to end. All conversations would remain confidential, if you prefer.

Thanks,

Roy

I put my phone number underneath. I'd left out some details on purpose. Didn't name my client. Didn't say what my line of work was. Made a vague allusion to restoring peace in the 'hood again. Maybe they'd get back to me, but I was betting they wouldn't. Being an HOA board member was hassle enough without having to address a sudden crime spree, or to answer random emails from people you didn't know.

Just as I was about to get up and go home, I got an alert that

Franco's Porsche had left Ski Shores and was on the move.

So I popped a third beer and watched his progress on my phone.

He followed Pearce Road to City Park Road, then took a right on 2222, and then went south on Loop 1. Was he alone? Was Olivia with him?

The Porsche exited on 35th Street and went east, then south on Oakmont Boulevard.

He was in the heart of Bryker Woods, a neighborhood of older homes that had skyrocketed in value over the years. Not just the homes, but the land underneath. An empty quarter-acre lot around there—if you could find one—might go for half a million dollars.

The car stopped at a home just south of 32nd Street, but less than sixty seconds later, it was on the move again. It went south to Jefferson Street, and further south on Hartford, and east on Enfield, and then over to Lamar, where it stopped at the parking lot for The Tavern, an iconic neighborhood pub that opened in the early 1900s. At least Franco had good taste in bars.

I figured Franco would be there for a bit, so I drove the short distance home.

Fifty minutes after the Porsche had parked at The Tavern, it returned to the house on Oakmont Boulevard, where it lingered outside for no more than thirty seconds. Then it proceeded to the Conlee house.

Strange. Who had Franco visited twice? I jumped over to the Travis County tax office website to see who owned that home on Oakmont Boulevard. I was surprised to see a name I recognized. Hadn't seen it in a while, but I knew the man.

Albert Strauss.

He was the historic preservation officer for the city of Austin, and Mia and I had met with him during a case involving a home scheduled to be demolished. He'd been helpful and friendly. As you'd guess, he'd been very passionate—almost fanatical—about protecting historic homes, to the point where he'd attempted to save the home in question, despite the owner himself wanting to demolish it and build a new home.

Was Strauss friends with Franco or his parents? Possibly. Or maybe he was friends with Olivia, via Evelyn and Norman. Strauss, in his line of work, tended to rub elbows with the Austin-area wealthy. Maybe Strauss had ridden with Franco to get a beer at The Tavern. Didn't seem likely, but who knows?

I still had Strauss's phone number, and I started to call him and make some discreet inquiries, but I decided that was premature. I needed to know more.

I did not hear back from any of the Mañana Street HOA board members that evening, which was not a surprise.

Franco's Porsche stayed at the Conlee house for the remainder of the evening. I had to wonder if he routinely spent the night with Olivia, or was he taking advantage of Norman's absence?

Speaking of Norman, I decided to check on his condition by texting Carmen at about eight-thirty. She replied quickly.

About the same. Also, Evelyn says she'd like to talk to you. Are you free tomorrow morning at nine?

13

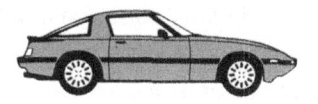

EARLY THE NEXT MORNING—THURSDAY—I SET out to dig deeper for any connection between Albert Strauss and Franco Keller, his parents, or the Conlees.

After a solid hour, I had nothing. No visible connection. Didn't mean there wasn't one.

I found Albert Strauss on Facebook and reviewed his friends list, which was visible to the public. No Kellers. No Conlees. No Carmen Romero, for that matter.

There's only so much time you can dedicate to these kinds of tangents, so I let it go for now. The Porsche stopping at Strauss's house probably meant nothing. It was unrelated.

"I'm very sorry about your husband," I told Evelyn Conlee an hour later. "I hope he improves soon."

"That's very kind of you to say. The house is so quiet without him around."

She appeared to be in her late sixties, maybe seventy, with short silver hair and flawless skin. She had a graceful manner about her and a thick West Texas accent. Her clothes were casual, but stylish and well tailored.

Her wheelchair was pulled up to a table near the swimming pool, and I was seated in a padded chair across from her. She had a tall glass of orange juice in front of her. A moment earlier, Carmen had offered me a glass, too, or coffee, after she had shown me out here, where Evelyn was waiting. I'd declined.

Franco's Porsche had left the house around 8:30, which was about the time I was leaving my house to come over here. I was glad he wasn't hanging around. I hadn't seen Olivia, either.

"Do you have any idea who might've wanted to harm him?" I asked.

"I really don't," she said. "But there is one thing I wanted to discuss with you. I felt it might be better if we did it in person. You work for the insurance company, correct? Just so I understand the situation."

"On a freelance basis, yes," I said.

"Can I speak confidentially with you?"

"Yes, ma'am," I said. "Although I should mention that if you have any information about any criminal activity, I wouldn't be able to keep that between you and me."

"Okay. Well. It's nothing like that—I don't think. I don't know who's responsible for the vandalism or the shooting, but I wonder…"

She hesitated, and I remained quiet.

She said, "Have you met Franco?"

Obviously Carmen hadn't told her about my encounter with Franco yesterday morning.

"I have, yes," I said.

"Did you have the chance to talk to him at length?"

"We only had a short conversation."

She nodded slowly and chose her words carefully. "Did you form any sort of opinion about him?"

"I did, and something tells me you have, too," I said. "I think that's why I'm here."

She smiled at me. "It's transparent, I know, but I just want to…get a second opinion."

"On what exactly?"

"I'm not sure what to make of him," she said.

"In what way?" I asked.

I noticed she had some bruises on her right arm, and it made me wonder if she had taken a fall recently.

"I would say two months ago—or at least six weeks ago—Franco and I were sitting right here beside the pool, having a conversation, just as you and I are doing right now. It was probably late February or early March, but it was an unusually warm day, and Franco and Olivia had just gotten back from somewhere. I don't remember where. Olivia went to take a shower, and Franco sat down with me. It surprised me, honestly."

"Why's that?"

"Since Olivia started seeing him, Franco hasn't shown any real inclination to get to know Norman and me. Don't get me wrong—I'd say that's completely normal for a man his age. Why would he want to visit with his girlfriend's aunt and uncle? And of course Norman is… well, he's not always the most approachable person. He can be intimidating. Brusque, even. I get that. Regardless, Franco sat down with me that day and it was the first real conversation we'd had. At first, I thought he was just being friendly, but it wasn't long before it felt like he was trying to steer the conversation in a particular direction."

She looked at me, as if hoping I wasn't thinking she was being silly.

"Steer it how?" I asked.

She thought about it. "I want to make sure I characterize this appropriately—to be fair to Franco. At first it was just general chitchat—with him doing most of the talking. He told me where he grew up, where he went to school, that kind of thing. He mentioned being on the wrestling team, and how much he missed that. Apparently he won a state championship."

Hearing that, I was glad I hadn't let him get a hold of me yesterday afternoon. A talented wrestler could take a person to the ground quickly, and keep him pinned there.

She said, "Then he said he originally wanted to be a financial advisor, with an emphasis on estate planning, because that's what his father does. So we talked about that for a bit, and then he mentioned that he'd had his own will drawn up just a few weeks earlier. I remember thinking, 'He's not married, has no kids, and he already has a will?' I mean, I guess it's all well and good to be responsible, but why was he mentioning that to me?"

"That is a little bit unusual," I said, to keep her talking.

"He stressed how important it is for everyone to have various documents completed—powers of attorney, DNRs, advance directives, all that sort of thing, and, of course, wills. He didn't come right out and ask, but I could tell he was trying to find out if Norman and I had all of that stuff in order. He was wanting me to volunteer that information."

"Did you?"

"I certainly didn't. I wasn't going to discuss that kind of thing with a kid I barely knew. And then—this is why I invited you over—he brought up the topic of life insurance."

She gave me a pointed look.

"Interesting," I said.

She said, "Since you're from the insurance company, you already know that I'm the beneficiary on that account. But if Norman should pass, and if something should happen to me after that…"

She left the rest unsaid, but I wanted no ambiguity.

"I want to respect your privacy," I said, "but since you have no children—"

"And no siblings anymore, since my brother died," she said. "Olivia's dad."

"So that means your only heir would be Olivia," I said. "Correct?"

"That's correct," she said.

"Is she mentioned in your will—if you don't mind me asking?"

"She is, yes. She would get almost everything of mine, and if Norman dies before me, that means virtually everything we own."

We both remained silent for a moment, pondering the implications.

"What if you should happen to die before Norman?" I asked.

"I don't believe Olivia is named in his will, but honestly, I'm not sure. Norman and Olivia are not close. Since she is not a blood relative to him, I don't think he really considers her an heir. He has two nephews, and they're both named in the will. I'm sure of that."

I said, "Are you and Olivia close?"

Evelyn stared toward the lake. "Yes, but not as close as we used to be, when she was younger. In fact, when she was in middle school and high school, she used to fly out here and spend several weeks with me each summer. But she got older, and our relationship changed, which is normal, I guess. She's also gotten into some trouble here and there, so I wanted to try to rebuild our relationship and see if I could help her get things back on track."

"Do you mind telling me what kind of trouble?" I asked.

You'd be surprised what some people are willing to tell a stranger, as opposed to a friend or family member.

"There was an incident in Sacramento involving a state senator," Evelyn said. "He and Olivia—just the two of them—were involved in a late-night car crash, and since he was married, there was all kinds of speculation in the media."

No reason for me to mention that I knew about it already.

Evelyn said, "But Olivia told me it wasn't an affair, it was just a… well, a date for money. I guess that's how you'd put it."

"Meaning she was a prostitute?"

"Oh, no! Nothing like that. There was nothing intimate involved. She said some men simply enjoy being in the company of a young, beautiful woman. She was an escort. That's what she called it."

Suddenly, I saw a possible explanation for Franco's Porsche stopping twice at Albert Strauss's house. As for the idea that no sex was involved in the "dates" Olivia offered, I saw no reason to quash Evelyn's naiveté. Maybe it was the truth. Doubtful, but maybe.

"Do you know if she still does that sort of thing?" I asked.

"No, that was just a harmless lark she did for fun in California. She told me she's moved on from that. Now she's on to this social media thing."

I had my doubts, but I wanted to get back to Evelyn's reason for calling me here.

I said, "About Franco—are you worried he had something to do with the shooting, or possibly just the vandalism?"

"I just don't know," she said.

"You should tell the detective about your conversation with him," I said.

"You really think so?"

"Absolutely. It will probably turn out to be nothing, but she needs to know."

"But if she talks to Franco, he'll know I told her about the conversation. He'll know I tattled on him."

"I'm guessing she won't even ask him about that specifically. That's the kind of thing she would hold back until she has a lot more evidence."

"That makes me feel better," Evelyn said. "I don't want him to think I'm accusing him of doing anything. I'll call her right after we're done here."

"I think that's a good choice," I said. "Another question—is there any chance Norman made any enemies when he served on the HOA board?"

She frowned, thinking about it. "I can't think of any person in particular who'd be angry with him for that. Obviously, there were times when he had to decline various building permits and the like, but that was the entire board, not just Norman."

"If you think of anything, please let me know," I said.

She nodded.

"One more thing I'd like to discuss with you," I said.

I told her about the disappearance of my hotspot phone, and the fact that Franco had appeared to be looking around outside in video footage prior to the theft. Then I told her about the driveway brawl yesterday morning. Her eyes got wide, but she asked surprisingly few questions.

But she did say, "Did you tell the police?"

"I told Lynann yesterday afternoon," I said. "It's good for them to know, but it might not be relevant to the shooting."

"I'll reimburse you for the stolen phone," she said.

"No need for that," I said. "But I would like to get your approval to put some more cameras out front. Is that okay?"

The truth was, new cameras would almost certainly be a waste of time. Now that Norman had been shot and was in the hospital, why would the shooter come back?

"Absolutely," Evelyn said. "I'd feel better if you did."

14

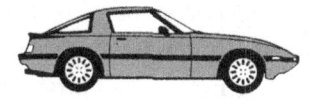

AFTER SETTING UP THE CAMERAS, I was driving away on Mañana Street when I saw Franco's Porsche coming my way. He passed slowly and glared at me the entire time. Olivia was in the passenger seat, but she was looking downward, probably at her phone. Probably posting something new on Instagram, or responding to a comment.

I wondered how quickly Franco would spot the new cameras. I'd used a fake rock again, but the rock was an actual camera, not just a hollowed-out hiding spot. I'd placed the rock camera next to a tree beside the driveway—somewhat conspicuous, by design. Franco should be able to spot it fairly easily, if he looked for it.

But I'd also strapped a camouflaged trail camera to a limb high above the rock camera, aimed downward. Then, for good measure, I'd hidden a second trail camera across the driveway, in a hedge. If somebody messed around with the rock camera, I'd likely catch it on one of the two trail cameras. These weren't your average trail cameras, either. These were high-dollar models that immediately sent photos to my phone via a cell subscription. So they weren't Wi-Fi security cameras, but they shared many of the same features and functions. I found Wi-Fi cameras to be more reliable, but cell-based trail cameras were handy in a situation like this one.

I checked the clock on the dashboard and saw that it was only 9:45. After my conversation with Evelyn, I decided I needed to visit The Tavern, but it wasn't open this early, so I drove to City Park and pulled the RX-7 under a large sycamore tree.

Franco Keller. All signs kept pointing to him.

Was he really Olivia's boyfriend or just her pimp?

Was it possible Olivia was still an escort and that she truly did have a no-sex rule? Unlikely, but not out of the question.

Had Franco and Olivia teamed up to plan Norman's murder? Regardless who'd planned it, why hadn't the shooter put another bullet or two into Norman to make sure the job was finished? Probably sloppy work by someone who'd never shot anyone before. They shot once and ran. But who was it?

Olivia stood to inherit the entire Conlee estate, but that could be years from now. Decades, in fact, depending on Evelyn's health.

If Franco had arranged Norman's shooting, hoping to eventually partake in Olivia's potential payday, he would have to trust her a hell of a lot. It would be easy for her to cut him out. Just tell him to take a hike. What was he going to do, tell the cops?

Wait a second. What if they'd created a bond stronger than trust?

I pulled out my phone and went to the county clerk's website. Clicked over to the marriage records. Entered the names.

Sure enough, Franco and Olivia had gotten married just seven weeks earlier—on a Tuesday. Obviously, they had not informed Norman and Evelyn Conlee. Or Carmen, for that matter.

I guess it was possible they were simply two crazy kids in love, and they'd chosen to keep the marriage secret for the time being, possibly because they didn't want to be judged for marrying so quickly. But there was also the fact that spouses can't be compelled to testify against each other.

At 11:45, I walked into The Tavern and found the place nearly empty. I grabbed a stool at the long, well-worn bar and was immediately greeted by the bartender, a slender woman with curly dark-brown hair. She was wearing jeans, tennis shoes, and a Tavern T-shirt.

"What can I get you?" she asked as she tossed a coaster in front of me.

"A Thirsty Goat Amber and some nachos, please."

"You want beef or chicken on those?"

"How about both? I like to live on the edge."

"You got it."

She poured the mug of beer, then went to see about the food. I checked the GPS tracker app on my phone and saw that Franco was back at the Conlee house now, after having gone to a nearby gym.

I drank some beer and waited. A minute later, the bartender came back and served another customer at the other end of the bar.

An English soccer game was playing on the TV above the bar. A Liverpool player named Mohammed Salah had just scored an amazing goal against Manchester City. The dude did things with his feet that most people couldn't do with their hands.

I checked the new cameras I'd placed in front of the Conlee house and saw that Franco had stood in front of the rock camera this morning and stared at it for a long moment. He knew what it was, but he'd left it alone.

A few minutes later the bartender came to check on me. "Those nachos will be right out," she said.

"No rush."

I checked my watch and looked at the front door, as if I were waiting for someone. Quite the thespian.

"You ready for another beer?" she asked.

"I'm fine right now. Hey, did you happen to see a tall, dark-haired guy in here earlier? I'm supposed to meet a buddy of mine, but he likes to stand me up, then laugh about it later."

"He does what?"

I probably could've skipped the forthcoming rigmarole and simply shown her a photo and asked if she'd seen him, but then she'd wonder why I wasn't just texting my buddy to see where he was. Plus the nonsense I was about to deliver was ridiculous enough to sound real.

"We make plans to meet, then he doesn't show," I said. "It's a prank we've been pulling on each other for a while."

She grinned—amused but puzzled. "More proof that guys are

weird."

"I'll admit it's kind of strange, but the upside is, I haven't actually seen him for three years."

She knew I was kidding. "So...let me make sure I understand. You say you're gonna grab a beer, and then one of you just doesn't show up?"

"That's pretty much it. Not always, but sometimes."

"Why?"

"Just for grins. The rules are, when one of us does it, the next time we meet, that person has to pay for everything, so I always order the highest-priced item on the menu."

"But what if he doesn't show up the next time, either?"

"It's a possibility."

"Sounds like a solid foundation for a lasting friendship."

I took my phone out and held it toward her with a photo of Franco on the screen. "This is the jerk right here."

She looked at it, then leaned closer and looked a little more closely. "Yeah, but it was last night."

"Oh, you're kidding," I said.

She shrugged. "Pretty sure it was him."

"Okay, so now he probably thinks I jerked him around instead. Did he act like he was waiting for someone?"

"He checked his watch a few times."

"Poor bastard," I said.

"But you're smiling."

"It's funny."

"How does he confuse last night with today?"

"He's not real bright," I said. "He graduated fiftieth in a class of forty."

She grinned again, even though my explanation didn't make a lot of sense.

"Was he alone?" I asked.

That question was the reason for this entire conversation. Had Olivia been with him?

"At first, but then another guy showed up after about twenty or thirty minutes," she said.

Now I knew that Olivia had not been with him. Who was the other guy? I figured I might as well get as much information as possible.

"Oh, really?" I said.

"I heard the name Brett, I think," she said.

"Yeah, Brett," I said. "Tall guy with an eye patch? Speaks Bulgarian? Has a silver tooth?"

"Yes," she said. "That's exactly him, except for the eye patch, the Bulgarian, and the tooth."

"So he was tall?" I asked.

"Nope. Average height. Do you really even know Brett?"

"I guess not. Maybe it's a different Brett. Could be a different Franco, for all I know at this point. Also, did I mention that Franco has a twin brother, and sometimes that brother likes to pretend he's Franco?"

"Did anyone ever tell you that you're a world-class bullshitter?"

"Coming from a bartender, I consider that a high compliment."

"As you should. I'll go get your nachos."

One question remained.

Had Olivia been with Franco at Ski Shores yesterday when I'd slapped the tracker onto his car? If she had been, there were only two possibilities: she'd walked home, or he'd dropped her at Albert Strauss's house. There was a way to find out.

Back in my car, I texted Scarlett. *Does Tammy know Franco and Olivia?*

She answered a minute later. *I'm sure she does.*

I said: *Do you have her phone number?*

Scarlett said: *Yes. What's up?*

I said: *If you asked her some sensitive questions, could she keep it to herself?*

Scarlett said: *Absolutely. No question.*

I said: *Franco was there yesterday afternoon, into the early evening. Would you ask Tammy if Olivia was with him? If she was, would you ask her if Olivia left with Franco?*

Scarlett said. *Will do.*

I waited five minutes. Then five more. Then I put the car into gear, and that's when I heard back.

Yes to both—Olivia was with Franco and she left in the Porsche with him.

I gave her a thumbs-up and told her I'd explain everything later.

Maybe I was on a wild goose chase, but I needed to follow it to the end either way.

I called Albert Strauss and he answered on the second ring.

"Mr. Strauss, this is Roy Ballard, the videographer. We met when Alex Dunn was trying to demolish his home."

"Oh, right. I remember you. How are you doing?"

"Doing great. I'm wondering if I could have a few minutes of your time sometime soon. Even today, if you can. In person, preferably."

"What's the case this time?" He sounded amused.

"If you don't mind, I'd rather talk about it in person. I promise it won't take more than a few minutes."

"I have a meeting at two, but I could do it right now if you're anywhere in the area," he said.

"That would be perfect," I said. "You're still in the same office?"

"I am."

"I'll be there in about ten minutes."

"You bringing your gorgeous partner?" he asked, with just enough lightheartedness that it wasn't creepy or out of place.

"It'll be just me today," I said.

15

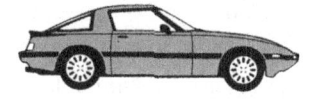

He hadn't changed at all. Still short and slender, with rimless glasses, medium-length gray hair, and a well-groomed goatee. He was in his mid-fifties, but the years had treated him well.

Today he was wearing black slacks, black leather loafers, and a crisp white button-down shirt. We were in his office on the fifth floor of the One Texas Center building. He offered coffee, which I declined, and then we sat in a couple of padded chairs near a large window looking down at the intersection of Barton Springs Road and South First Street.

I thought there was a pretty good chance he wasn't going to enjoy this meeting, but I'd do what I could to make it as painless as possible under the circumstances. He'd been very helpful when Mia and I had met with him during the Alex Dunn matter—enough that I'd considered giving him a pass on this conversation entirely. But there was too much at stake. I had to see if my suspicions were true. Maybe there was an innocent explanation. I almost hoped there was, even if it meant my case would still be stalled.

"So...what can I help you with this time?" he asked, smiling.

I was glad he asked nothing more about Mia.

"I need to ask you a delicate question," I said.

"That sounds intriguing," he said. "It's not often that this office elicits delicate questions. Contentious questions, sure, or complicated questions. But not what I'd called delicate questions."

"Well, to be frank, my question isn't connected to this office," I said. "It's more personal than that. And before I ask, I want to assure you that anything we talk about will remain between you and me. Period. I won't tell a soul. The Pope could ask me about it and I'd tell him to take a hike."

"I'm afraid I'm fairly confused at this point," Strauss said.

"I have that effect on a lot of people," I said. "So I'll just get right to the question, then."

"Please."

"You mind telling me your connection to Olivia Reed?"

"I'm sorry, who?"

The reaction appeared legitimate.

I took my phone out and showed him a photo of Olivia. His expression instantly froze in a tight grimace. A long moment passed. He looked at me, and then away. I put my phone away.

"I don't know what to say," he said.

I said, "Let me reiterate that I will not tell anyone what we discuss today. And I'm not here to judge. I just need some information."

"About what?" he said.

"About the services she offers," I said. "And how much she charges. Things like that."

"This is terrible," Strauss said.

"No, it really isn't," I said. "We all make mistakes, and if that's the biggest mistake you make in life, you're a saint compared to most people."

"I don't understand why you're looking into this," he said.

"I was working on a case and I happened to learn about, uh, Olivia's sideline. I would bet it's unrelated, but I need to make sure."

"What questions do you have?"

"If you didn't know her real name, how did you connect with her?" There was no reason for me to mention that she was an influencer on Instagram.

Strauss took a deep breath and said, "A friend—I won't give you his name—told me about her. My wife and I are separated right now and it appears we'll be divorcing. Her choice, not mine. I just wanted you to know that. I wouldn't have done this if we were still together."

"You don't have to explain any of that to me," I said.

"I feel so stupid. My wife and I had not had…had not been physical in a very long time. Years, in fact. So I did something impulsive."

"What name did she give you?"

"Gwendolyn," he said. "No last name."

"Did the two of you talk at all?"

"About what?"

"Anything," I said.

"Not beyond what you'd expect in that type of situation," he said.

"She asked what you wanted, and you told her."

"Right."

His face was a deep red. Now I knew that Olivia's no-sex rule was bogus.

"How much did she charge you?" I asked.

He hesitated. "I'm embarrassed to say, but I will. It was a thousand dollars for an hour."

"Does the name Franco Keller mean anything to you?" I asked.

"I don't think so, no."

"He was the man who dropped Olivia off," I said.

"I never met him. I saw him pull into the driveway and that's it. I didn't get a good look at him. He drove a blue Porsche, I know that much."

There was no point in telling Strauss how stupid it was to arrange the hook-up at his house, as opposed to a hotel. Too late now. But I did need to warn him about what might be coming.

I said, "Did you hear about the man shot in his driveway two nights ago?"

"The one at the house on Lake Austin?"

"Right. That was Olivia Reed's uncle."

Now he went pale, because he was smart enough to understand how far and wide an investigation into a shooting might spread. "Does that mean the police will want to speak with me?"

"It's possible," I said. "Or they might not. The trail might never lead to you."

"How did you find out about last night?" he asked. "If you did, they will."

I hesitated. "As much as I appreciate your help, I can't answer that.

But I can tell you that the police won't be able to follow the same path I did to get here, and there might not be another path. How did you contact her? Text or phone call?"

"I texted at first, and then she called," he said.

"Did you use your own phone?" I asked.

"Yes. Was that a mistake?"

"Well, it wasn't the best way to go about it," I said. "But she probably has a throwaway phone she uses just for business—or Franco does—so I doubt the cops will be able to connect you to her that way. What did your text say?"

"I just said I'd like to meet her, which is what my friend told me to say."

"No discussion of money or anything else?"

"That was all on the call," he said.

"I'll need that phone number," I said.

His discomfort was obvious. "What for? Are you going to talk to her?"

"I'm not planning on it right now. I'm going to do a search and see what pops up. If I do need to talk to her at some point, I won't mention your name or tell her where I got the number."

He reluctantly checked his phone and wrote a number down on a slip of paper that he slid across the desk to me. The area code was 916, which was for Sacramento, if I remembered correctly from a trip I'd taken out there several years earlier. That told me it was probably Olivia's phone, not Franco's.

When I looked up, I saw that Strauss had placed his elbows on his desk, then cradled his head in his hands. He was the picture of despondence. I felt bad for bringing this anxiety into his life. Or maybe it had been percolating under the surface since last night, after he'd succumbed to temptation.

"It's not the end of the world," I said.

"I can't believe I did this," he said softly. "If this gets out..."

I gave him a moment, but he didn't raise his head.

I said, "I've made a lot of mistakes in my life. I'm talking doozies—and I used to beat myself up about it all the time. Then a smart person told me I should use them as an incentive to do better in the future. In other words, sure, take responsibility, but then give yourself a break and just learn from it."

He raised his head again and looked at me. "I appreciate your discretion," he said.

"Can I give you another piece of advice?"

"Please do."

"If the cops do make contact, which doesn't seem likely, talk to your lawyer first. I know the investigator, and she'll expect you to do that, under the circumstances. She won't give you a hard time. She'll just want to interview you and see what you know, which isn't much, and then she'll move on. Nobody else will ever know."

He nodded slowly. "Thank you."

I got up to leave.

He said, "Does your partner know about this?"

"No."

"Can I ask you a favor?" he said.

"What is it?"

"Please don't tell her," he said. "It would be humiliating if she knew."

"I won't," I said. "You have my word."

16

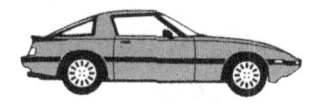

"SO IF YOU CAN SEPARATE *your feelings about the shooting from your feelings about Roy, where does that lead?"* Beth asked.

That was a good question, and Mia thought she knew the answer, but she remained quiet for a moment to think it through.

Then she said, "It's possible..."

Beth waited.

Mia said, "It's possible that I could...bring him back into my life, without bringing the anxiety back, too."

She was beginning to cry freely now.

Beth didn't say anything.

Mia sniffed, then wiped her nose with a tissue. "But the way he works—what he does—that won't change."

Beth didn't reply.

"I don't know if I'm ready to deal with that," Mia said. "The risk. I don't know why he does it."

Beth said, "Let's talk about that for a minute. If you could understand why he does it—why he won't do something else instead—would that change anything?"

Mia could see a wren hopping from limb to limb in an oak tree in the small backyard.

"Maybe. I'm not sure."

"Did you ever ask Roy that question?"

"You mean, why he does what he does?"

"Yes."

"Not in so many words," Mia said.

"Then in what words?"

"At one point he suggested I could work on cases that don't have much risk associated with them, but later when I suggested it for him, too, it was obvious he had no interest in that."

"That's not really asking him why he does what he does."

Mia sat quietly, trying to remember some of the conversations they'd had.

"I guess I didn't want to put him on the spot," she finally said. "And I still don't want to. It's obvious that his work is extremely important to him."

"Why do you think that is?"

"You tell me."

"You don't have any thoughts?"

"No," Mia said. "Beth, please."

"Please what?"

"I don't know the answer, and I'm not going to pretend I do."

"I'm not asking you to pretend, I'm just —"

"I want you to tell me what you think," Mia said. "It's obvious you have an opinion on it. Please just tell me what it is."

Beth considered the request for a long moment. Then she said, "How long has it been since his daughter was abducted?"

"Ten or eleven years. Somewhere around there."

"Do you think he's over the trauma from that?"

"Of course not. He's told me he still feels guilt. And shame. He thinks it was his fault."

"Was it?"

"I wouldn't say that. He was a victim, too. I blame the person who took her."

"But Roy left her alone, right? She was, what, five years old? And he left her alone in the car?"

"Just for a few minutes."

"So it wasn't his fault? He was blameless?"

Mia didn't reply.

Beth said, "If you heard that same story about a person you didn't know—some random mom or dad—and that person left a child that age alone in a car, would you say it was that person's fault?"

"You're trying to get me to say it was Roy's fault," Mia said. "It was a mistake. Everybody would agree to that, I think. But his fault?"

"And look how hard you're resisting, because it's terrible, isn't it? To think it might've been his fault, at least partially. And using denial is one way we cope with something like that. Another way—we go the other direction. We blame ourselves more than we should. We never give ourselves a break, even years later."

"That's Roy," Mia said. "But what does this have to do with—"

She stopped cold. Suddenly the answer was right there in front of her. So obvious. How had she never seen it?

"That's what he does for redemption," she said quietly. "Catching bad guys. That's how he keeps those terrible feelings of shame at bay. He thinks he's atoning for what he did. It's not that he won't make the sacrifice for me. It's that he can't bear to give it up."

They sat in silence for a long moment.

"He probably doesn't realize any of this himself," Beth said. "He thinks he's just doing a job that makes him feel productive and valuable."

"But if he stopped doing it..."

"It could have a psychological impact on him—possibly a significant one—if he lost that coping device."

17

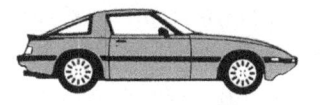

AS I RODE DOWN IN the elevator, I checked my phone and saw another text from Scarlett.

The shooting is all the talk on Nextdoor, but nobody seems to know anything.

I said: *Thx. Let me know if anyone confesses.*

She said: *One lady mentioned possibly seeing a prowler on the night of the shooting, but she posts about prowlers several times a month, and wolves, and mountain lions.*

I said: *Mushrooms will do that.*

She said: *Did that info from Tammy help?*

Maybe. Not sure. Which was true.

Any other progress?

The elevator opened. I stepped out and found an out-of-the-way spot in the lobby to stand for a minute. *Met with Carmen yesterday, then the detective on the case. Not much progress there. Met with Evelyn this morning.*

I stopped typing for a moment and contemplated how much more I should share. No reason to tell Scarlett about the GPS on Franco's Porsche and how it led to Albert Strauss, and I'd pledged to keep that to myself, anyway. I planned to keep my word. Then there was the conversation Franco had had with Evelyn about wills and other estate-planning documents. Should I mention that?

She had some interesting comments, but nothing earth shattering, I said.

I waited a moment and Scarlett said: *Would love to hear more.*

I said: *Get together again soon?*

She gave that a thumbs-up.

I said: *How about dinner tonight at my place? I know it's short notice.*

She said: *Going to a movie with a friend.*

I said: *Tomorrow night?*

She sent a GIF of Napoleon Dynamite dancing, which I took to be a yes.

Any dietary preferences or limitations?

Nope. I have an adventurous palate. But simple is good, too.

Wine? Beer?

Any white wine would be wonderful.

Will touch base later, I said.

I went outside, got into my car, and drove west on Barton Springs Road.

Where was this case going? Was I getting sidetracked?

My job was to determine who'd vandalized the Conlees' property and shot Norman, and I was willing to make the assumption for the time being that it had been the same person or persons. Who?

I now knew that Olivia Reed sidelined as a high-priced call girl, and Franco was probably her pimp and definitely her husband, but so what? That might have nothing to do with the vandalism or the shooting.

On the other hand, it opened up some possibilities. What if Olivia had done something to make one of her johns angry? Would she and Franco ever be forthcoming with the cops about it? Of course not. But if something like that was at the root of the case, it meant Norman Conlee was an innocent bystander.

Traffic was backed up from the light at Lamar. I stopped just short of the railroad trestle overhead. My car was shaded by massive pecan trees arching over this stretch of the road. Somebody had spray-painted *Unbridled* on the trestle, and in a different color, *Convy Rules*. Whatever. Traffic moved for about ten seconds, and then I had to stop again, right in front of Peter Pan Mini-Golf.

Who was Brett? Just a friend that Franco had met at The Tavern? Probably. I didn't have a last name, so there wasn't much I could learn about him.

Five minutes later I made it through the light, and a few minutes after that, when I passed under MoPac, traffic was backed up from Bee Caves Road, so I swooped right onto Rollingwood Drive without much thought. Then, more deliberately, I took a right on Riley and a left on Pickwick Lane. The street arced gently to the right and then straightened out. I eased off the gas. I hadn't planned to stop, but I did, just for a moment, staring at the house to my left.

It was in that house that a man named Sean Hanrahan had hidden with an abducted six-year-old girl named Tracy Turner. Hanrahan was the girl's step-uncle, in fact, and he'd collaborated with the stepfather to take her. This was no ordinary custody tiff; the stepfather, who loved Tracy as his own, planned to flee the country with his mistress and his stepdaughter, who would never see her mother again. I'd eventually figured out where she was stashed, and then I'd busted through the front door to get her out, paying a price in the form of a round from a .357. The patrol cop who came in behind me killed Sean Hanrahan.

I'm not sure I would've had the guts to do it if my own precious girl had not been abducted many years ago. Worse, I'd allowed it to happen by leaving her in the car alone. Just a minute or two, but that was enough. Came back and she was gone. So when I'd told Albert Strauss that I'd made mistakes, well, that hardly even covered it.

I sat quietly and remembered a moment from two nights ago. In the dim light of Scarlett's bedroom, she'd noticed the round, faintly purple scar on my rib cage and touched it.

"What happened here?" she asked.

"Got attacked by a unicorn," I said. "They can be feisty, despite their easygoing reputation. They're a menace, to be honest. A scourge."

She hadn't seen the exit wound on the back yet, which was bigger and uglier.

Scarlett propped herself on one elbow and looked closer. She looked at me, then back at the wound. "I'm not exactly sure what a bullet wound looks like, but I'd guess it looks like this."

"You would guess right," I said.

"You got shot?"

"I did."

"On purpose? Somebody shot you?"

"Yes, and it was kind of rude."

Her expression told me something had just changed in her perception of me. Not necessarily for the worse. Just seeing me in a different light.

"What on earth happened?" she asked.

So I told her everything—not just about the shooting, but going many years back to my own nightmare with Hannah, so she could have some context. Then I told her about Tracy Turner, and how my investigation connected to her abduction.

As I talked, Scarlett nodded, getting excited, and said, "I remember hearing about that."

We talked for a long time about all of it, and I realized it had been some time since I'd told the entire story to someone new. It didn't hurt as much as it used to.

"How is your daughter now?" she asked.

"She's good, but she lives in Canada," I said. "Edmonton. Her mother got remarried and they moved up there, so Hannah and I don't see each other as often as I would like. In fact, we don't talk much, either. I text or call, but she doesn't respond very often."

"How about your ex?"

"I think Hannah responds to her," I said.

Scarlett elbowed me. "Smart-ass. What I mean is, are you in touch with her? What is she like?"

"She's a great mom," I said. "We talk a couple of times a year, and she sends me a photo of Hannah occasionally. The truth is, we had a happy marriage, until I screwed it all up."

"When your daughter went missing, did your ex..."

"Did she blame me? Wouldn't you?"

"I don't know what I would do."

"She was furious," I said. "There's one little bit of information I haven't shared yet. When we were at the park—Hannah and me—the reason I left her alone in the car was to go back, just for a minute, and get the phone number of a woman whose brother had some puppies available for adoption. She was an attractive woman. Laura got the idea that I was—"

I stopped talking. I had to, because my throat was getting tight. Maybe it wasn't so easy after all. Scarlett gripped my forearm.

A moment later, I said, "She would've been angry anyway, even without that little detail, and who could blame her? I left our five-year-old daughter alone. Who does that? Who is that stupid?"

"You were young."

"Old enough to know better than that."

"Do you think your ex has impacted how your daughter responds to you?" Scarlett asked. Then she quickly added, "I don't mean that to sound critical of her, and I don't mean to pry into your business."

"That's okay," I said. "I don't think Laura would intentionally try to sabotage our relationship. I think Hannah and I aren't close because of the distance, and she's a teenager, and the fact that I'm not the type to win any father-of-the-year awards. I know that. I've accepted that."

Scarlett was intuitive enough to let my self-assessment stand without argument, and instead she just held me. It's what I needed at the moment.

Now, sitting in my car, I could see a person moving about inside the Pickwick Lane house. I wondered if they knew what had taken place in their home. Probably. How could they not? Wouldn't it be difficult to live there, given that history? The person, an older woman, came to a window and looked out at me, no doubt wondering why I was lingering at the curb, so I let the clutch out and moved along.

18

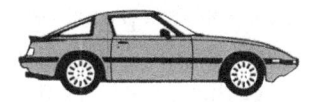

I TOOK BEE CAVES ROAD to Cuernavaca, then swung left at the Y onto Mecca Road and went under the Austin Lake Estates arches. As I approached my house, I saw that a beat-up Chevy truck with a lawn mower in the bed was parked in front. There were no curbs, and the truck was half on the street and half on the lawn.

I passed the Chevy slowly and saw a man sitting behind the wheel, looking at his phone. I turned into the driveway, but instead of raising the garage door, I parked outside.

By the time I'd exited my car, the man was walking down the short driveway to meet me. He was probably in his mid-twenties, medium height, unshaven. Wearing faded blue jeans, work boots, and a denim shirt. His dirty ball cap had a Colt logo on the front.

"Howdy," he called out.

My alarm bells were clanging big time. I didn't know why.

"Help you with something?"

"I'm out here mowing lawns and I wondered if I could cut yours. Ain't very big, so I'd say thirty bucks. That includes trimming and blowing."

I looked at the lawn, which I'd mowed no more than five days ago, and then back at him. No way this guy had been waiting for me to get home so he could make that offer. There were plenty of other houses he could have approached.

"It doesn't really need it right now, but if you'll give me your name and number, I'll call you when it does."

"Sure will," he said. "You got anything else you need done around the place? Plumbing? Electrical. I'm sort of a jack of all trades."

"You live around here?" I asked.

"Not far," he said.

"I haven't seen you around," I said. "Or your truck."

"I get up real early and work all over town," he said. "I can paint, too, if you need it."

"It's a rental, so I won't be doing any painting."

I wish I'd had a little more notice that this guy was waiting for me. I have a security camera mounted on the porch and it covers the area where he was parked, but it only sends me a notification if a vehicle pulls into the driveway or a person steps onto the porch. If I set the range this far out, it would alert me to vehicles passing on the street all day long.

"How about the deck around back?" he asked. "How's that holding up?"

Of course, the obvious question now was, how did he know there was a deck? It was a red flag, and he knew that as well as I did. He was trying to send me a message, without actually saying it. He wanted to intimidate me.

"I never caught your name," I said.

"Johnny Morris," he said.

"Johnny, how did you know there was a deck back there?"

"I peeked over the fence to see how big the yard is."

"You do that a lot—peek over fences?"

"Didn't mean no harm," he said. "Just looking for work."

"Are you?"

"Pardon?"

"I think you're trying to rattle me," I said. "You wanted to let me know you know where I live. Or maybe you wanted to check the house out and look for weak spots."

He grinned. "Kinda paranoid, ain't ya?"

"Well, let's find out. Why don't you show me some ID and we'll see if it says Johnny Morris?"

He stared at me for a long moment. Then he finally gave up the pretense.

"You need to mind your own business," he said, but it came out as *bidness*.

"If you work on it, you might be able to come up with something more clichéd," I said. "I guess I'm supposed to follow up with 'Who sent you?'"

"I heard you had a smart mouth," he said.

"Who told you that? Some other brain-dead redneck?"

I was trying to cajole him into saying or doing something rash. He had the eyes of a man who'd do cruel things just for fun. It appeared from his body language that he wanted to take a swing at me, or maybe pull a weapon. But right here, right now? No chance.

"Just let it go and you'll be all right," he said.

"Let what go? Are you talking about the Jack Johnson hit and run?"

"You know what I'm talking about."

"I have a lot of cases," I said. "So if you're going to threaten me, you need to be specific."

He opened his mouth, but I said, "Please don't say, 'It's not a threat. It's a promise.' I don't think I can take you seriously if you say that."

He looked like he was just about to boil over, but he tried to mask it with a fake laugh.

"You're a clever guy," he said.

"If I didn't have halitosis, I'd be quite a catch."

"You think about what I said," he replied, and he turned for his truck.

"Does this mean you aren't going to mow my lawn?" I asked.

He kept walking. When he drove away, I snapped a photo of his truck, including his license plate.

For obvious reasons, the man in the Chevy truck became my top priority.

I went inside and ran his plate. It came back to the Chevy—so the plates weren't stolen—and the registered owner was Paul Murtaugh.

That name meant nothing to me. So I checked various social media and found a Paul Murtaugh on Facebook, the only person by that name in Austin. His most recent visible post was from two months earlier. His profile photo was a Dallas Cowboys logo, but I found an older shot and it most definitely was not the guy who'd just been here. Paul Murtaugh was tall, skinny, pale, and balding.

I dug around on Murtaugh's Facebook page some more and got nowhere. I was hoping to see a photo of the Chevy or the man who'd been driving it, but no such luck. Who was the redneck in my yard in relation to Paul Murtaugh?

I checked the tax rolls and saw only one Murtaugh, but it was a woman named Marian. She had an exemption for being over 65, so she might be Paul Murtaugh's mom or aunt. Or not.

I ran Paul Murtaugh's criminal history and saw that he'd been busted for theft of property between $100 and $750, driving while intoxicated, and driving with his license suspended—all misdemeanors. He had no felony record.

The archives for the *Austin American-Statesman* finally gave me the answer I was seeking. A sixteen-year-old obituary for a man named Perry Murtaugh told me that his widow was Marian, his older son was Paul, and his younger son was Brett.

Boom.

The man who'd met Franco at The Tavern was named Brett, according to the friendly bartender. Couldn't be a coincidence. That Brett and this Brett were the same. Had to be. Right now, I had an advantage—Franco Keller would have no way of knowing I'd connected him to Brett Murtaugh. That might prove useful later.

I found several mugshots of Brett Murtaugh and all doubt was removed. This was the guy. His criminal history was long and varied.

Possession of a controlled substance.

Resisting arrest and resisting transport, in the same incident.

Falsifying a prescription.

Two counts of burglary.

Criminal mischief.

Unlawful possession of a weapon.

Deadly conduct.

Assault with a deadly weapon.

And many more.

He'd been released from county jail just three weeks earlier, after serving sixteen months for his latest charge—burglary of a building.

How had he or Franco learned where I lived? My address was nowhere online, nor would it have been found in any documents my client would have shared with Norman Conlee. For that matter, even my client didn't have my address. All of my business mail went to a post office box.

Obviously, Franco or Brett could have run the license plate on my RX-7, and they might have tried that first, but that wouldn't have gotten them anywhere, because I had all my vehicles registered to the address of a tract of land I owned on Fitzhugh Road.

I kept thinking and arrived at a theory. Yesterday, after my altercation with Franco in the Conlee driveway, I'd walked Scarlett back to her house, then drove home. Somebody could have tailed me and I might not have noticed. Careless of me, but at that point, I had no reason to think anybody associated with this case would have any reason to follow me.

I dug around some more, and I was able to determine from one of those classmates websites that Brett Murtaugh and Franco Keller both had gone to Dripping Springs High School. Murtaugh was two years older than Keller.

At this point, I decided it was time to give Lynann Chukwueze an update. Then she could bring Murtaugh in for an interview, if he'd cooperate. She could also get a warrant for Murtaugh's cell phone and check his location when the various incidents of vandalism and the shooting had taken place.

I started with a text. *You are a brilliant investigator, so you've probably already discovered that Franco Keller and Olivia Reed got married seven weeks ago and apparently haven't told anybody.*

I waited for a moment, but she didn't reply right away.

So I sent another one. *Franco has a friend named Brett Murtaugh who just came to my house to deliver a veiled threat. Wants me to back off. As you will see from his record, Murtaugh is no choirboy. I always wanted to use that phrase. It didn't feel as good as I thought it would.*

Still nothing. Maybe she was in an interview.

I sent a third one. *Evelyn Conlee probably contacted you with some information about a conversation with Franco. I suggested she do that. So you're welcome. I'm a giver.*

I didn't mention anything about Olivia Reed being a call girl. Maybe Evelyn would mention it, or maybe she wouldn't. Or maybe Lynann already knew.

She hadn't replied in ten minutes, so I moved on to other things.

A Google search for the phone number Albert Strauss had given me for Olivia turned up nothing of relevance. Some hits, but it was all old stuff, when the number belonged to other people. If she was advertising her services anywhere online, I couldn't find it.

If Franco Keller had ever won any sort of championship in wrestling, in any state, I couldn't find any mention of it online. That told me it probably never happened. No surprise that he'd made that up, but it didn't prove anything else. The lie was insignificant, but if I had another run-in with him, it was good to know he didn't have any special skills.

Now what?

I grabbed a bottle of beer and sat on the deck in my backyard. It was a heavily treed lot, which gave me some privacy, even though the neighbors weren't far away. Better than the apartment I'd lived in prior to moving in with Mia.

I thought about this guy Brett Murtaugh. Was he the vandal? The shooter? Is that why he'd threatened me? Had Franco put him up to it? Pretty stupid to threaten me and put himself on my radar. They probably figured some random videographer would be easy to intimidate.

There was the possibility Murtaugh had nothing to do with the events at the Conlee house, but Franco had recruited him to scare me off. Or maybe Franco simply wanted some payback for the throat punch. Whatever the arrangement, I assumed that's what they had discussed at The Tavern last night.

I finished my beer and just as I was getting up to grab another one, Lynann Chukwueze called.

"Oh, good, you're still alive," she said. "I hope you don't think I've been ignoring you."

"My ego would never permit such a thing."

"Evelyn Conlee called me about an hour ago and told me about her conversation with Franco Keller."

"Glad to hear it."

"I appreciate you sending her my way on that. It was the right move."

"No problem. What did you make of it?"

"Maybe Franco's just a curious guy," she said. "Or he's driven by money, so that's what he talks about. There are plenty of people like that."

"But you don't necessarily think that explains it," I said. "Especially when you throw in the fact that he and Olivia got married."

"Clever of you to figure that out," she said. She had a particular tone in her voice.

"But you already knew, didn't you?" I asked.

"I checked it yesterday," she said.

"Damn," I said. "You beat me to it."

"This isn't a competition," she said.

"That's exactly what you'd say to throw me off my game and gain an advantage."

"Tell me exactly what happened with Murtaugh. Word for word, if you can."

I had the sense that she had some news about Murtaugh, but to hear it, I'd have to answer her questions first. So I patiently recounted the incident as best I could. I had to paraphrase in a few places, but I didn't embellish or exaggerate.

When I was done, she said, "'Brain-dead redneck.' Nice touch."

"And as an added bonus, it was accurate."

"How do you know it was Brett Murtaugh?"

"The truck he was driving came back to his brother Paul. Then I found mugshots of Brett online and it was definitely him. One hundred percent. No question."

"You know, you're pretty good at digging stuff up," she said.

"That's awfully nice and accurate of you to say."

"You planning to report the threat to the sheriff's office?" she asked.

"You know as well as I do that they couldn't do much about it."

"Agreed. So what's your morning like tomorrow?"

"I'm flexible."

"I'm gonna need you to come down and make a sworn statement."

"Why's that?"

"Brett Murtaugh is the prime suspect in a murder a few weeks ago. Ugly one in South Austin. Guy got beat to death with a hammer."

19

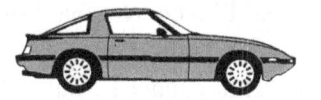

AFTER MIA SHOT AND KILLED a man named Damon Tate—who tried to use his truck to shove our van in front of an eighteen-wheeler—she experienced anxiety, insomnia, and nightmares. PTSD, essentially. She began to see a therapist, and it seemed to help a little at first, but then she regressed. She made a game attempt at one point to return to work, but she couldn't stop feeling the effects of the trauma. She decided she couldn't do it anymore.

I suggested that she could get a PI license, then accept cases that weren't likely to involve much risk. Computer forensics, for instance. Missing persons. Corporate espionage. Interesting stuff, for some people. I thought it might be the ideal solution. She said she'd think about it.

Then she asked if I was planning to continue with fraud investigation. The question caught me off guard. She'd been expressing concern for my safety, but this was the first indication that she'd been wondering if I might make a change myself. If I didn't continue specializing in fraud, my options as a legal videographer would be limited—chiefly recording depositions, scenes of accidents, and so on. I'd be bored to tears.

Nor could I obtain a PI license—not for at least seven more

months—because of my criminal record. When I'd worked as a camera operator for a local news channel, I'd impulsively popped my obnoxious and sexist boss in the face with a microphone stand and broken his nose. Even if I did eventually get a PI license and work on the kinds of cases I'd suggested for Mia, well, that probably wouldn't cut it for me.

When all of this was happening, I was on a case that seemed perfectly benign—attempting to confirm that a man named Caleb Dimmick worked at a motorcycle dealership owned by his father, as opposed to simply riding the payroll and never actually showing up. But it grew into more, and it became violent. Several people died. I narrowly avoided that fate myself, and I think that's what pushed Mia over the edge. She couldn't bear to live with the possibility that I might not make it home one night, but she didn't want to ask me to stop doing what I loved. Not that I didn't offer. I did.

And now, here I was again, wrapped up in a case that involved a level of danger I wouldn't have anticipated.

I asked Lynann to tell me more about the murder.

"It's not my case, but I recognized the name Brett Murtaugh. He served sixteen months for a burglary. He and a kid named Manuel Solis broke into a body shop that was supposed to keep a lot of cash on hand, but they didn't find it and got caught in the process. Solis turned snitch and helped put Murtaugh away."

"And Solis is your victim," I said.

"Yep."

"Murtaugh settled the score when he got out."

"That's the theory, but we don't have squat so far. No witnesses and no DNA or forensic evidence. Either he got lucky or he planned it out pretty well. Considering that it was an attack with a hammer right outside Solis's house, I'd say it was mostly luck."

"What time did it happen?"

I couldn't imagine that sort of attack in the daytime in a residential area.

"Middle of the night, after Solis left the little beer joint where he worked. We think Murtaugh followed him home."

"Did Murtaugh have an alibi?"

"His brother said he never left the house that night, and he'd have known if he did."

"Who's working the case?" I asked.

She named two detectives I didn't know.

"Do they trust the brother?"

"They pushed him hard, but he wouldn't change his story."

Another call was coming in from a number not listed in my contacts, so I let it go to voicemail.

"You planning to bring Brett in?" I asked.

"We tried already and he won't talk. He knows the system."

"You've got enough to get a warrant on his phone," I said.

"Look at you, stating the obvious."

"Sorry."

"It would almost be cute if it weren't annoying," she said.

"It'll never happen again."

"You know that's not true."

"I know. I can't help it."

"Right now, Murtaugh doesn't know you've connected him to Franco Keller. I think it's best to leave it that way for the time being. So I'm not planning to approach him about the incident at your house. But that also means you need to be careful. If he thinks you didn't report the threat…"

"He might think he's free to try something, because you won't know who did it," I said.

"Yup. Hey, if it's any comfort, if you should get shot, stabbed, or run over by a truck, I'll talk to him first."

"Oh, thanks," I said.

"It's the least I can do."

Now I got a voicemail notification.

"I'm going to send you video footage of the whole thing," I said. "You can't really ID him from it, but you can make out the truck pretty well."

"Can you see the plate?"

"No, but I got a photo when he drove away and I'll send that, too."

"Good," she said. "I'll see you tomorrow morning."

Now I listened to the voicemail someone had just left.

Mr. Ballard, this is Amanda Fielder with the Mañana Street HOA responding to your email. Why don't you give me a call back at your convenience? Thank you.

I called Amanda Fielder back and she answered on the second ring.

"Mr. Ballard, how can I help you?"

"Please call me Roy," I said. Then I explained my interest in the vandalism on Mañana Street. "Would you be willing to meet with me?"

Face-to-face interviews are always better than conversations over the phone.

"I'm sure that would be no problem," she said.

It was 4:15 right now, so I said, "How about 5:30?"

"I'm afraid that wouldn't work," she said. "I have my Bunko group coming over at 7:00 and I still have to get some things ready."

"It wouldn't take more than fifteen minutes," I said. "Then I'll clear out."

"I might be drinking wine by then," she said.

"I would encourage it," I said. "Many people have told me alcohol makes my company more bearable."

She opened her front door wearing olive-colored yoga pants and a white square-necked tank top. She was perhaps fifty, with shoulder-length blonde hair and red-framed eyeglasses. I declined a glass of chardonnay, and we sat on a sofa in her living room.

Much like Scarlett's house and the Conlee house, Amanda Fielder's home also featured enormous walls of windows looking onto Lake Austin. Well, of course. If you're going to pay for that view, might as well maximize it. She had a two-story dock on the lake, with a blue speedboat on a hydraulic lift.

Several tables in the living room and an adjoining den had been prepared for the upcoming evening of Bunko. I saw notepads and pens, plus several trays and bowls of snacks, including M&Ms, almonds, and popcorn. Almost made me want to hang around and join the fun.

"I've already talked to the police," Amanda Fielder said. "A uniformed officer, and then that tall detective named Lynann. I'm afraid I can't pronounce her last name."

"Chukwueze," I said.

"Impressive," she said. "You must know her."

"I do, yes. She's one of the best."

"Then she probably already told you everything that I told her."

"Unfortunately, she isn't always at liberty to share that kind of information with me—but you certainly can."

Amanda Fielder stared at me for a long moment. "You look like that actor," she said. "You know which one I'm talking about?"

"Ernest Borgnine?" I said.

She laughed sharply. "No, of course not. He was in that sitcom, and then he started making movies."

A long-stemmed glass of white wine rested on the coffee table, and I got the sense that Amanda had already emptied it more than once before I'd gotten here.

"I don't think Ernest Borgnine ever did a sitcom," I said.

"Funny you mention him, because my husband loves Ernest Borgnine. He's several years older than us, so he—meaning Jerry, my husband—saw a lot of his movies. He's out of town right now—Jerry, not Ernest Borgnine." She laughed at her own confusing train of thought. Then she said, "What exactly is it that you do?"

I had already explained it on the phone, but I told her again as briefly as possible. I wasn't positive she completely understood.

I asked specifically about any conflicts that might have arisen during Norman Conlee's tenure on the HOA board.

She said, "Oh, our neighborhood has its share of drama. I guess they all do. Loose dogs, missing mail, people driving too fast. But the vandalism and the shooting? I can't imagine anyone would resort to anything like that. I was hesitant to even discuss it with the detective, because I wouldn't want anyone falsely accused."

"That's understandable," I said. "I'm sure Lynann won't make any rash accusations. That's just not her style. She's very methodical."

"I hope not. I mean, I hope so."

"Is there any particular person or incident that stands out?" I asked.

She stared at me again. "You really do look like him," she said. "And you sort of talk like him. I can't remember his name. This is driving me crazy."

By now I had arrived at the conclusion that this meeting was going to be a waste of time. Maybe if I played along, we could get this out of the way and move on.

"What was he in?" I asked.

"Hmm," she said as she reached for her glass and took a large gulp.

I think she was even more in the bag than I had originally surmised. "I can't remember," she said. "And I know you didn't come here to talk about that. You want gossip about the neighbors."

"I don't know if I'd call it gossip, but if there were any residents who had a beef with Norman, it would be helpful to hear about it."

"He was the president of the board for two years, you know," she said.

Yes, I know. That's why I'm here.

"Right," I said. "Do you remember anything he did, or didn't do, that might've made somebody angry?"

She waved a hand. "Oh, hell, everybody's angry all the time nowadays, even without a reason. I'm not talking about our neighborhood, either, but everybody. Just look at all the fights on Facebook."

"That's true," I said.

"As far as your question, I can think of only one person who got really mad one time and started yelling at a quarterly board meeting. That was Jeremy Olson. He was planning to build a deck, but it didn't pass approval by the architectural control committee. Norman was also the head of that committee."

"Was Jeremy yelling specifically at Norman?"

"Yes. Exactly."

She drank more wine.

"How did Norman respond?"

"He got pretty heated, too. Jeremy threatened a lawsuit and then stormed out."

"How long ago was this?"

"Maybe six months. And the weird thing is, Jeremy is the one who found the gun."

"Wait a second. He found a gun?"

20

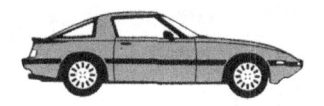

"YOU DIDN'T HEAR ABOUT THE gun?" Amanda Fielder asked.

"No, I didn't."

"Oh, I figured you'd have heard about it," she said. "Everybody's been talking about it."

I was doing my best to remain patient. "Please tell me more."

"Like I said, Jeremy found a gun," she said.

"When?"

"He was taking his garbage cart out. He has a thick hedge running along the street, and he saw it under that, in the grass."

"When was this?"

"He posted about it just a little while ago."

"But when did he find it?"

"This morning."

"Where did he post about it?"

"Nextdoor," she said. "He said he found a gun and that he called the police, and that they came out to get it. I remember seeing a cop down there before lunch."

"Which side of the street is Jeremy on?"

"Lakeside."

"So it was APD?"

"Right."
"A uniformed cop?"
"That's what I saw."
"Just one?'"
"I think so."
"Did he say what kind of gun it was?"
"Jeremy or the cop?"
"Jeremy."
"You mean, like, the brand?"
"Yes, or whether it was a revolver or a semi-automatic," I said.
"I don't think so. Hang on a second."

She leaned forward and grabbed her phone off the coffee table. A moment later, she said, "His post says, 'I just wanted everybody to know that I found a gun under my hedge this morning. I have no idea if it's related to the recent shooting, but I notified the police and they came to get it.' That's all. Several people asked questions, but he never replied."

"Did you talk to the cop?"
"Why would I do that?"
"I was thinking the cop might've knocked on a few doors to ask questions."
"Not my door."
"What time was this?"
"Oh, maybe eleven thirty."

Lynann hadn't told me about the gun two hours ago on the phone, but I couldn't blame her for that. Sometimes detectives wind up with information they don't even share with other people in the department.

"Tell me more about Jeremy," I said.
"Like what?"
"Just whatever you can tell me. Describe him for me."
"Well, he's probably sixty years old. Divorced. Lives alone. I don't think he has any kids. He doesn't mingle much with anyone from the neighborhood. We occasionally have happy hours or parties and there's the Halloween hayride, but he never takes part in any of that."
"How long has he lived here?"
"I'd guess maybe eight years."

She drained her glass.

"When he started yelling at the board meeting, did that seem out of place?"

She appeared puzzled. "We never yell at our board meetings," she said.

"No, I mean did that seem out of place for Jeremy, or is that the kind of guy he is? Is he the type who loses his temper?"

"I don't know him well enough to answer that. I wouldn't call him a friendly guy, I can tell you that much."

"Did he ever file the lawsuit?" I asked.

"Fortunately, no. He would've lost, but it could've been costly for the HOA and raised all of our monthly dues."

"What was the problem with the deck he wanted to build?"

"He wanted to elevate it, to give him a better view over the lake and the hills on the other side. It would've created some privacy issues—looking right down in the backyards of the neighbors on either side of him—so they objected."

"Did Jeremy know that?"

"He did, yes."

"Did he have any kind of falling out with them?"

"Nothing out of the ordinary," she said, rising from the sofa. "I'm going to get some more wine. You sure you don't want a glass?"

"You know what? That would be nice."

I didn't really want any wine, but I wanted to keep the conversation going. I'd surpassed my fifteen minutes, and if I didn't keep her talking, she might realize it was time to shove me out the door.

"Chardonnay's okay?" she asked as she walked over to a credenza, where an open bottle was chilling in a bucket.

"That's fine."

"I have others."

"No, I like chardonnay."

She grabbed a fresh glass and poured it nearly to the top, did the same with her own, and then brought them over to the sofa. She handed mine to me, and we touched glasses.

"Here's to that actor whose name escapes me," she said, sitting again, and taking another large gulp.

"That actor is quite a guy," I said. "He has a certain *je ne sais quoi*."

"He does."

"Sort of an indescribable quality," I said.

"I wish I could put my finger on it," she said, grinning.

"Who are the neighbors, if you don't mind me asking?" I said.

Now she appeared puzzled again. "My neighbors?"

"No, I mean Jeremy Olson's neighbors," I said.

She laughed so hard she had to cover her mouth to stop herself from spitting wine. When she recovered, she said, "Sorry. I've had two glasses on an empty stomach. I'm not driving, so what the hell? But I should have a snack soon." She looked at me, already having forgotten the question, then remembered it and said, "Oh. It's the Chamberlains and the Grays."

Was this angle worth exploring? Or was I going down a rathole? I try not to make many assumptions while working a case, but knowing everything I did about Franco Keller, I couldn't help feeling this was a dead end. Still, I committed those last names to memory.

"You mind telling me about them?" I said.

"You sure are thorough," she said.

Her phone pinged with a text. She looked at it, typed a quick reply, then put the phone down again.

"Are they good neighbors?" I asked, then added, "the Chamberlains and the Grays."

"They're great," she said. "Actually my friend Lizzie—Lizzie Chamberlain—will be here in a few minutes to help me finish setting up. You can stay and talk to her if you want."

Lizzie arrived ten minutes later, carrying a small soft-sided ice chest and a plastic bag filled with more snacks. She was about the same age as Amanda Fielder, with short black hair, pale blue eyes, and a friendly face. Amanda introduced us and went into the kitchen to take care of some things.

I explained as briefly as possible who I was and why I was there. When I asked about Jeremy Olson, her expression became somewhat guarded.

"I wouldn't say he's a bad guy," she said, "and all of us are capable of having moments when we're a little unreasonable."

"I agree completely," I said. "Does your spouse feel the same way?"

I'd noticed a wedding ring on her hand.

"Mostly, yeah, he does, but he was more upset by the deck plans than I was. Anyway, we got past it and everything's fine now."

"So you're on friendly terms with Jeremy?"

"Well, I wouldn't quite say that."

"Unfriendly terms?"

"Not that, either. He basically ignores us, and that's fine. We've tried to wave and make peace, but he isn't having it. He just acts like we aren't there. It's kind of sad."

"Was he friendly before the deck disagreement?"

"Friendlier," she said. "He'd at least wave back."

I felt that she was still a bit apprehensive about this discussion, so I tried to loosen her up a little more. "Sounds like a gregarious fellow. Life of the party. I mean, to actually wave back? That's my kind of congeniality."

That earned a wry smile.

"I think he's sort of an introvert," she said. "Anyway, what exactly does this have to do with Norman getting shot?"

"Apparently nothing," I said. "But my client pays me to chase down all the details."

"And to drink wine while you're on the clock," she said.

"That's just a bonus."

"You're not thinking Jeremy did it, right? I mean, all these questions…"

"I have no reason to think that," I said. "But when I heard about the deck controversy and the shouting at the board meeting, I decided I should at least hear the story."

"And then Jeremy found a gun this morning," she added.

"Right," I said. "Have you seen him today?"

"I have not."

"Were you there at the board meeting?"

"For the first part, yes. It made me uncomfortable."

"Did Norman shout back?"

"Not when I was there, but I left in the middle, and I heard it got pretty heated after that. Have you talked to Sandra and Ed? They were there for all of it."

"Are those the Grays?"

"Right."

"Not yet, no."

"You should do that—if they're willing. They sort of drove the objection to Jeremy's deck more than we did, because the deck was going to be closer to their side. Jeremy would've been looking right down on their pool. No privacy at all. Ed is sort of a stickler for privacy and security, especially since—"

A crash came from the kitchen as Amanda had obviously dropped some sort of large metal plate or dish that bounced and clattered.

"I'm okay!" she called out. "Just clumsy. Nothing broken."

Lizzie grinned at me and mimed drinking from a wine glass. "Need any help?" she called back to Amanda.

"No, I'm good."

"Since what?" I asked.

"Someone broke into Ed's truck a couple of weeks ago. Actually, 'broke in' isn't accurate, because his truck was unlocked. They stole a bunch of hunting stuff."

"Did they catch the person who did it?"

"I don't think so."

"Did any other vehicles get burglarized that night?"

"That was the only one, as far as I know. They were in Cancun when it happened."

"Do the Grays have security cameras?"

"Not then, but I think they put a couple up."

"Any other problems since then—I mean, other than the problems at the Conlee house?"

"I don't think so. This is generally a very quiet street. It helps that it's a dead end and there's a sign that tells people that before they drive down it. Everybody knows just about everybody, and if a strange vehicle shows up, it stands out."

Amanda appeared in the doorway to the kitchen. "You think I should start heating up the enchiladas now or wait until everyone gets here?"

"I'd start them," Lizzie said. "They'll take about thirty minutes. You sure you don't want some help?"

"No, no. Y'all keep visiting." Amanda looked at me. "You need more wine?"

"I'm all set, thanks."

My glass was still nearly full. Plus, I was ready to leave. I figured

I'd followed this trail far enough. Besides, it was 6:40, and the rest of the Bunko group would be arriving shortly.

"Are you figuring out whodunit?" Amanda asked.

"I'm pretty sure it was Mrs. Peacock in the library with the candlestick," I said.

"Ha!" Amanda said, and she ducked back into the kitchen.

"She gets sort of manic when she hosts," Lizzie said quietly. "Hell, I do, too."

"Do you have a phone number for Sandra and Ed?" I asked.

"Sure, I'll text it to you," she said. "It's Sandra's number."

I gave her my phone number, and when I checked to see that the contact information had come through, I noticed I'd received a text from Carmen ten minutes earlier.

I thought you'd want to know that Norman passed away about an hour ago.

21

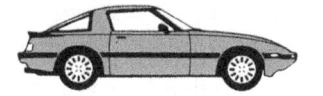

THAT NIGHT I HAD ONE of those dreams where a noise wakes you up, but you aren't sure if the noise is in the dream or in real life. I couldn't identify the noise. Just a loud bump or thump. I checked the clock and saw that it was 4:19. I lay quietly for a long moment and simply listened.

In my dream, I'd been shopping at one of the large home-improvement stores, buying lumber to build a higher fence around my house. Ironic, when you thought about it. Had I dropped a two-by-four in my dream?

I wasn't concerned enough to get up and look around, but I did grab my phone off the nightstand and check my security cameras. Back deck, front porch, garage, living room. I saw nothing to be concerned about. None of my motion-activated lights had come on.

There were only three doors into the house, and all of them were covered by a camera. Anyone attempting to enter through a window—which would make considerable noise—would have to go through the living room to come upstairs to the master bedroom.

Could've been a neighbor coming home late, closing a car door. A raccoon scurrying across the roof. The wind blowing a limb against the side of the house.

Ten minutes passed and I heard nothing more, but I was wide awake now. I'd been in this position before, the night I shot Nathaniel Tate. I'd trusted my instincts—along with my security cameras and my Mossberg pistol-grip shotgun—and had lived to see another day.

My instincts now said I was feeling a bit shaken up by Brett Murtaugh's visit. Normal. Who wouldn't be? Murtaugh was obviously a violent man. Was he a two-time murderer? Now that Norman Conlee had died, Murtaugh very well could be implicated in a second homicide, if he'd been the shooter.

I'd spoken to Carmen after I'd received her text, of course. I'd excused myself from Amanda and Lizzie and gone out to my car, where I'd texted Carmen back.

Sorry to hear that. Thanks for letting me know.

She'd replied: *This makes it murder, right?*

I said: *Almost certainly, but the prosecutor would need to know all the facts first.*

I couldn't imagine many scenarios in which the shooter would not be charged with at least second-degree murder, but you never know. The shooter could claim that they'd had a struggle and the gun went off accidentally. Lame, but it happened all the time, and it sometimes led to a plea deal on a lesser charge.

There was no use in trying to sleep anymore, so I got out of bed, quietly went downstairs, and checked the doors. All locked tight. No sign of any trouble. I started a pot of coffee. It was now 5:03.

While the coffee brewed, I went into my office. I'd texted Scarlett about Norman last night, but she hadn't replied before I'd gone to bed. Now I saw her response, time-stamped at 11:34 p.m. *I was at a movie and dinner with Glenda and just saw your text. That's terrible. He was kind of a jerk, but he didn't deserve to die the way he did. Everybody is talking about it on Nextdoor. Let's talk tomorrow, okay?*

I didn't text back yet, because I didn't know if she was the type to leave her text alerts audible overnight. I didn't want to wake her.

I placed my phone on the desk and sat quietly.

My mind was a jumble, so I typed a list of everyone with a possible motive to want Norman Conlee dead.

Olivia Reed.

Franco Keller.

Brett Murtaugh.

Jeremy Olson.
Evelyn Conlee.
John Doe.

John Doe could be anybody who held a grudge against Norman Conlee and his pharmaceutical company for pricing their drug out of reach of those who needed it to survive. If a John Doe shot Norman, well, he'd done a damn good job of building a vandalism ruse and covering his tracks. Right now, there was no evidence to suggest that a John Doe had done it.

I figured Evelyn was the least likely suspect on the list, considering her immobility, but I wasn't prepared to strike her off just yet.

Olivia had an alibi in the form of Carmen, but I left her on the list anyway. Right now I was focusing on motive, not opportunity.

Six people, but considering recent developments, my money was on Brett Murtaugh. Obviously, if Murtaugh had done it, Franco had put him up to it. Unfortunately, I didn't have any evidence to back this up.

I checked the security cameras at the Conlee house and found nothing out of the ordinary. They were online and working as they should.

I checked the tracker on Franco Keller's car and saw that last night at seven o'clock, he had driven to a restaurant called Contigo in East Austin. Seriously? He'd gone out to eat just a few hours after Norman Conlee had died? Had Olivia been with him? I guess there was a small chance they hadn't known about Norman yet, although that seemed unlikely. Evelyn or Carmen would have informed Olivia. On the other hand, I could imagine Franco and Olivia arriving at the restaurant, then learning that Norman was dead, and finishing their dinner nonetheless.

I poured a cup of coffee and waited for my meeting at nine o'clock with Lynann.

"Hey, why didn't you tell me Jeremy Olson found a gun yesterday morning?" I asked.

Lynann was setting up the camera for my sworn statement. I was seated at a small table in a claustrophobic interview room with no windows.

She gave me a look that said I was silly for even asking.

"Revolver or semi-auto?" I asked.

She ignored me.

I knew it was time consuming and difficult, and sometimes nearly impossible, to trace a firearm's serial number to find the owner, because there was no searchable database with that information. Like it or not, the gun lobby had ensured that it wasn't easy to connect a gun to its owner. But there was one exception.

"Was it stolen?" I asked.

"Roy," she said.

"Not gonna talk, eh?" I said in a James Cagney voice.

She didn't reply.

"How did your date with Eleanor go?" I asked.

"Very well, thanks."

"Glad to hear it. Seeing her again?"

"That's the plan."

I waited for her to add more, but she didn't.

"I guess you know about the bad blood between Olson and Norman Conlee," I said. "Then there's the fact that Ed Gray had some hunting gear stolen from his truck, but that could be coincidental."

"You've been a busy boy," she said. "Now hush." She turned the camera on and joined me at the small table.

I knew the drill, so I began my statement without any further prompting. I gave my full name, address, and date of birth. Then I described my encounter with Brett Murtaugh. No detail was too small. I gave the date, time, and place where it happened. I described Murtaugh's appearance and the vehicle he was driving. Next, I recounted the conversation as best I could. In places where I was paraphrasing, I so indicated. When it was word for word, I mentioned that, too. I said that I had security-camera video of the incident, along with a photo of the truck's license plate, "Both of which I've already provided to the formidable investigator currently seated at the table with me."

Lynann glared at me but remained quiet.

I said, "After the man left, I ran the license plate through a database available to the public and learned that the vehicle is owned by a man named Paul Murtaugh. I found photos of Paul and it was not the same man. But I also found mugshots of his brother Brett and I can tell you with one hundred percent confidence it was the man with whom I had just had the unpleasant encounter. That's right—'with whom.' I'm no grammar slouch. In conclusion, I am giving this statement freely and can attest that all of the facts are true."

I must have done a decent job, because Lynann didn't have any follow-up questions. She rose from the table and turned the camera off, then said, "You just couldn't help being a wise-ass, could you?"

"But you *are* formidable," I said. "What's more, I hope this statement was helpful. In fact, I hope it turns out to be a crucial element in finding and convicting Norman Conlee's murderer."

"Here we go again," she said.

"What? You doubt my sincerity?"

"You're fishing. You know I can't just tell you everything, no matter how helpful you are."

"So I am helpful?" I asked.

She sat down again. "A little, but your obnoxiousness almost outweighs it."

"Almost," I said.

She put one hand on the table, drummed her fingers, and stared at me.

I said, "You know it won't go any further."

"Um-hmm," she said.

I kept quiet, because I was pretty sure I had her now.

"If the gun was stolen, it hasn't been reported," she said quietly.

"That sucks," I said.

"Could be completely unrelated," she said. "Just a lost gun. Maybe somebody opened a car door and it fell out."

I nodded and waited.

"That's all I got," she said.

"Thanks," I said. "I mean that. Hey, let's talk about Jeremy Olson."

"Nope."

"Just tell me if there's anything there," I pleaded.

"I'm not playing that game," she said.

"Have you interviewed him?"

She stared at me.

"He sounds like a volatile guy," I said.

She didn't bite.

"I wonder if he has an alibi," I said. "Actually, I guess he'd need several alibis, when you consider all the different incidents of vandalism and then the shooting. I bet a guy like that would be easy to crack, if he has a temper. Especially with your interview skills."

She said nothing.

I said, "Hey, did you get the cell-phone records for Murtaugh yet? For that matter, you should get Franco Keller's records, too, so we can see if there are texts between those two geniuses."

Lynann checked her wristwatch.

"Those records might break this case wide open," I said. "And I'm sure we both want that. A wide-open case. I know you're busy, but you've probably started on the affidavit. Right?"

Not a word.

I said, "Why, thank you, Roy. I'm overloaded as it is, so I appreciate that gentle, yet respectful, reminder."

She laughed hard and said, "It's a good thing you're sorta cute." Then she pushed back from the table and got up. "I gotta go." She turned the lights out and waited for me just outside the door.

"Wait a second," I said. "Sorta?"

"Thanks for coming in, Roy," she said. "Now take off."

22

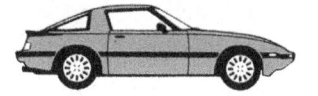

I STOPPED AT MAUDIE'S ON Lake Austin Boulevard for breakfast tacos, then remained at my table for a few minutes afterward, trying to decide what to do next.

It was tempting to contact Jeremy Olson and see if he'd talk to me, but that would piss Lynann off if she hadn't interviewed him yet, and it was unlikely Olson would cooperate, based on what I'd learned about him.

What about Ed and Sandra Gray? Might they know something useful? What would they know beyond what Lizzie and Amanda had already told me?

It wasn't even eleven o'clock. What else was I going to do until Scarlett joined me at the house tonight for dinner? The case was at a standstill, and when that happens, sometimes you have to give it a shove, or at least try.

I sent a text to Sandra Gray, explaining who I was and what I wanted. I was hoping Lizzie had already informed her that I might be getting in touch.

No immediate reply. I went to the men's room, then went out to my car. She called me just as I was about to turn the key.

"Lizzie told me you might want to ask me some questions," she said. "Or Ed. Frankly, I'm glad anyone is interested in the theft at all. I got the sense that the police are so overwhelmed with these kinds of cases, there's not much they can do about it."

"Unfortunately, that's true," I said. "And they sort of do triage—the greater the value of what was stolen, the higher priority it receives."

"That's what we've discovered. A couple of years ago, somebody managed to steal my purse and started writing checks all over the place. I think it was nearly three thousand dollars before they were done. Of course, my banks reversed it all and I didn't have to pay, but when I filed a police report, the investigator said she had something like four hundred active cases. So I said, 'I guess I probably won't ever hear from you again,' and she just laughed. I knew for a fact that they had video of this guy at Walmart and a few other places, but nothing ever came of it."

I rolled the window down because the interior of the car was getting warm.

I said, "You mind if I ask about your experience with Jeremy Olson?"

"Oh. Yeah, sure. I think Lizzie and Amanda told you most of it, but Jeremy wanted to build an elevated deck that would've basically looked right into our backyard. I mean, it's not like we're skinny-dipping back there, but we'd like a little privacy, you know? First, we talked to him directly about it, but he said it was his property and he could do whatever he wanted. He was pretty rude, to be honest. So then we filed a complaint with the HOA. We never had much of a relationship with Jeremy before that, but *after* that, he won't even make eye contact."

"Tell me about the board meeting," I said.

She went into detail, but I didn't learn anything I hadn't already known. Apparently, Norman did end up raising his voice in response to Jeremy's provocations, but neither man made any threats or said anything wildly inappropriate. It was just a heated debate about a mundane issue.

"You mind telling me what was stolen from your husband's truck?"

"Sure. It's like they just grabbed everything they could, with the idea of sorting it out later. The glove compartment was almost empty, but there wasn't really anything in there of value. Ed said it was all just paperwork and the owner's manual for his truck, and maybe a couple of charging cables for his phone. Junk like that. But in the back he had some of his hunting gear, and they took a bunch of that."

"What kind of stuff?"

"The biggest loss was a thermal rifle scope I had just given him for his birthday. That alone was worth nine thousand dollars. It was still in the box. I don't know why he left it in his truck, but that's what happened."

A rifle scope that cost nine grand? I had no idea any scope could cost that much.

"What brand was it?"

"Trijicon. I bought it at Academy."

"What else was in there?"

"Several trail cameras and some fairly expensive binoculars. I think a range finder. I'm sure I'm forgetting some stuff. I can get you a list if you want one. In total, it was nearly thirteen thousand dollars worth of merchandise."

"Any idea at all who might've done it?"

"Not a clue. I'm sure we'll never see any of it again. Thank goodness for insurance, right?"

Libraries are great places to stop and do a little research when I don't feel like driving all the way home. That way I can use my laptop in an environment more comfortable and accommodating than any of my vehicles. This time, I stopped at the Westbank Community Library on, of all places, Westbank Drive. Of course, this particular street used to be called Westlake High Drive when I was a kid, but things change.

The library was mostly empty, but I found a table near the back, where I had plenty of privacy.

Sandra Gray was right about the overwhelmed police investigators. They did their best, but there were only so many hours in a day and resources were tight. Many cases got filed and that was as far as they went. No investigation at all. But a case that involved more than $13,000 worth of property had to have received some effort. Most likely the investigator had hit a dead end.

The chances that the thief would have any use for a high-end thermal rifle scope himself were essentially zero, so he would try to pawn it or fence it or otherwise sell it. But chances were good an item like that would be tough to unload. It wasn't as common and generic as, say, a television or jewelry.

I clicked over to the Austin page for Craigslist and searched for rifle scopes. Half a dozen scopes were listed, ranging from $50 to $900, but none were Ed Gray's stolen scope.

I jumped over to eBay, entered "rifle scope," and was hit with more than 23,000 listings. So I narrowed it down by the brand name, which still gave me more than one thousand listings. I tried a new search for "trijicon thermal rifle scope" and got thirty-five results, with the highest one costing $7,499.00. I slowly went through them, hoping to see one from a seller located in Austin. Then I realized the thief could've shipped the scope to a friend anywhere in the country or around the world, and that would make it even more difficult to identify the stolen scope. Most of the scopes seemed to be from sellers who operated "stores" on eBay—legitimate optics supply companies or sporting goods outfitters.

My phone vibrated with a text from Scarlett. *Can I bring anything tonight?*

I said: *Just an appetite for whipped cream.*

She sent an emoji of a face with a raised eyebrow.

I said: *Get your mind out of the gutter. I'm making strawberry shortcake for dessert.*

That earned a laughing-face emoji.

I clicked through the various eBay listings and determined that none of the available Trijicon scopes exactly matched the one stolen from Ed Gray's truck.

Maybe the thief had sold it right after he'd stolen it. I couldn't imagine a fence would accept such an easily identifiable high-end item, but you never know. And today's pawnshop owners didn't run things the way they did thirty or forty years ago.

There were literally hundreds of other sites where the thief might've been able to sell the scope, and there was simply no way for me to check them all.

What time should I be there? Scarlett asked.

How about 6:30? I said. Then I added: *You can stay as long as you'd like.* Subtle, huh?

I focused on my laptop again. I was overcome with the feeling that I was wasting my time. What did the burglary of Ed Gray's truck have to do with the problems at the Conlee house? Probably nothing. And what did it have to do with the bad blood between Jeremy Olson and Norman Conlee? Again, probably nothing.

Jeremy Olson. Maybe I should rank him second on the suspect list, right behind Brett Murtaugh. I went through my regular routine when I wanted to know more about a person, which means I started with a criminal background check.

He had some speeding tickets, but that was it. Boring, but about what I expected.

I spent at least thirty more minutes looking for dirt on Olson, but I came up empty.

I learned that Amanda Fielder was right—Olson was divorced and had no children.

He owned his home on Mañana Street, plus a home in Houston, from where he had moved. He was probably keeping that one as a rental.

He had never sued anybody or been sued. He had never filed for bankruptcy.

I learned that he had once applied for a patent to cover the design of a pill dispenser that apparently had never gotten anywhere.

I found nothing else.

It was just now noon and I was getting drowsy from having woken up so early. I leaned back in the chair and closed my eyes for a moment.

When I woke up thirty minutes later, I had an idea.

I returned to Craigslist, but this time I went to the page for San Antonio. I was working under the theory that the thief might be willing to list the scope in a different city, to make it less likely that the victim or the cops would find it.

I went to the for-sale section, clicked "sporting," and searched for "trijicon thermal scope."

One result. One item. The right one.

23

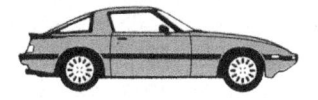

IT WAS THE SAME MODEL, but without the serial number, I couldn't be certain it was the stolen scope. The ad featured all of the selling points of the scope, which were obviously cut and pasted from a bulleted list on a sales website somewhere.

But I read further and saw two things that clinched it.

First, the price—$2,000. This was a $9,000 scope. Even a person with more money than sense wouldn't discount it that much. The type of person who owns a $9,000 scope would be more likely to stick it in a closet, planning to do something with it later, and then forget about it. But thieves often sold items at bargain-basement prices, usually to feed a drug habit as quickly as possible.

Second, the ad said that the scope was "lightly used for one deer season." And that's what tipped the scales and made me send a reply.

The seller said he would only accept texts—no emails or calls. It was possible he'd bought a throwaway phone solely for this sale. For him, it would be worth a few bucks and a minor hassle to maintain anonymity.

Still have the scope? I texted.

He replied one minute later. *Yes.*

You firm on price? I asked.

I could come down to $1800 but that's it. This scope is worth a lot more.

I checked the clock. It was still early—only 12:45—so I had time to check this out.

When could I see it?

Where are you coming from? he asked.

It would make him nervous if I said Austin, so I said, *San Marcos. I could leave here in one hour.*

Another minute passed. Then he said: *Can you meet me at the Target at 35 and 1604 at 3:00?*

I got there at 2:42. He'd told me his name was Jake and he'd be driving a maroon Buick Encore, but I didn't see one in the lot.

I parked where he'd asked me to—in the row directly facing Five Guys, the fast-food joint that specialized in burgers and hot dogs. Something told me he'd met here before, which could be true even if he were a legit seller. Some people made a decent living, or boosted their income, by selling stuff online. But why hadn't he listed it on eBay? An item as uncommon and expensive as a Trijicon scope would probably sell more quickly on eBay.

I'd told him I'd be in a black RX-7. If this guy was a thief and had any sense, he'd be scoping me out right now from a distance, and possibly even running the plate. Then he'd google my name. Spend a few minutes trying to determine if it was a trap.

At 2:55, I got out of the car and leaned against it, the picture of nonchalance. I wasn't sure if I looked like a hunter or not, but I was wearing a baseball cap with the logo of a feed store in Johnson City. This was a special hat, with a tiny camera built in.

When 3:15 rolled by, I wondered if he was standing me up—but I resisted the urge to text him. I didn't want to seem overeager.

At 3:21, a reddish crossover type vehicle turned off the highway feeder road and came in my direction. The driver started to go past me, but then he braked and abruptly whipped it into a spot two spaces over.

When he climbed out, he said, "You Roy?"

"Yep."

He looked to be in his early twenties, with unkempt brown hair. His clothes were dirty and he needed a shave. He was roughly six feet tall, but I doubt he weighed more than one-forty. He had small circular sores on his face and his forearms. This was not a healthy specimen.

"I had no idea what an RX-7 was until I saw it on the back. I thought it was an SUV."

"I get that a lot," I said with a warm smile, but he didn't smile back.

Instead, he leaned into his vehicle and came out with the scope in its original box. Then he walked over and said, "There's nothing wrong with it, but I like the scope I already have."

"What kind do you have?" I asked.

"Huh?"

"What brand of scope are you using now?"

"Oh, it's one of these, too, but I forget which model."

"You like it?"

"Yeah, they're good scopes. The best you can get, actually. Normally I would've returned this one for a refund, but my mom didn't give me a receipt and I didn't want her to know I didn't need it."

I held my hand out. "May I see it?"

He handed me the box. I gently lifted the lid and removed the scope from its cradle in a Styrofoam insert. I had already looked at photos of these scopes online, so I knew exactly where the serial number was—and it matched the number Sandra Gray had given me. This was the stolen scope.

I put the scope back into the Styrofoam, then put the lid back on.

"Why so cheap?" I asked.

"I started at a higher price, but nobody was replying, so I kept lowering it. Hard to sell such an expensive scope."

"You used it during deer season last fall?" I asked.

"Yeah, but I like my other scope better. Not that this isn't a great scope, but I'm used to my old scope."

"You got a record?" I asked.

"A what?"

"I'm just wondering if you have a criminal record, seeing as how this is stolen property," I said.

"What are you talking about?" he said, but his voice suddenly had a slight tremor in it.

"You couldn't have used it during deer season last year," I said. "This scope wasn't available until two months ago. It's the latest, greatest model." It was the truth.

"That's wrong," he said.

"I called the manufacturer and confirmed it," I said, which was a lie.

"They told you wrong," he said. "Give me the scope."

"When is deer season?"

"What?"

"When is the first day of the general deer season? Every hunter knows that by heart."

"I don't have to answer your stupid questions."

"It's the first Saturday in November."

"Who the hell cares?"

"This scope was stolen in Austin," I said.

"No, it wasn't," he said.

"I'm not here to give you a hard time," I said. "So relax."

"I'm totally relaxed, because it's not stolen property," he said.

"Where did you get it?"

"I told you, it was a gift from my mom."

"So your mom stole it?"

"Nobody stole anything," he said.

"Why don't you call your mom right now and let's talk to her about it?" I suggested.

"What the fuck is your problem, bro?" he asked.

"Ah, yes," I said. "Now is when you pretend to be offended. Morally outraged! The gall of me to accuse you of theft!"

"Give me the fucking scope back," he said, with his hand out.

"I'm not planning to jam you up, as long as you cooperate," I said. "I just want some information."

He looked skeptical.

"You a cop?"

"Nope."

"Then who the hell are you?"

"I'm a legal videographer. There have been some other crimes in the neighborhood where this scope was stolen, so I'm trying to find out who's responsible. Now I'm wondering if it was you. Ever vandalize a house and a car in Austin?"

"Fuck that, man. I have no idea what you're talking about."

"Then now's your time to come clean before you get dragged into something much bigger. A guy got shot and killed on that same street."

His face was pale now. It appeared he knew nothing about the incidents on Mañana Street.

"I just want my scope back," he said.

"You're not leaving me any choice but to call the cops."

"Hey, I'm the one that should call the cops," he said. "*You're* ripping *me* off. You're the one that'll get busted."

"Then call them. If it's not stolen, go ahead and call."

He reached for the scope, but I pulled it back.

"You can't just keep it," he said.

"*Au contraire*," I said. "You know the law that allows security guards to stop shoplifters with stolen merchandise? Same thing applies here."

He was getting frustrated. "I'm gonna fuck you up bad," he said.

"Is that a joke?"

"You're gonna find out."

Normally, I wouldn't assume that a man smaller than I am wasn't a threat, but this guy—well, he was too scrawny and thin to worry me.

I said, "I have trouble taking that seriously, seeing as how a light breeze might carry you away at any minute."

It turned out that he was, in fact, stupid.

He took a swing, but like most people who don't know how to fight, he didn't throw a clean jab or a hard, straight right. He threw an amateurish looping punch that gave me plenty of time to lean backwards. His right fist came close to my face, but it missed by an inch, and the momentum carried him around and to my right, as I stepped left.

He spun quickly toward me, but I was ready, and I snapped a fast left jab that caught him square in the nose. He yelped with surprise and pain. I had the scope cradled in my right arm like a football.

Blood was beginning to trickle from his nose when he said, "Give it back!"

I took a quick step forward and popped him again, directly in the nose for the second time. I couldn't get much power behind it, since my right hand was occupied, but I'm sure it stung.

"Damn it!" he said, cupping his nose with both hands. When he lowered them, his palms were red, and blood had dribbled down his chin and fallen onto his shirt.

"Just tell me where you got it," I said.

"Fuck off."

"That's one way to look at it," I said.

He edged closer, so I threw another jab, but he was just out of reach. It made him take a step back, and it appeared he'd had enough. My concern now was that other people in the parking lot might've noticed the fracas, and somebody might call the cops. I needed to wrap this up soon.

"Where did you get the scope?" I asked. "Answer that question and I won't call the cops."

"My mother gave it to me," he said.

"Really?" I said. "We're back to that again?"

He wiped his nose with the back of his hand, but it was continuing to flow.

I said, "Just tell the truth and I won't tell anybody what you told me, including the cops. You have my word as a former Girl Scout."

"Girl Scout? What the hell is wrong with you?"

"It's levity, Jake. Trying to put you at ease, so you'll cooperate. See, what you need to understand is that you don't have any other options. I've got copies of your Craigslist ad, our texts, and I have your license plate number. Now I also have the scope, and the serial number matches the stolen one. So let's stop screwing around. You're in possession of stolen property, which is a crime. Any chance you're on parole or probation right now? If you are, this will screw you up bad. Now's the time to take the break I'm giving you, before this gets out of hand."

It wasn't a bad little impromptu speech. Would it work?

He shook his head, as if wondering how the day had taken such a miserable turn. "I got it from a friend of mine," he said. I could tell he was disgusted with himself for cracking. "I don't know where he got it."

"You didn't know it was stolen?"

"Hell, no."

I didn't believe him, but that was unimportant, especially now that he was talking.

"Who's the friend?" I asked.

"Man, I can't tell you that."

"Sure you can. You have lips, a tongue, and vocal cords."

"I'm not gonna rat him out."

"Rat him out? You just said you don't know where he got it. Maybe he didn't know it was stolen, either. You wouldn't be ratting him out."

"All I know is he gave it to me to sell it, and we were gonna split the money."

"Where does he live?"

"Austin."

"You do, too, right?"

"Yeah."

"What's your friend's name?"

He took a long breath, trying to decide if he was going to adhere to that whole "honor among thieves" notion.

Finally he said, "Clancy."

I was elated that the name was familiar, but it took me a moment to place it. Then I remembered. The Conlees' yard guy was named Clancy.

24

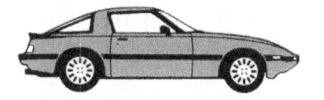

I TOOK 1604 OVER TO 281 and went north in heavy traffic. Passed through Bulverde, Spring Branch, and then Blanco, where I turned northeast on 165, which took me toward Henly.

I'd explored the theft of the scope to determine if Jeremy Olson had anything to do with it, and it appeared the answer was no. That was a dead end. I wouldn't strike Olson off the list yet, but I wasn't going to waste any more time on him unless something changed.

Now I had to focus on this guy Clancy. Jake had insisted he'd met Clancy only once, at a party in San Marcos, and Clancy had sold him the scope for $300. Jake knew it was worth a lot more than that, so Clancy followed him to an ATM and they made the deal. Jake said he never asked Clancy where he got it. He didn't have Clancy's phone number or know where he lived. I kept pushing, asking questions, until Jake wouldn't talk anymore. He turned for his car, and I had to either let him leave or physically restrain him. I let him leave.

Had to be the same Clancy—the Conlees' yard guy. I needed to know more about him. I couldn't do in-depth research until I got in front of my computer, but that didn't mean I couldn't be productive while driving. I made a hands-free call to Scarlett.

"Hey, there," she said.

"I have a question for you."

"What's up?"

"Do you happen to know the Conlees' yard guy?"

"Clancy? I've talked to him a couple of times. He always smiles and waves when he sees me."

"Wait a second. You mean he's friendly when a beautiful woman passes by? Imagine that."

"You're sweet. What's up with Clancy?"

"Can we speak confidentially?"

"Absolutely."

I quickly brought her up to speed about my conversation with Sandra Gray, her husband's stolen rifle scope, and the ad I found on Craigslist in San Antonio. I described my meeting with Jake and the way he had finally coughed up the name Clancy. I'm not sure why, but I left out the part about popping Jake in the nose. She didn't need to know about that.

Scarlett said, "I can't believe you figured all of that out so quickly. Or at all. That's pretty clever."

"True, when you consider the fact that I can barely tie my shoes."

"I wondered why you wore slip-ons. Where is the rifle scope now?"

"I have it."

"You didn't give it back?"

"Hell, no."

"Didn't this guy Jake throw a fit?"

"He wasn't happy, but what could he do? The scope was stolen, so he couldn't call the cops. He gave me a harsh glare, but I somehow survived it."

"You think Clancy stole the scope from Ed Gray?"

"I have no idea. You know if Clancy does the Grays' yard, too?"

"I don't think so," she said. "I've never seen him there."

"Do you know if he does any other yards on the street? Any of the Grays' neighbors?"

"I've only seen him at the Conlees' place."

"And you don't recall whether Clancy is his first or last name?"

"I just know he goes by Clancy."

I could call Evelyn Conlee or Carmen and get all of this information, but I didn't necessarily want them to know where the investigation was headed.

"Anything else you can tell me about him?"

"Like what?"

"Anything, really. Approximate age, height, shoe size, favorite color. Does he enjoy long walks on the beach?"

"He's maybe thirty years old. Average height, and thin. I've seen him sitting in his truck, eating lunch, so I guess he brings it with him. Honestly, from what little I know, he seems like a nice, hardworking guy, so I hope he isn't involved in all this mess somehow."

"Do you know his company name, if he has one?"

"I've seen it on his truck, but I can't remember what it is. Something cute. Oh, it's The Other Side of the Fence. Hang on a second."

Now I was approaching the huge, steep hill halfway between Blanco and Henly. The RX-7 climbed it with no problem, and even gained speed when I downshifted to fourth.

Scarlett said, "I'm looking at his website and his name is Clancy Finn. It looks like it's just him. No employees."

"That's helpful. Thanks."

"No prob. I'll see you in a little bit."

In Dripping Springs, I stopped at the HEB grocery store to grab a few things for dinner—a couple of prime ribeyes, potatoes, and the makings for a fresh tossed salad. Several bottles of white wine from various vintners. And dessert, of course.

I took Ranch Road 12 north, then went east on Hamilton Pool Road, then took Highway 71 to Bee Caves Road. I got home at about six o'clock, and although I knew I should clean up around the house and get ready for Scarlett's visit, I couldn't resist doing some quick background research on both Clancy Finn and this guy Jake.

Clancy Finn first. He was twenty-eight years old. A criminal background check showed that he'd been busted for trespassing nine years ago, but I couldn't find any additional details on that charge. Seven years ago, he'd written a bad check. That was the extent of it.

I saw his mugshot, and he did indeed look like a friendly guy, the type who might wave innocently at a pretty woman walking down the street. Appearances can be deceiving, of course. I surfed around for anything else I might find about him—say, somebody accusing him of theft, or vandalism, or a violent act. Zilch.

I was just about to run Jake's license plate when the doorbell rang. The clock read 6:31. I hopped up and opened the door, to find Scarlett looking magnificent in a sleeveless black-and-white sheath dress that ended mid-thigh.

"Wow," I said. "Just wow."

"Thanks," she said. "It's nice to put on a little makeup and get out of the house on occasion."

"Let me offer the profound appreciation of everyone outside your house," I said. I stepped aside and swung the door wide. "Come on in."

She did, and when I closed the door and turned around, she was right there waiting and stepped forward to give me a long kiss—the type of kiss that often derails other plans.

"There," she said. "That means the other night was officially *not* a one-night stand."

I said, "Maybe we should, uh, forget about dinner for the time being and—"

"Nope," she said. "Not yet."

"You sure? We could always—"

"How about a glass of wine?" she said.

"No, I'm fine. Oh, you mean for you! Sure. Why don't you take a seat and I'll proffer you a variety of vintages."

"That would be lovely. What's on the menu for tonight?" she asked as she gracefully propped herself on a bar stool.

"Ribeye steaks, baked potatoes, and a salad," I said, as I went around the end of the bar and into the galley kitchen.

"Yum."

"Nothing fancy."

"Perfect."

I showed her three bottles of white wine. She chose one and I poured her a glass. I was drinking bourbon on the rocks.

"I hope you don't mind that I didn't make the strawberry shortcake from scratch," I said. "I sort of ran out of time."

She laughed. "Were you really planning to make it from scratch?"

"No, but I was planning to pretend that I was. I've never made one in my life. Probably better that I don't start now."

"I'm sure it will be wonderful."

"How do you like your steak?"

"Medium rare."

"What do you like on your potato? Butter and sour cream?"

"Sure."

"Cheese?"

"No, thanks."

"Bacon bits?"

"Real bacon?"

"Yes, ma'am."

"Then yes."

"Chives?"

"You really have chives?"

"I do. I got some just in case. I can't even tell you what they are—green tubes of some sort—but I have some."

"Then by all means, yes, chives. I wouldn't want your effort to be wasted. They're related to onions, by the way. And scallions."

"Oh, okay," I said.

"You're not sure what a scallion is, are you?"

"Anything like a rapscallion?"

"*You're* the rapscallion."

"I'm related to an onion?"

"More likely a chive."

"Well, now I understand why I like baked potatoes so much," I said. "Speaking of which, why don't we adjourn to the back deck as I scorch us up some, uh, I mean, as I grill us a fantastic dinner?"

"Works for me. I'm starving."

25

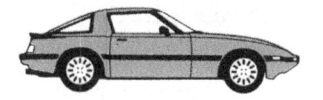

AFTER DINNER, WE STAYED ON the deck with our drinks and enjoyed a balmy evening. I could hear somebody running a lawn mower a few houses over, even though it was almost dark. The temperature was mild, the humidity was low, and somehow there weren't any mosquitoes buzzing about.

"That was excellent. Thank you. I can't believe I ate that entire steak."

"I hope you saved room for dessert," I said.

She looked at me. "Oh, I think so. I might even be able to eat some strawberry shortcake after that."

I could tell she was giddy from the wine.

"You're a bit of a minx, aren't you?" I said.

"Occasionally. With the right person."

"I like it."

"I'm glad." She was grinning, but it slowly faded and she said, "I wanted to mention something to you. Some news I need to share."

"What's up?"

"Remember that project I turned in on Wednesday morning? It was for a very prestigious design firm in San Francisco. They've been my client for about a year, and they keep sending me more and more work, which has been great. This latest job was packaging design for a family of car-care products."

"That sounds pretty cool," I said.

"It is, and fortunately, they loved it, and so did their client. Based on that, well, they offered me a job."

"Wow," I said. "In San Francisco?"

"Yep. I would have to relocate."

She waited for my reaction.

"Oh. That's amazing. I mean, it is, right? If that's what you want."

"It's very flattering, I can tell you that much. I would be the creative director. Not *a* creative director, *the* creative director. I would be leading the creative department of one of the top firms in the world."

"That's damn impressive," I said. "Congratulations."

"Of course, I haven't decided yet whether I'll take it. They wouldn't need me there for three months. That's when the current creative director is going to retire."

Of course, the subtext of the conversation—obvious to both of us, I think—was *What about us? Where are we headed? Should this budding relationship, if it even qualifies as one, be a factor in her decision?*

Or maybe she wasn't thinking about that. Maybe I was simply a hook-up, as the kids say nowadays. Truth was, I had no problem with that, because I honestly had no idea where I wanted this to go. Maybe nowhere. Right now, I was just letting it go wherever it went of its own accord. I couldn't decide if that was smart or stupid.

"Roy?"

I looked at her. I'd been lost in thought for a moment.

"We don't need to think about it right now. Or at all, I guess. I just wanted you to know the situation. I didn't mean to assume that—"

"No, that's fine," I said. "I'm glad you told me."

"I didn't mean to put a damper on the evening."

"I'm not dampered," I said. "Not even close to dampered. Are you dampered?"

"Now that I know you're not, neither am I."

"Good to know," I said. "So we're having a fine, undampered evening."

"We are. Let's continue that way."

"More wine?" I asked.

"I would love some, but if I do, I probably shouldn't drive."

"I would say that's a good option, wouldn't you?" I said.

"Not driving?" she said.

"Right."

"I *am* enjoying the wine," she said.

I grabbed the bottle and filled her glass.

"I guess that settles that," she said.

Thirty minutes later, after some pleasant conversation, she said, "Is it time for dessert?"

"The shortcake or—"

"You decide," she said.

"The way you look in that dress," I said. "This is an easy one."

Upstairs, we stood beside the bed and kissed until we both couldn't wait any longer.

She unbuttoned my shirt, swept it over my shoulders, and let it drop to the floor.

I reached for the zipper on the back of her dress and slowly pulled it down to the small of her back.

"You smell good," I whispered into her ear. "That perfume."

She lifted the strap off her left shoulder, then the right, and began to lower the dress.

Black panties. Black bra.

She stepped out of the dress and tossed it onto the foot of the bed. Her stomach was toned and tan. My breathing was shallow. My heart was beginning to beat heavily.

She reached for my belt, loosened the buckle, and popped the button of my jeans.

She reached for my zipper, but then she stopped. "Oh, wait. We forgot something."

"What?"

"I'll be right back."

She went downstairs and a moment later I heard the refrigerator opening.

The whipped cream.

I smiled. She hadn't been kidding. This was going to be fun.

It was.

Ninety minutes later, we came downstairs for strawberry shortcake. The clock on the microwave read 10:44. We sat on the leather couch in the living room and ate with spoons.

"It's very good," Scarlett said. "If you'd told me it was homemade, I would've believed you. These strawberries are amazing."

Now she was dressed in one of my longer T-shirts. She hadn't brought along any overnight clothes.

"I'm a master at choosing strawberries," I said. "I usually go for the red ones, because I'm wise that way."

"Did you find anything else out about Clancy?" she asked.

I set my empty bowl on the coffee table.

"His record is pretty clean," I said. "I didn't see any red flags."

"What was there?"

"Little stuff. A bad check. A trespassing charge."

"That's it?"

"Yep."

"I'm glad. I don't feel like I got fooled. Maybe he really is a nice guy. I would've been disappointed if he had a long rap sheet."

"A long rap sheet?" I said, grinning.

"Hey, I watch the cop shows. I know the lingo. Rap sheet. Do they talk that way?"

"Most of them just say 'record' or 'CCH.'"

"Which is what?"

"Complete criminal history. Keep in mind the site I used isn't one hundred percent accurate. Some charges fall through the cracks, especially older charges, or they never make it into their records to start with. But there are other sites I check, too, including city, county, and state sites, and when you put them all together, you can generally get a complete picture."

"It's kind of fascinating, to be honest," Scarlett said. "I never knew all of that was out there."

"Public records," I said. "If you get busted, people can find out. Then there are all the mugshot sites, which show you in all your glory. I should know."

"You should know?"

"Yep."

"About having your mugshot taken?"

"Uh huh. I've been arrested a couple of times."

"Seriously?"

"Yep."

"What for?"

I told her the story about breaking my boss's nose with a microphone stand after he called my female colleague a terrible name, and the other story about the time I'd gotten caught with some uppers I'd been using on a late-night stakeout.

"I'm proud of the first one, but not so much the second," I said.

"Have you, uh…"

"Have I used any since then? Nope. Not once. I took literally maybe ten pills over the course of a week. It was stupid. Haven't done it again."

"Good to hear. I'll have to find those mugshots someday. I bet you look like a total hunk."

"Oh, totally. And that orange jumpsuit is so fashionable."

"Okay, back to this other stuff. Did you look up that guy Jake?"

"Not yet."

"Ooh, we should do that!"

"Right now?"

"Sure. Why not? I'd like to see how you go about figuring these things out. Unless you'd rather do it in the morning."

"No, we can do it now. Let me get my laptop."

I went into my office, and when I returned, Scarlett was in the kitchen, rinsing the dishes we'd just used.

"You don't have to do that," I said.

"I don't mind." She even put them into the dishwasher. What a guest.

Then we both sat on the couch again and she leaned in close as I tapped on the keyboard.

"Since we don't know his name, we'll start by running the license plate," I said. "I use this site right here. They've got all kinds of criminal and civil records. Sometimes I can get it all done on this one site."

"Just for Texas?"

"No, the entire country. Well, most of it. For criminal records, for instance, they probably cover forty states. Same with property tax records, corporate records, and professional licenses. For license plates, it's only five states, but Texas is one of those, fortunately. Makes my job easier. So let's see what we've got."

I pulled the photo of Jake's license plate and entered the number into the search bar on the website. The result came back.

"Thomas Zachariah Buckley," I said.

"Is that Jake?" Scarlett asked me.

"Maybe. We'll try to find out. Now I'll go over to the criminal records page and run that name."

I did, and the result was...nothing.

"I didn't expect that," I said.

"He has no record?"

"Nope, which makes me think that Thomas Zachariah Buckley is not our buddy Jake. It's just a hunch, but if Jake hasn't been busted before, I'm Mother Teresa."

"So where do you go from here?"

"Let's google 'thomas zachariah buckley' and see what we get," I said, typing it in.

There were several hits. The seventh was a link to an obituary.

Thomas Zachariah Buckley, a native of San Antonio, had died four months earlier at the age of sixty-seven. He'd been a truck driver and a member of the Rotary Club. He left behind Marian, his wife of eleven years, and two sons, Barry and Jacob.

"I guess it has to be Barry," Scarlett said. Then, when I looked at her, she said, "Kidding. Duh."

"I'm embarrassed I fell for that."

"Score one for me," she said. "I'm surprised Jake used his real name."

"Some of these guys aren't real bright, as you might guess. Let's see what kind of citizen ol' Jake is."

I returned to the site that offered criminal background checks and entered the name "jacob buckley."

As I typed, I said, "I imagine we'll have to weed through several

Jacob Buckleys, since we don't have his middle name or date of birth. But we'll probably be able to narrow it down by location and a rough estimate of his age. I'm choosing records from Texas only, and that will help."

The resulting hits gave records for three Jacob Buckleys. One of them was currently forty-eight years old, so we ruled him out. The second one was nineteen and appeared to live in North Texas, so we struck him, too. The third Jacob Buckley was the right age—twenty-three—and his middle name was Zachariah, just like his dad.

"That was easy," Scarlett said.

"I know, right? My job is a total cakewalk."

"Seems that way. Why do they even pay you?"

"Excellent question. But let's set that aside for later and review Jacob Zachariah's criminal pedigree, shall we?"

"Let's."

There were several separate records for Jacob Zachariah Buckley from different arresting agencies, so I started with the Texas Department of Public Safety.

"Possession of stolen property," I said. "There's a shocker. That was three years ago."

"Possession of marijuana," Scarlett said, reading the next one down.

I scrolled farther.

A speeding ticket that turned into a warrant when he ignored it.

Another ticket for failure to maintain financial responsibility, also known as not having liability insurance.

Nothing too serious. Nothing violent.

I jumped over to a newspaper archive website and searched his name. I saw an article with the headline *Teens Arrested On Water Tower*. Five years ago, Jake Buckley and some of his pals had crawled under a fence and climbed a water tower on a Saturday night in the town of Lockhart, just outside Austin. I'm guessing there was booze or pot involved, but the article didn't mention it.

"Bored teenagers," Scarlett said. "I did that once—climbed a water tower. It wasn't a real tall one, but the view was still amazing. I was maybe sixteen."

"I tried once, but a friend of mine was climbing the ladder ahead of me and he froze. The height got to him. So we had to talk him back down."

"In hindsight, it's pretty dumb. I'm surprised we don't hear about drunk kids falling off water towers more often. How come that arrest wasn't listed on the other site?"

"The charges probably got dropped," I said.

There was another article about Jacob Buckley making the all-district soccer team when he played for Reagan High School.

I scrolled lower and saw an article about the stolen property charge. The second paragraph mentioned that two people had been arrested—Jacob Buckley and his stepbrother, Brett Murtaugh.

Imagine that.

26

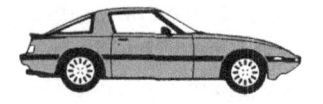

AT EIGHT O'CLOCK THE NEXT morning, after Scarlett had gone home, I sat on the deck again with a mug of coffee and contemplated what we'd learned.

Clancy Finn.

Jacob Buckley.

Brett Murtaugh.

Had Finn really sold the stolen scope to Buckley, or had Buckley made that up on the fly? How did he know Finn? Was there really a party in San Marcos? How did Brett Murtaugh fit in? Murtaugh was Buckley's stepbrother and Franco Keller's school classmate.

Scarlett had pointed out last night that it was interesting that Brett and Paul Murtaugh had not been mentioned in Thomas Buckley's obituary, considering that they were his stepsons. I was impressed that she'd picked up on that. I speculated that Thomas wasn't real tight with his second wife's two boys.

Did any of this have anything to do with the crimes at the Conlee house?

I was feeling physically rested but mentally restless. Impatient. At times like this, I always had to avoid the temptation to do something rash in an attempt to make progress.

On this particular occasion, I didn't have to resort to an impulsive act.

My phone rang and I saw that it was Lynann Chukwueze calling.

"This can't be good," I answered. "You calling on a Saturday morning."

"How can you get into so much trouble in one day?" she asked.

"Um, what did I do?"

"That's what I'm calling to find out. Where you were yesterday afternoon at about three o'clock."

"That's very specific," I said.

"Don't bullshit me, Roy. You know I already know the answer."

I couldn't imagine what had happened for her to know where I was, but the best approach with Lynann is always to shoot straight.

"I was in San Antonio meeting a guy named Jake about a rifle scope he advertised on Craigslist. The scope is worth about nine grand and I suspected it had been stolen from Ed Gray's truck. Turned out the guy's name is Jacob Buckley, and he is Brett Murtaugh's stepbrother. He was unable to withstand my withering interrogation, and he quickly divulged some critical information—if he wasn't lying his ass off."

"What kind of information?"

"He said he got the scope from someone named Clancy, which also happens to be the name of the Conlees' yard guy."

"Were you planning to share any of this with me?"

"Absolutely. Yes. Of course. You know me. I'm the sharing type."

"When?"

"I've always been that way."

"No, when were you planning to share it with me?"

"I was going to call you this morning. I didn't get back from San Antonio until about six last night, and I didn't want to disturb your evening. I'm thoughtful that way."

"Jacob Buckley is dead, Roy."

That I hadn't expected.

"What happened?" I said. I was hoping he'd gotten hit by a bus or slipped in the bathtub.

"Where is the scope right now?" she asked.

"I have it."

"You need to come in and talk to me again," she said. "Like right now. And bring the scope with you."

"Last night we found him shot in the head and dumped in Barton Creek," she said.

We were in the same interview room. It was much quieter in the office today, it being a weekend.

"That's terrible," I said. "Barton Creek is usually so pristine."

She gave me a look. "That was pretty low, Roy."

"Yeah, you're right. I'm just in a mood."

"Poor baby," she said. "You gonna be okay?"

"It's possible Jacob Buckley killed Norman Conlee, or that he was somehow involved, so I'm going to hold my remorse until we know for sure. Even if he wasn't involved in that, he was probably doing something stupid and it got him killed. That's the type of guy he was."

"Man, Roy, you've gotten jaded."

That remark stung a little.

"I'll work on it," I said. "Any idea who shot him?"

"If I knew, I wouldn't be talking to you."

"You got any leads? Any suspects? Any persons of interest?"

"Just you," she said.

"In that case, you're in bad shape, because I didn't do it."

"Tell me about yesterday afternoon."

I spent the next ten minutes updating her on everything I'd learned since I'd given my statement to her yesterday morning. I told her about talking with Sandra Gray about her husband's stolen scope, then finding the ad on Craigslist and arranging a meeting with Jacob Buckley in San Antonio.

She said, "Now walk me through your conversation word for word, as best you can remember."

"I can do better than that," I said. "I recorded it all on video. I was wearing a hat with a camera built in."

She laughed. "You are so ridiculous. A hat with a camera?"

"But it works," I said.

"I guess it does."

"There was, uh, a little bit of violence," I said. "He took a swing at me and I had to pop him a couple of times."

Now she was shaking her head. "Again? One of these days, that's going to catch up with you."

"Maybe so, but not with this guy."

"He could've been carrying."

"I was watching for that," I said.

"Let's see the video," she said.

I'd brought along my laptop for that purpose, so I played it for her. She watched it without expression, then asked me to play it a second time. When we were done, she asked me to email that video to her, so I did that, too.

Then she said, "I hate to point out the obvious, but if you'd told me all of this yesterday, after it happened, Jacob Buckley might still be alive."

"How so?"

"I probably would've tried to track him down and call him in for an interview. Whatever happened last night—that might've been avoided."

I knew a lot of city, county, state, and even federal investigators, and Lynann was right near the top of the list of those I respected most, but she was starting to piss me off.

"You're saying that if I'd called you last night at about, oh, six or seven o'clock, about a stolen rifle scope that might have nothing to do with Norman Conlee's murder, you would have immediately jumped on that?"

She started to answer, but took a deep breath instead. Then she said, "I need you to share important information when you have it. That's what I'm asking."

"What's up with those cell-phone records for Franco Keller and Brett Murtaugh?" I asked.

"What about them?"

"You get those back yet?"

"You need to get past the idea that this is a two-way street," she said. "You know it can't work like that, and that's just the way it is."

I was getting a little heated, but I decided it was time to ease the tension, especially since I was implying, during a recorded interview, that she might normally share information with me.

"You're right. I apologize. What else do you need to know?"

"Did you ever see Jacob Buckley again after he left the Target parking lot?"

"I did not."

"No further contact?"

"Nope."

"No texts, no phone calls?"

"Nothing."

"Tell me what you did after that meeting," she said.

It didn't matter that she knew me and trusted me. She couldn't give me any special favors. She had to get my alibi, just as if she didn't know me at all.

"I drove home, but I stopped at HEB in Dripping Springs along the way."

"Did you go anywhere after that?"

"I did not."

"You stayed home all night?"

"Sure did. What time was he killed?"

"Were you all by yourself?" she said.

"No, I had someone over for dinner."

"Who was that?"

I paused. "I'd rather not drag her into this right now, but if you still need her name later, I'll give it to you. Is that fair?"

"We'll see. What time did she leave?"

"Is that really important?" I asked.

"Well, that's an answer in itself. Come on, Roy. I'm not going to judge you." Then she added, "And I'm certainly not going to tell anyone."

She was alluding to Mia, of course. If she had the occasion to talk to Mia anytime soon—which wasn't likely—she wouldn't tell her that I'd had an overnight guest. Why would I care about that, though, right? I mean, it had been three months.

"She left at seven o'clock this morning," I said.

Lynann kept it professional. No wisecrack. No raised eyebrow. No smirk.

She simply said, "I might need to talk to her, but we'll wait on that."

"Thank you."

"I want her name now, though," she said. "That's the compromise."

I figured that was fair. "Scarlett Bishop. She lives down the street from the Conlees."

She wrote down Scarlett's name and said, "Anything else you need to tell me?"

"I feel like we're not excited enough about Jake Buckley and Brett Murtaugh being stepbrothers. That ties everything together."

"Let's hear why you think that," she said.

"Okay, well, we have this group of punks who are all connected—Franco Keller, Brett Murtaugh, and Jacob Buckley. Franco somehow hooks up with Olivia, and so now he's rubbing elbows with the Conlees. The two of them—Franco and Olivia—figure out that Olivia could inherit the entire Conlee estate, assuming Norman dies before Evelyn does. So they recruit Murtaugh or Buckley or both of them to commit the vandalism and the eventual shooting. It's also possible that Franco acted alone, and Olivia knew nothing about it."

I stopped, but she still didn't say anything.

"I don't know how—or if—Clancy Finn fits in," I said. "Maybe Jacob Buckley just threw Finn's name out there to distract me. Or maybe Finn is involved somehow. The only hitch in the plan is that Evelyn could be around for many more years. If Franco and Olivia are expecting to get everything, they might have to wait a long time. That, or they're planning to do something to her, too. But that would be so blatantly obvious, they can't possibly be that stupid. Or maybe they can. Regardless, it seems like somebody should warn Evelyn."

Lynann finally said, "We've spoken to her in broad terms about a wide range of possibilities. Yesterday, in fact. She knows she needs to be careful."

I took that to mean that Lynann had reached all of the same conclusions I'd just described, or close.

"Glad to hear it," I said.

"Anything else you want to add?"

"Not that I can think of."

"Do you have any evidence or information you haven't shared with me?"

"Such as what?"

She actually smiled. "Well, how would I know, Roy, if you haven't shared it with me?"

"I can't prove my theory, if that's what you're asking. Not yet. But I'm a tenacious bastard. Just ask anyone."

"I don't have to ask," she said.

She got up and turned the camera off, then sat back down.

I said, "I didn't mean to get testy earlier."

"Don't worry about it."

"How did you connect Buckley to me?"

"We got location data for his cell phone, saw that he'd stopped in that parking lot, then found video from a camera. And there you were. It wasn't real difficult."

"Where did he go that night?" I asked.

She shook her head no on that one.

"I've got something to share with you," I said.

"I'm listening," Lynann said.

"Maybe you already know it, but Olivia Reed is a call girl."

I could see that I'd finally told Lynann new information.

"Where'd you get this?" she asked.

"Evelyn told me the other day," I said. "Olivia's affair with that state senator wasn't an affair, it was business. And I have recently confirmed directly with a john that Olivia is still in that line of work. I promised to keep the john's name out of it, but I can tell you that this isn't a hunch or a guess, it's one hundred percent fact. The going rate is one thousand bucks an hour."

"Per *hour*?" Lynann said.

"Yes, ma'am."

She whistled, then glared at me. "You've had two days to tell me this."

"Honestly, I wasn't sure it was relevant."

"But, see, it might explain why Franco came after you in the driveway. It's possible he was trying to stop you from finding that out, rather than finding out he had anything to do with shooting Norman. In other words, it gives him a different motive for wanting to punch you in the face."

She was right, of course. I waited patiently. She had something else to say.

"We got those cell records you keep yammering about, and Murtaugh was nowhere near the Conlee house during any of the incidents. Doesn't mean he wasn't there. He's street smart and would know to leave his phone at home or turn it off. But I'd call it a big strike one. Same thing with texts. He and Franco texted quite a bit, but none of it was significant. Maybe they used burner phones. Or maybe they had nothing to do with any of it."

"Okay, but why did Murtaugh threaten me?" I said. "It makes no sense."

"Well, again, you punched Franco Keller in the throat, and maybe that was enough for him to send Murtaugh after you. I've seen a lot worse over a lot less. Or maybe Franco is involved in the shooting, but Murtaugh is simply hired muscle. He might not know anything about it."

I had to concede that those were possibilities.

She added, "On the other hand, there's one other little detail that gives this theory some legs."

I could tell from her expression that something big was coming.

"Yeah?"

"Yesterday when I talked to Evelyn Conlee, she shared more information about her health. She has a disease called corticobasal degeneration, which is terminal. Her doctors say she has about a year to live."

27

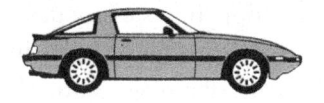

AS I DROVE, I CONTEMPLATED what I'd just learned.

Evelyn Conlee's diagnosis was sad and tragic, but it fit well into my theory.

If Olivia wanted the entire Conlee estate, all she had to do was wait. It certainly magnified her motive, or Franco's motive, acting on her behalf, whether she knew it or not. Unfortunately, so far I had zero evidence to support my theory that Franco—or he and Olivia working together—had orchestrated the vandalism as a means to cover up the shooting to come later.

What now?

Franco Keller wouldn't talk.

Neither would Olivia Reed.

Brett Murtaugh would just as soon take a hunting knife to my soft underbelly.

Jake Buckley had talked, but it was difficult to know what was true and what was a lie, and now he couldn't clarify.

Should I take a run at Clancy Finn? Tempting, but my gut said no. I didn't think he was really involved, and if he was, I wanted to hang on to the element of surprise for a bit longer. Jake Buckley damn sure wouldn't tell Clancy he'd given me his name. Clancy, for now, would have no idea he had been implicated.

Who did that leave?

There had to be some way to approach this from a new angle.

Of course there was.

But I waited twenty-four hours out of respect for the grieving.

Barry Buckley, Jake's younger brother, led a wide-open life on social media—Instagram, Twitter, Tiktok, Facebook, and a few other platforms. Privacy didn't appear to be a big concern. You could scroll through his posts and learn just about everything, and he posted multiple times every day.

He was born in Austin, went to Reagan High, where he had played on the lacrosse team. Barry had then attended Austin Community College for some period of time, but did not graduate. I guessed he was maybe twenty-one or twenty-two years old.

He had a pretty girlfriend named Maxxinne, which couldn't possibly be her real name, could it? They'd been dating a little over one year, because he mentioned it on the anniversary of their first date. They were a cute couple.

He worked at an auto parts store on Slaughter Lane in South Austin. He was currently restoring a 1977 Ford Bronco he'd bought six months ago. The body was in decent shape, but the engine needed a lot of work. At least he had it running, after rebuilding the engine.

He worked out. Marched for various causes. Was always smiling and laughing and having fun with a tight circle of friends.

In short, he seemed nothing like his brother Jacob.

He was easy enough to find, because his latest post on Facebook was just 37 minutes earlier: "A customer just told me his car was overheating even though he'd had the radiator replaced. I said it might be a bad thermostat, and he said, no, the air conditioner was working fine." Several people laughed about that one.

So he was at work, even though his brother had been killed just two nights earlier. And he hadn't said a word about it in his posts. That told me a lot about their relationship.

I wondered if I should give it another day or two. I didn't want to be a ghoul. Ah, screw it.

I parked the RX-7 in front of the parts store and walked inside at 10:56 on Sunday morning. Barry Buckley had come around the counter and I could tell he was looking past me, at my car. The store was otherwise empty.

Barry Buckley said, "Cool ride, man. What year is it?"

"Eighty-two."

"Nice. Still got the 12A in it?"

"Yep. You know these cars?"

"A little bit. They're classic nowadays. How long have you had it?"

"Just a couple of months."

"You like it?"

This was going well.

"Love it. Obviously it's pretty slow by today's standards, but it's so much fun to drive."

"Hard to find anyone to work on them, though, so be ready for that. Or learn to work on it yourself."

"Will do," I said. "You're Barry, right? I cleverly picked that up from your nametag."

"That's me. What can I help you with today?"

I was glad there were no customers in the store right now, and if any other employees were here, they were in the back.

"My name is Roy Ballard," I said sticking out my hand. He shook it. "I'm a legal videographer and insurance companies hire me to get evidence of fraud. That's my specialty. And I'm working on a case right now that, well, long story short, I met your brother on Friday afternoon."

Barry's easy smile slowly faded. "You met Jake?"

"I did, and want to say I'm very sorry for your loss."

"Thank you. What did he do?"

"Pardon?"

"If you're working a fraud case and you met my brother, I figure he did something stupid."

"Uh, well, he did, but it might not even be connected to the fraud case. You mind if I ask you some questions?"

"Tell me what he did first."

"Fair enough. He was in possession of a stolen rifle scope."

"Oh. Okay. I mean, theft sucks, but that doesn't seem like a huge deal."

"Well, it was worth about nine thousand dollars, so that makes it a state jail felony, and with your brother's record, he could've served up to ten years and a fine of ten grand."

"There are rifle scopes that cost nine thousand dollars? That's crazy. Not that I'm excusing what he did. He was always in and out of trouble. Do you work with the cops or what? Do you know who killed him?"

"I'm afraid I don't, but that's one of the reasons I wanted to ask a few questions. You mind?"

"So you're sort of a private investigator?"

"Usually I'm the guy who follows people around with a camera to prove they aren't really injured. Or sometimes they are. Other times, the case turns into something more complicated, and that's what happened here."

"So how was Jake involved?"

I described the vandalism and subsequent shooting at the Conlee house, and how the scope had been stolen on the same street earlier. By the time I was done, Barry had a nauseated expression.

"Are you saying Jake had something to do with all of that?"

"Again, I just don't know. Does that sound like something he'd do?"

"Not really. He wouldn't just vandalize something for the thrill of it, or to be spiteful. That's not the way he was. He had problems, but deep down, he was a decent guy."

I'd learned long ago that you can't shy away from awkward or intrusive questions.

"What were his problems?" I asked.

"Mostly drugs," Barry said. "I tried to help him over the years, and so did Dad, but it never worked. If he killed somebody, man—I don't even want to think about that."

"On Thursday afternoon, a man came to see me at my house and made some vague threats, trying to scare me off the case. I later identified him as Brett Murtaugh."

"Oh, Jeez."

"What can you tell me about him?"

"I haven't seen him in three or four years. That's by choice."

"You don't get along?"

He paused for a moment, then said, "You know what? Let's go in the back and get some coffee."

"He was terrible," Barry said. "A sadist. He took a lot of pleasure in tormenting me when we were kids. He did it to Jake, too, to some degree, but Jake sort of looked up to him—who the hell knows why?—and Brett could sense that, I think, so he didn't hassle him as much."

We were seated at a small, round table in a windowless break room. On the way in here, we had encountered another employee, Tony, and Barry had asked him to watch the front for a few minutes.

"Brett is older than you both?"

"Three years older than me and two years older than Jake."

"What about Brett's brother Paul?"

"He was old enough that he had his own apartment, so he never lived with us. I hardly knew him."

"How old were you when your dad and Marian got married?"

"I think I was eleven."

"So Brett was about fourteen?"

"Right. I was much smaller than he was, so I was an easy target. Brett seriously didn't have an ounce of kindness in him. Everything he did was about inflicting pain and misery and stealing and lying. I caught him stealing from my dad's wallet once."

"That's pretty low."

"There were times when I prayed that Brett would just die. I would seriously fantasize about him getting hit by a car or something. The worst part was seeing Jake slowly change because of Brett. I mean, Jake was a fairly normal kid until Brett showed up. But then he became more withdrawn and angry and I just felt like we kind of lost him slowly over the years."

It was obvious he was still carrying a lot of resentment, and I felt a bit guilty for forcing him to dredge it all up.

"Do you know if Jake stayed in touch with Brett?"

"He did, yeah, and that's one reason I hadn't talked to Jake much in the last couple of years. I hate to say it, but I finally got tired of all the lies and the excuses. Ever heard that phrase 'Not my circus, not my monkeys'? When you realize trying to help is doing nothing but stressing you out, that's when you have to stop. But I tried hard for a lot of years, I really did."

"Sounds like you were a pretty good brother."

"I don't know about that. There were times when I felt like I'd abandoned him, and now—well, I feel really guilty, because he's dead."

"I don't know if it helps, but I've known a lot of people like Jake, and you can't help them until they're ready for help. From what I saw on Friday afternoon, he wasn't ready. I realize I'm a total stranger, but I can assure you that you have nothing to feel guilty about."

Barry looked down at his clasped hands on the table. "I appreciate that."

I gave it a moment, then asked, "Can you picture Brett shooting a man if someone paid him to do it?"

Barry looked up now. "Oh, absolutely. In a heartbeat. Do you think he did it?"

He seemed somewhat excited at the prospect of Brett getting nailed for murder.

"I just don't know, but I'm hoping to find out. Do you know Franco Keller?"

"Yeah, one of Brett's buddies in high school. Kind of an asshole. Rich kid. I don't know why he hung out with Brett, unless Brett was selling him drugs."

"You know a guy named Clancy Finn?"

"Never heard of him. Who is he?"

"A guy who does landscaping on the street where the scope was stolen. I don't think he was involved, but Jake told me he got the scope from Clancy. I think he was trying to throw me off the real trail."

I asked some other questions, but none of it led anywhere useful.

When I was done, I thanked him for his help.

"No problem, man. Hey, enjoy that RX-7."

"Will do." Then I said, "Ever driven one?"

"Never had the chance."

"Want to drive mine?"

His face lit up. "That would be a blast, and I still have a few minutes left on my break."

So we went out for a quick spin, and he was smiling when we pulled back into the parking lot.

I went home and took a nap.

When I woke, a text had arrived from Scarlett. *Hey there. Just wanted to say I really enjoyed Friday night. And yesterday morning.*

Not as much as I did, I replied.

Even though we hadn't known each other for long, I found myself somewhat melancholy at the idea she might move away.

See you again soon? she asked.

Absolutely, I replied. *Later this week?*

She sent a thumbs-up.

Then I opened the GPS tracker app to see if Franco had gone anywhere interesting lately. The gym once. A liquor store. A gas station. Several restaurants. And Albert Strauss's house again last night.

What the hell?

28

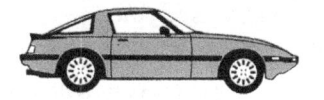

FOR A MOMENT, I THOUGHT I must be mistaken, or that the app was somehow screwing up and showing me data from earlier in the week.

I believed Strauss when he said he wouldn't be seeing Olivia anymore. I still believed him. So what was going on?

I noticed that Franco's car didn't stop for a moment, then leave and come back later, as it had last time. This time it stayed there for eleven minutes, then left and did not return.

Eleven minutes. No way was that enough time for a "date" with Olivia, even if Strauss was a hasty client.

I was baffled, so I decided to give Strauss a call. I was prepared to leave a voicemail, but he answered.

"It's Roy Ballard," I said. "How are you this afternoon?"

"Just fine," Strauss said, sounding anything but fine.

I hadn't really planned what to say, so there was a pause. Then I finally said, "I'm not trying to intrude into your life, and as I said on Thursday, it doesn't really matter to me what takes place between two consenting adults, but I'm...wondering if you changed your mind."

"About what?"

"About seeing Olivia Reed."

He didn't answer.

"Mr. Strauss?"

"Yes."

"Is there anything you want to tell me?"

I could hear movement on the other end, as if he were pacing.

"How do you know these things? How do you know who comes to my house?"

"That's my job," I said. "I'm not going to share my tactics."

Mostly because I don't have the legal authority to put a GPS tracker on anyone's car.

"Did you follow Franco? Is that how you do it?"

So now I knew it was Franco, not Olivia, who had come to his house.

"Mr. Strauss, let's focus on what's important. Why did Franco come to see you?"

"I don't know what to do," he said.

"Maybe I can help you," I said. "What's going on?"

"This needs to stay between us," he said. "No matter what. Can you promise me that?"

"Assuming you aren't about to confess to murder or spying against our country, yeah, I can do that," I said.

"You cannot tell the police. You can't tell anyone. I will deny I ever said it."

At this point, I was pretty sure I knew what he was going to reveal, so I was willing to make that commitment. "I give you my word I won't tell anyone, unless at some point you give me permission to tell someone."

Another long silence.

"Are you recording this call?" he asked.

"Absolutely not."

"It would be illegal to record me without my consent."

That wasn't true, but I said, "I'm not recording the call. You'll have to take my word for that. Or I can come talk to you in person."

"No. I trust you."

I waited patiently.

Then he said, "He's blackmailing me."

That was exactly what I had suspected. It was an old scam, but it was still popular because it worked.

"Tell me what's happening," I said. "Give me the details."

"She carries a purse, which, I don't know why, but that seemed odd to me. A woman who does what she does for a living—I just didn't expect her to carry a purse. Not when she comes to someone's house. I don't know if that's ridiculous or not. I guess she needs a place for her things, like anybody else. But in hindsight, now I realize that's where the camera was hidden. She set it on the dresser and...it caught everything."

"Franco showed you video?"

"He did, yes."

"And how much money does he want?"

"Fifty thousand dollars."

That was a lot of money, but I muted my reaction. The poor guy was already dispirited enough.

"Is the video clear?"

"What do you mean?"

"Is the quality good? Are you recognizable?"

"Very much so. She isn't, though. You can tell she intentionally kept her face obstructed or kept her back to the camera."

"Is there anything in the video that, uh, would cause undue embarrassment?"

"You mean beyond the fact that I paid a woman for sex and she was perhaps one-third my age? No, other than that, it would not be embarrassing at all."

I couldn't blame him for being sarcastic and ill-tempered. He felt trapped and desperate.

"How did you leave it with Franco?"

"How could I leave it? I said I would pay him."

"Are you planning to actually do that?"

"I don't know. I'm not naïve enough to think he won't come back for more, again and again, until I have nothing left to give. Do you have other options to suggest?"

I didn't have extensive experience with blackmail or extortion. I could think of only a couple of legal ways to address the situation.

"You could talk to the police—unofficially—and see what they suggest."

"No. I can't. He'll post the video on YouTube and a bunch of other sites. That's what he said—the moment I go to the police, the video gets shared."

"But he wouldn't have to know you talked to them. Or you could hire an attorney to handle that conversation for you, without revealing who you are—at least initially."

"I'm not willing to take that risk. He might find out somehow."

"You understand he's counting on you to be fearful like that."

"Well, yes, because it works! I *am* fearful."

"Do you believe he'll release the video?"

"Of course! Why wouldn't he?"

"Because if he posts the video, he'll never see a cent from you. He loses all his power over you if he posts it."

"I know how it works. Even if he doesn't post it, what could the police do? I can't prove Franco did anything. It's my word against his. Plus, I would have to confess to everything. It's humiliating."

"Trust me, they've heard a lot worse. So much worse. Something like this, to your average detective, would be downright mundane. Just another day at the office."

"Out of the question. I'm not contacting the police. My understanding is that if I report it, it will all be public record. They would create a report, and if they ever managed to arrest Franco, there would be a probable cause affidavit and a lot of other documents that anyone can access."

"You've really looked into this," I said.

"I was up all night. If I go to the police, I might as well let him release the video, because the end result would be the same."

"Not if your lawyer talks to them for you."

"I'm not doing it."

I don't know why I was trying to help him. It made no difference to me what he decided to do. If he were a close friend or family member, I might be willing to try some tactics that would be a bit questionable from a legal standpoint.

"Maybe I should just pack my things and move to Alaska," he said. "Or Europe."

"When are you supposed to give him the money?"

"He gave me three days."

"All I can suggest at this point is that you try to record any phone calls or in-person conversations you have with him. If you can gather enough evidence to prove what he's doing, that should be enough to make him stop before you ever have to go to the cops. After all, he's committing a serious felony. They would go after him pretty hard for that, and Olivia, too."

I had a pretty good idea how I might react if I were in a similar situation. I'd convince the blackmailer that I'd inflict serious physical harm if he continued. Unfortunately, a guy like Albert Strauss could never pull it off. He couldn't come across as threatening. That meant the poor son of a bitch had no way out.

"I need time to think," he said. "This is terrible. I was so stupid."

29

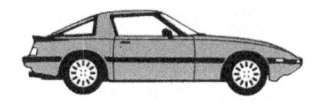

DESPITE MY PROMISE TO KEEP the information confidential, I badly wanted to tell Lynann Chukwueze what I'd learned. If Franco and Olivia blackmailed one person, might they have blackmailed others? What if one of those victims had learned where Olivia lived?

I sat on my living room couch with a notepad and once again tried to create an updated list of suspects and persons of interest, hoping it would clear my head and give me some inspiration as to how to proceed.

Franco Keller.
Olivia Reed.
Brett Murtaugh.
Jacob Buckley.
Clancy Finn.
Jeremy Olson.

Those were the top suspects, but I had to add a couple more names, just like last time.

Evelyn Conlee.
Carmen Romero.
Eight people. Ridiculous.

Surely there had to be a simple answer. Most crimes are not very complicated. Most are not planned well. Most criminals are incompetent and leave a trail of clues and evidence. If they somehow don't, it's usually dumb luck, or because they commit the crime at random.

What was I missing?

Or what had I added that needed to be subtracted?

What had I taken for granted that needed to be viewed through fresh eyes? I could think of only one thing.

I'd been operating under the assumption that the vandalism was a ploy to make it appear the shooting was random, that Norman went out to investigate another incident.

What if that was wrong?

What if Norman really had surprised the vandal, who had no intention of shooting anyone? What if there had been no devious plan to kill him?

Or, to muddy the waters even further, what if the vandalism and the shooting were totally unrelated and committed by different people?

I heard car doors, greetings, and laughter at the house next door. Friends getting together for dinner and drinks. No worries.

I put the pad down and let it go for the rest of the night.

I was woken at 4:47 a.m., but I wasn't sure by what. A noise again? A vibration? A change in air pressure? A scorpion crawling along my leg? For some reason, it felt different this time than it had when I'd woken up early Friday morning.

Once you've gotten into a shootout with a killer who comes for you in the middle of the night—as I had with Nathaniel Tate—it becomes more and more difficult to dismiss those awakenings and go back to sleep. As it should. Even when you know it's nothing, you wake completely and stay that way for an hour or two.

I eased out of bed and retrieved my pistol-grip shotgun from the second drawer of my dresser, where it always lay in wait underneath a stack of sweaters. Then I quickly pulled on a pair of shorts and a dark T-shirt.

I returned to the bed and sat down, the shotgun nearby on the mattress, and opened the security-camera app on my phone. Checked the front-door camera first and saw nothing out of the ordinary, meaning it had caught several clips of deer crossing the yard, and a few clips of branches blowing in the breeze, but mostly a lot of clips of insects flying directly in front of it. The bugs were always annoying, but there wasn't any practical way to prevent them from being attracted to the infrared light.

Then I checked the back-door camera and, other than insects, there were only two clips. One was from three hours earlier—a fat possum nosing around on the deck, looking for a free meal, and ambling away disappointed.

The second was from just six minutes earlier, when the motion-activated light on the back porch had come on—but I couldn't see what had triggered it. I'd set the sensitivity fairly low on that light, so it wouldn't be turning on all the time. It would take something larger than a possum to set it off.

The problem was the range of the light's sensor extended farther into the backyard than the camera could see. Deer jumped the four-foot-tall chain-link fence almost every night, which was why I hadn't placed another camera in the yard itself. Right now I was wishing I'd been willing to put up with that inconvenience. Had a deer triggered the light?

I was reassured by the fact that my alarm system would've alerted me if anyone had tried to breach a door or a window.

I rose from the bed and moved to the window. From here, I could peer down into the backyard and see places the camera couldn't see.

There were a lot of shadows cast by a nearly full moon. Lots of places for a person to stand motionless and wait.

I stared for a long time and let my eyes adjust. I didn't see any deer. The deer triggered the light often enough that it no longer spooked them, so it didn't cause them to run away. But there were a few corners of the yard I couldn't see from here, which could explain why I wasn't seeing a deer, or it could've hopped back over the fence and moseyed along.

Then I saw something that puzzled me at first. Deep in a clump of cedar trees, there was a sudden light. No, not a light. More like a glow. That was the best way to describe it. It lingered for maybe three seconds, then disappeared.

It hadn't been my imagination.

Then I realized what I'd seen. A cell phone in a pocket, the light from the screen muffled, but still showing through the fabric. The person carrying it might not have even been aware that the phone had lighted up.

If it was really a phone.

I watched and waited, hoping to see it again.

By now, my eyes had adjusted and I was fairly certain I could make out a person standing in the trees.

I could imagine what had happened. The person had planned to try the knob on my back door, but the motion-activated light had spooked him. He'd made a run for the trees. Now he was trying to decide what he should do next. Ironically enough, so was I. But I knew I didn't have much time.

I should call 911. Let the sheriff's office handle it. Right? Not a chance. It would probably take a deputy ten or fifteen minutes to get here, unless one just happened to be nearby.

I grabbed the shotgun and quickly descended the stairs. There, I waited near the front door with the app open, watching both the back and front cameras. If the person came to the back door or passed in front of the house, which was the direct route out of the neighborhood, I would see him. If he went toward the lake—meaning he wouldn't pass in front of the house—I would not see him. But he had to have gotten here in a vehicle, and I doubted he'd parked in that direction.

Three minutes passed. Slowly.

I began to question myself. Had I really seen anything? That light—the glow of the cell phone—probably had a reasonable explanation. Maybe I'd moved slightly and suddenly seen a reflection off the window. Or it had been moonlight filtering through the trees and hitting the ground. Or it had been a lightning bug. Or a reflection from an airplane overhead.

Didn't matter now. I was in it until I knew for sure. I'd sit here until dawn if that's what it took.

It crossed my mind that the person—if there had been one—could've hopped the fence at the rear of the lot and cut through the neighbor's property. They could've slipped away and avoided both cameras.

Five more minutes passed.

If there really was a person in my yard, he had to be wondering whether the lights had been activated by motion or by me flipping a switch.

I moved from my spot near the front door to the couch. Might as well get comfortable. Now it had been nearly ten minutes since I'd been upstairs.

Would a person attempting to ambush me have the self-discipline to wait longer than ten minutes? I doubted it.

Two more minutes passed, and the front-porch camera showed a dark figure moving from right to left on the far side of the street, heading out of the neighborhood. He was walking fairly quickly, but not hurrying. He appeared to be average height and weight, but it can be hard to judge such things on a grainy nighttime video.

I watched until he was out of camera range. I waited ten seconds. Then I rose from the couch, eased my front door open, and slipped into the night, the shotgun cradled in my arms.

30

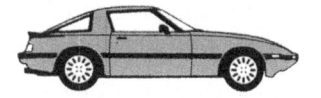

LAST YEAR, WHEN I SHOT a man named Nathaniel Tate, I was on rock-solid legal ground. He was trespassing, and he was armed. He tried to trick me by playing a recording of cats fighting just outside my bedroom window. Wanted me to part the curtains and take a look. Then he would've shot me through the glass from just a few feet away.

But I'd already seen him on one of my cameras. Didn't know who it was, because he was wearing a ski mask. Didn't matter.

When that cat recording began to play, I flipped my bedroom lights on—to make him think I might open the curtains any second—and hurried down the hallway and out the back door. Came to the corner of the house and peeked around. There he was, handgun extended toward my window, still waiting. Moron.

I told him not to move, and of course he moved, swinging the revolver toward me. So I shot him. Double-ought buckshot did the job.

This time, right now, was different. I didn't know if this person was armed. He was no longer trespassing. He wasn't threatening me. In fact, I was pursuing him. I had to be careful. I knew that.

Maybe it was some drunk kid who'd hopped my fence to take a leak. That didn't make a lot of sense, but drunk people sometimes don't make sense. I've been there myself. Or maybe the person I was following wasn't the person who'd been in my backyard.

I was wearing some rubber-soled moccasins I keep near the front door for trips to the mailbox, and those let me walk quietly. I followed the concrete driveway to the street and went left, moving slightly faster than the person I'd seen on camera a moment ago.

After forty yards, I stopped and listened. Nothing. I kept moving, even faster now.

I didn't want to confront him. I wanted to follow him to his vehicle and get a plate number. Possibly make an ID, ideally without him knowing he'd been made.

Unfortunately, after another sixty yards, I still hadn't laid eyes on the shadowy figure, and I couldn't hear any footsteps in the darkness ahead of me.

I reached the iron arches that mark the entrance to Austin Lake Estates and paused for a moment. It was time to give up. The person was gone. Either he'd begun to trot before I'd even stepped out of my house, or he'd turned on one of the side streets I'd passed.

The neighborhood was remarkably quiet in the middle of the night. Not one vehicle had passed. No dogs had barked. Some porch lights were on, but most were not. I could hear a motorcycle far in the distance, probably on Bee Caves Road.

I began to walk back toward the house, and halfway there, I caught movement to my right, in a yard, something coming out from behind an oak tree.

Could've been a deer or a dog or my imagination, but I was on edge and reacted without thinking.

I dove and rolled on the pavement—and just in time, because a shot thundered in my ears.

Somehow I managed to hang on to the shotgun, and as I came up on one knee, I leveled it at the man fifteen feet from me and pulled the trigger. It kicked hard.

The man staggered backward and dropped his gun. I couldn't see it clearly, but I could hear it thud to the ground.

A moment later, he collapsed onto his butt, and then he lay backward, fully prone. I could hear him moaning. A few nearby porch lights snapped on, but not as many as you'd expect.

I moved closer, slowly, shotgun at the ready.

"It hurts," the man said.

I recognized the voice. Pure redneck.

"I'm sure it does," I said. "That's why people try to avoid it."

I took a few more steps, and now I was looking down at the face of Brett Murtaugh.

I called 911 and said there'd been a shooting. I gave the approximate address and said I needed to put the phone down to assess the man's injuries.

I scooted Murtaugh's handgun several yards away with my foot, then knelt down beside him, placing the shotgun within arm's reach—for me, not for him.

"You're an idiot," I said.

"What's going on out there?" a man yelled from a house across the street.

"Do you have a flashlight?" I called back. "Everything is under control, but I need a flashlight."

I tore Murtaugh's T-shirt off with my hands, and he groaned with pain in the process.

"You wanna tell me why you tried to kill me?" I asked.

"Fuck off."

I couldn't see well in the moonlight, but it appeared the buckshot had kept a tight pattern, catching him in the right biceps and shoulder. But there was one errant hole on the left side of his chest. There wasn't much bleeding from any of the wounds, but that didn't necessarily mean anything. The hole in the chest was the biggest concern, even though it wasn't bleeding at all. Maybe he'd be fine. Maybe it had nicked an artery and he'd be dead in five minutes. I used his torn shirt to apply pressure to the wounded biceps, which was bleeding the most, and he yelped with pain.

"Why were you in my backyard with a gun?" I asked.

"The fuck're you talking about?" he said.

He seemed a little out of breath, but that was to be expected. I could smell whiskey each time he talked. Liquid courage.

I said, "Why were you coming after me? You working for Franco?"

"Gonna kill you later," he said.

"Like you killed Jake?" I asked.

"Exactly like that," Murtaugh said.

"Why'd you kill him?"

"He was stupid as you."

"You shot your own stepbrother in the head?"

"Gonna do it to you, too."

"Where'd you put him?"

"In the creek."

I was pretty sure the location of the body had not been shared with the public. Murtaugh also didn't realize this conversation was being recorded on the 911 line. I only hoped he was speaking loudly enough.

"Did you kill Norman Conlee?"

"Fuck you."

The man from across the street was approaching with a flashlight. I turned and saw that he had stopped at the edge of his yard. I couldn't see him well, but I could make out the apprehension in his body language.

"I promise it's safe," I called. "Can you bring the flashlight over here?"

He reluctantly came closer, but stopped ten feet behind me, still on the pavement. From there, he shined the light on Murtaugh. "Who is he?"

I looked for any wounds I hadn't spotted earlier, but there were none. "How does your chest feel?" I asked Murtaugh.

His eyes were glazing over. I didn't know if it was shock or something worse.

"Brett?"

He mumbled something and then lost consciousness.

"Jesus, is he dead?" the man behind me asked.

I grabbed Murtaugh's wrist with one hand and felt a weak pulse. Steady, though. Using one hand, I gently rolled Murtaugh onto his side. I thought that's what you were supposed to do when somebody had a penetrating chest wound, but I wasn't positive.

"Did you call the cops?" the man asked.

We were outside the Austin city limits, so the sheriff's office would be handling this one.

"Did you shoot him or did somebody else do that?" the man asked. "Did he shoot at you first? Was there somebody else here?"

I said, "Can you go get some gauze and medical tape? If you don't have those, just grab some towels and duct tape."

"You want me to use my towels?" the man asked.

I finally heard a siren, still at least a mile or two away.

"And something for a tourniquet—a belt, a rope, or even an electrical cord." He didn't move, so I barked, "Now!"

He turned and hurried back to his house.

I remained crouched there in the dark, continuing to apply pressure to the wounded arm. I would've felt a lot better about this situation if the shooting had taken place at my house, rather than well down the street.

Still, it was going to be a long night, followed by a long morning. I was going to get grilled long and hard. That was standard procedure.

I just hoped Ruelas didn't catch the case. Let it be somebody else—somebody without an axe to grind. Anybody but Ruelas.

31

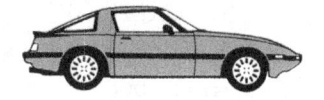

"YOU'RE A REGULAR ONE-MAN SHITSHOW," Ruelas said ninety minutes later. "Everywhere you go, people die or get maimed. Vehicles and buildings get damaged. Nothing good happens."

"I'm clumsy," I said.

It was nearly seven o'clock in the morning. We were in an interview room at the substation on Hudson Bend Road, and we'd probably be here for a long time to come—if I continued to cooperate. I had the option of ending the interview anytime I wanted.

"Who is Brett Murtaugh to you?" Ruelas asked.

"I met him on Tinder and we had a good time at first, but then he got kind of clingy," I said.

"Joke all you want, but it looks like you stalked this guy and gunned him down."

"It looks like you cut your hair with gardening shears. Sometimes appearances are deceiving."

It was not in my best interest to goad him, but damn it, I couldn't resist. He was always so smug. Even more irritating, he never appeared to be bothered in the slightest by my jabs. Years as a cop will give you a thick skin.

"Why was he coming after you?" Ruelas asked.

As far as I knew, Murtaugh was still alive, and there was no reason to think that would change. I'd monitored his pulse until the EMTs had arrived, and it had remained steady.

"It's kind of complicated," I said.

"Boil it down for me."

I started at the beginning and told him everything—or almost everything. I didn't mention anything about Scarlett. I told him about Franco Keller and Olivia Reed and Brett Murtaugh and Jacob Buckley. I talked for nearly fifteen minutes.

At one point, he said, "How do you know Olivia Reed is a call girl?"

Both times I'd visited Albert Strauss, I'd promised confidentiality, so I said, "I spoke to one of her johns. He confirmed it. That's all I can share about that."

"Somebody I know?"

"The john? Highly doubtful."

I continued with my statement, and he stopped me with a couple of questions, but not as many as one might think. After all, it wasn't his job to figure out who shot Norman Conlee. That was on APD. Ruelas was only concerned with my shootout with Brett Murtaugh.

When I was done, he said, "Why didn't you call 911 when you spotted a person in your backyard?"

"First, I couldn't be positive there was really anybody out there, and second, because I knew he might be long gone before a deputy could arrive."

"So you followed him down the street with a shotgun?"

"I did."

"That's pretty aggressive."

"And totally legal. I can walk down the street with a loaded shotgun, day or night."

I drained a bottle of water he had given me before we started.

"Not necessarily, if you're intending to kill a fleeing suspect," Ruelas said. "There was no threat to you. He didn't have any of your property."

"I just wanted to see if I could ID him. I thought I'd lost him, so I turned around to go back home and he was hiding behind a tree. He fired a shot and I fired back in self-defense."

I'd been in this position—explaining why I'd shot someone—more times than I would care to share at a dinner party. *"Oh, I'm up to three now. How many people have you shot?"*

"Did you know who it was when you shot him?"

"I didn't, but it wouldn't have mattered, obviously. Anybody who shoots at me is going to get return fire. My life was threatened, so I responded accordingly."

He was asking all the questions one would expect in a post-shooting interview, but because it was Ruelas, I could feel myself losing patience. Not because the questions were inappropriate, but because he was enjoying grilling me.

"Walk me through the shooting itself," he said. "Give me the details."

"Okay. Well, gunpowder was invented by the Chinese in the ninth century. After that—"

"Skip the bullshit," he said. "You woke up, and then what?"

I spent ten minutes describing the incident as completely as I could.

Something woke me. I grabbed the shotgun. Checked the cameras. Saw that the motion-triggered light had come on. Went to the window and eventually saw a glow, which I took to be a cell phone in somebody's pocket. Went downstairs. Watched on the camera and saw a figure walking past the front of the house. Waited a moment, then followed.

"I was almost to the arches when I gave up and turned around. I took a few steps and I saw movement, so I dove, and then I—"

"If you dove, that means you knew there was danger," Ruelas said.

"Yeah? So?"

"I just don't get why you wanted to place yourself in danger, unless you were hoping to confront him. You had plenty of time to call 911, but you never did."

"Was I or was I not within my rights to follow the guy?" I asked. "That's a rhetorical question, because we both know the answer."

His face looked sour, but he had no reply.

I said, "I dove and rolled, and then I came up on one knee and fired a shot."

"You dove and rolled and held on to the shotgun the whole time?"

"Right."

"What're you, an acrobat?"

"Yes, exactly. I'm an acrobat. It's one of my many hobbies. I also carve soap and collect ashtrays."

He shook his head impatiently, because he has no discernible sense of humor.

"You got any way to prove Murtaugh shot first?"

"I don't have to prove that. I mean, it's true and everything, but I don't have to prove it. If you think it didn't happen that way, the burden of proof is on you."

"That's weak," Ruelas said. "You know how things work in the real world."

"Maybe, but it's that whole 'innocent until proven guilty' thing. Bet you've heard of it."

"So I'm supposed to take your word for it?"

"Oh, hang on," I said, pulling my phone out. I opened the app for my security cameras, and after a minute, I was able to play footage from the exact moment of the gunshots. Obviously, the video wasn't relevant, but the audio was valuable. The gunshots were muffled from a distance of several hundred yards, but still audible. I played them twice. They sounded nothing alike.

Ruelas looked at me. I looked back at him.

"So what?" Ruelas said.

"That's Murtaugh's handgun, then my shotgun."

"Is it?"

"You know it is."

"Hard to tell," Ruelas said. "Could be the other way around."

"You need to get out to the gun range more."

"Recordings can get distorted."

"I'm sure you have people on your staff who can confirm it. Recreate the scene if you have to, with the same guns and my camera. Compare the recordings. That'll prove it."

He let it drop.

"What happened after you shot?"

"He fell and I approached him. His gun was on the ground, so I moved it with my foot. The man living across the street came out, so I asked him to bring a flashlight. He did, and I assessed Murtaugh's injuries. The wound to his biceps was the worst, so I put pressure on it. The others weren't bleeding much. The hole in his chest concerned me, but there wasn't much I could do about that. From his breathing, it didn't appear to be a sucking chest wound. I turned him on his side. Then I sent the neighbor back for a tourniquet."

"Earlier you said you started treating Murtaugh's injuries before the neighbor came with the flashlight," Ruelas said.

I realized he was right. It was a discrepancy.

"That's right," I said. "Just a minor point."

"But it means your memory is shaky."

"He shot first," I said. "That's what you're getting at. I'm not wrong about that. He came there to shoot me. Have you checked his cell phone? The light I saw meant he'd gotten a call or a text." I could tell from his expression that I was on to something. I said, "Bet it was a burner. Was there anything on it?"

Ruelas hesitated, then said, "There was an ambiguous text."

"Just one?"

"Yep. That's all."

"What did it say?"

He stared at me for a long moment, deciding whether he wanted to share it. "*You get it done or what?*"

"That's what the text said?" I laughed. "Well, there you go."

"There I go what?"

"It's obvious what that means."

"Why don't you tell me?"

"Seriously?"

"I look like I'm joking?"

"The person was asking if he'd killed me yet."

Ruelas shrugged.

"You don't agree?" I asked.

"Could mean a lot of things."

His disingenuous attitude was intended to irritate me. Why was I letting it work?

"You need to figure out who sent that text," I said. "I'd say Franco Keller is a strong candidate. Talk to Lynann Chukwueze. She can fill you in on a lot of the details."

"So you're still doing that thing where you tell people how to do their jobs?"

"Have you listened to the 911 call? He admitted he killed Jacob Buckley."

"He might've been talking big to put a scare into you."

"He's also a suspect in a murder that took place earlier this month. That's why you should talk to Lynann."

He shrugged, as if he couldn't care less about any of this.

"I'm going to leave now," I said, putting my palms on the edge of the table.

"I'm not done," he said.

"I am."

"You want to hear what I think?"

"If I can make popcorn first."

"I think you pissed Franco off when you punched him in the throat, and he was trying to get some payback by sending his buddy Murtaugh. Beyond that, you don't have a clue what you're doing, as usual."

"I appreciate the vote of support."

"Unless you're holding something back, you've got zero evidence that Franco Keller or Brett Murtaugh had anything to do with the murder of Norman Conlee."

"Well, since Lynann is handling that case, you don't need to worry about it, right? Bet you're thrilled." I pushed back from the table and stood up. "Let me know if you have any other questions."

I moved past him and headed for the door, but he couldn't resist one last stab.

"Why are you working alone on this one?" he asked.

I turned back around. "What did you say?"

"Why isn't your partner helping you?"

Now he was goading me. Taunting me—about Mia. There was no way in hell he hadn't heard about our breakup, but he was pretending he didn't know. And he knew I knew that.

I could feel the anger rising in my chest and throat, but I did my best to hide it, despite wanting to come around the table and tear him apart.

"I guess she came to her senses, huh?" I said. "Decided she could do better."

If I was putting myself down, what could he say in response? Maybe I was mistaken, but it appeared, for a quick moment, that he regretted asking the question.

"You'll get your shotgun back when the techs are done with it," he said. "If I need anything else, I'll call you."

Out in the hallway, I realized I was clenching my teeth and my palms were sweaty. I'd come very close to losing it in there.

Stop thinking about it. Let it go.
I glanced down at my phone and stopped dead in the hallway. Mia had called four minutes earlier. She'd left a voicemail.

32

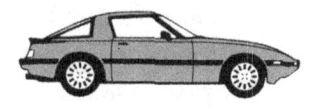

"It could have a psychological impact on him—possibly a significant one—if he lost that coping device," Beth said.

"Meaning what, exactly?" Mia asked.

"I want to remind you that this is all speculation."

"Please, Beth. I know that, but this conversation is helping me. Even if it never applies to anything outside this room."

Beth thought about it for a long moment.

"Assuming what we've discussed is accurate, if he lost his work—that daily sense of purpose that helps him atone for his past, even if we agree he doesn't have anything to atone for—well, it could really put him in a bad spot. His self-esteem could suffer. He could sink into depression."

"So he might feel the way I felt two months ago."

"It's possible."

"I wouldn't want that."

"At a minimum, I think he'd feel restless and anxious for a good long while. Of course, it's possible none of that would happen. He might find other ways to cope, or he might be fine without any replacement at all. And, as I've said several times now, this could all be wrong. I haven't talked to him, so I don't know. I can only go by what you've told me."

Mia glanced at the clock and saw that she had ten minutes left in the session. Beth was a stickler for ending sessions on time, so subsequent clients would not be inconvenienced.

It was time to say it. Quit beating around the bush and just say it, instead of waiting for the next session.

"I want to try again," Mia said, and she'd never felt such relief. "I want to try getting back together with Roy. Assuming he's willing."

Beth didn't reply.

"But I don't want to try and then realize I can't handle it," Mia said.

"I'm glad you're being honest with yourself about what you want, and whether it's even realistic. That's important."

"There's also the chance he might be seeing someone."

"True. He might be."

"I wouldn't interfere in that," Mia said.

Beth made no comment.

Outside, a squirrel was attempting to reach the bird feeder, but Beth had recently moved it to a new place, hanging it ten feet off the ground with a long piece of fishing line. The squirrel would probably find a way to reach the feeder eventually, or he'd leap for it and bring it crashing down. A win either way.

Five minutes left in the session.

"What if I can't handle it?" Mia said. "I think I can, but what if I'm wrong?"

"You don't have to answer that question right this minute," Beth said. "You can give yourself time to think about it. I wouldn't advise rushing anything."

The squirrel was chattering loudly, plainly irritated or excited.

"I have another idea," Mia said. "What if we worked together again—Roy and me—and that's it for now. I become his partner again as a test. If I can't handle that—the job—then there's no way I can handle us together again."

Beth didn't offer an opinion.

"He might not like that arrangement at all," Mia said.

"Are you sure you would?" Beth asked.

"I don't know."

Beth glanced at her wristwatch.

"Is this all a terrible idea?" Mia asked.

"You should think about it some more and we'll talk when you get back from Oregon."

33

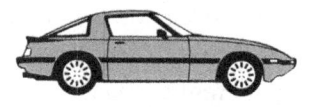

I DUCKED INTO AN EMPTY break room, held the phone tight to my ear, and listened to her voicemail.

Hey, it's me. I just now heard what happened. Are you okay?

There was a lot of background noise, including some other people talking.

You can call me back if you want, but I'm at the airport, going to see my brother, and I think we're about to board.

When she said *we*, did she mean the other passengers, or was somebody making the trip with her?

But at least please text me, okay? I'd like to hear from you. I'm worried about you. Take care.

And she hung up. I listened to it again. And again. Hearing her voice simultaneously lifted my spirits and put an ache in my heart.

I'd like to hear from you.

Did she mean in general, or about the shooting?

I'm worried about you.

That was the problem, wasn't it? I made her worry. If I wanted her back, all I had to do was stop making her worry. Right?

Unless it was too late. How far had she moved on? Was someone boarding that plane with her? I thought I'd fully let her go by now, but perhaps I was wrong.

I started to hit the button to call her back, but I hesitated. Did I really want our first conversation in three months to be a hurried call while she was surrounded by strangers and possibly a new boyfriend? Bad idea.

So, instead, I did as she asked and sent a text. *I'm completely fine. Wasn't as bad as it probably sounds. Good to hear your voice. Enjoy your trip. Will you call me when you land?*

Then I wondered if that sounded desperate. *Will you call me when you land?*

Call me about what? I'd already told her I was fine.

Her brother lived in Bend, Oregon, which meant she might be in the air for three or four hours or more, depending on whether she had a connecting flight. It was going to be a long wait, unless she decided to call right now, before boarding.

I waited several minutes, just standing in the break room, but she didn't reply. I made sure my ringer was on, then went out to the parking lot. Stood there for a moment, looking around, and then it dawned on me. A deputy had brought me over here hours ago. I had no car.

Well, hell. What a hassle.

I could go back inside and demand they give me a ride. Or I could call an Uber.

Or what about Scarlett? Would she have gotten word about the shooting yet? Apparently not, since she hadn't texted or called while I was being interviewed. Which meant I needed to call her anyway and let her know what had happened, before she heard about it. Then I could tell her my predicament, and if she offered a ride, great. It was now eight o'clock, so I probably wouldn't be waking her.

I texted first. *You got a minute for a phone call?*

She replied immediately. *Sure. What's up?*

So I dialed her number. When she answered, I said, "You're not going to believe the night I had."

"That's insane," she said forty minutes later, from the driver's seat of her car.

I'd given her the short version of events on the phone, and now I'd just finished describing the shooting in more detail. We were headed east on Bee Caves Road in her Land Rover Discovery. We had the sunroof open and the windows down, but the car was designed well enough that the noise was minimal and it was easy to hold a conversation.

She said, "How could he not have known you'd have cameras in place, and an alarm system, and that you'd be armed? How stupid is he? I mean, he has to know what you do for a living, right? You use cameras!"

"I don't know."

"What an idiot."

"Agreed."

If Scarlett was shaken up by what had happened, she didn't show it. She drove and asked questions, and of course she expressed relief that I wasn't harmed, but she didn't look at me like she was worried that my time on earth was limited.

"Maybe he was hoping you'd come outside," she said. "That he could lure you out there somehow."

"I figure that was the idea."

"What an idiot," she repeated.

"Yep."

"Do you know if his shot came close to hitting you?"

"I don't really know. He was pretty close, so I'd say he probably would've hit me if I hadn't dove."

"How close?"

"Maybe fifteen feet."

"Wow. I don't know much about guns, but that seems like an easy shot."

"Usually, yeah, even under pressure."

She was coming up on Cuernavaca Drive and had to stop in the left-turn lane and wait for a green light.

"Do you think he'll die?" she asked.

"He was stable when they took him away."

"That's good," she said. "I guess. I mean it *is* good, right? He's not going to come after you again, is he?"

"He said he would, but I doubt it."

The light changed and she made the left.

I said, "Before you picked me up, I called my client and gave him an update."

"What did he say?"

"He put the case on hold."

She glanced over at me. "What for? Because of the shooting?"

"Pretty much. You have to understand he doesn't want me as a hired gun. He just wants video footage of the person who was committing the vandalism at the Conlee house, and he said that seems extremely unlikely at this point. Plus, I'm a valuable part of his team and he doesn't want me injured or killed."

"That was nice of him to say."

"He didn't say that, but it's true."

She laughed. "So what now?"

"I'll go home, type up my case notes, and send them in. In a day or two, I'll contact Evelyn Conlee or Carmen about getting the cameras back."

She passed the small convenience store on the left, then the larger convenience store on the same side. A moment later, she swooped into a hard curve and glided under the metal arches.

After we passed the first cross street, I pointed to my right and said, "Right there. That's where he was. Hiding behind that tree."

She eased off the gas a little bit.

"It looks so different in the daylight," I said. "You'd never know what happened in that spot less than twelve hours ago."

By the time the EMTs and the first deputy had arrived last night, neighbors had come outside from almost every house within a hundred yards. Some of them had approached the scene, and several of them recognized me as the new guy who'd moved in a few months earlier. I wondered what kind of reception I'd receive in this neighborhood in the coming days.

Your average Joe doesn't like to be woken by middle-of-the-night shootings. Would neighbors avoid me? Pretend they didn't see me? Or be more direct and ask me what had happened? After I shot Nathaniel Tate, one neighbor told me I was a danger to the neighborhood and I should move away. I was angry, but I couldn't say he was wrong. Was that true here, too, in this new house?

Twenty seconds later, Scarlett pulled into my driveway and put the transmission in Park, but she left the engine running.

"I'm glad you're okay," she said. "I've grown rather fond of you."

"Likewise," I said.

"You're fond of you?"

"Very much so," I said. "I mean the world to me."

There was something about the way the light was angling in through the sunroof that cast her in a flattering glow.

"You want to come in?" I asked.

She smiled. "Roy, you've been up all night. You can hardly keep your eyes open. You should get some sleep."

I nodded. "Thanks for the ride."

"You bet. Call me later?"

I said I would, and we shared a quick kiss, and I went inside.

She was right—I was exhausted, but still keyed up from the shooting and subsequent interview. I found myself looking for things to do, starting with a security check. All the windows were locked. The alarm system was in working order. My Glock nine millimeter was fully loaded and would remain within arm's reach for the time being.

I took a shower, then sat on the couch and turned on the TV just for the company, but my mind wandered. I was thinking of Scarlett. And Mia.

Mostly Mia, to be honest. She hadn't called or texted me back. She was in the air, on her way to Bend. Would I hear from her when she landed?

After a while, I began to feel drowsy, so I went upstairs to bed. As I slipped from wakefulness to sleep, my mind replayed a pleasant memory.

34

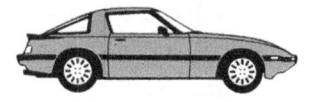

"GET YOU ANOTHER ONE?"

I swiveled my bar stool away from the TV and toward the bartender, and I bet my eyes gave me away immediately. Surely they widened in surprise. After all, you don't expect to suddenly have the most beautiful woman on the planet appear in front of you without any warning. She was tall—maybe five-ten—with long red hair pulled into a ponytail. High cheekbones.

But she wasn't talking to me, or offering me a drink. She was addressing the guy to my left.

"Absolutely," the guy said. "I never turn a beautiful girl down."

She smiled and I noticed the dimples. Good lord, the dimples.

"Jameson rocks?" she said.

"He sure does," the guy replied. "Hell of a whiskey maker. He also turns a five into a seven, if you know what I mean. But a ten like you doesn't need any help in that department."

I cringed on this man's behalf. I'd never seen him in here before. Not that I was a regular, but I frequented the place often enough to know who some of the regulars were. This guy was perhaps forty, but he was dressed like he was still in a fraternity. Madras shorts? Really?

The bartender smiled again, but this time it was the kind of manufactured smile that said *Please don't make me put you in your place.*

She grabbed a fresh glass, filled it with ice, and turned for the bottle of Irish whiskey behind her.

"Damn," the guy said. "Are you a runner? Those legs. I don't blame you for wearing shorts."

She came back around with the bottle and poured a generous amount over the ice in the glass. She placed a napkin in front of the aging frat boy, then set the drink on top of the napkin.

"You're on thin ice," she said.

"Hey, you might be the prettiest gal I've ever seen in this place," the guy said. "Then again, this is my first time here."

It was hard to tell whether that was a joke that didn't land or simply drunken babbling.

The bartender said, "I'm not sure how to reply to that."

"Well, it was a compliment, so..."

"Hard to tell."

"No, it really was!"

"You should work on your material."

She turned her attention toward me, plainly hoping I would need a fresh drink, and that would end the conversation with this guy, but no. He spoke before she could ask me anything.

"My name's Jack. What's yours?"

She looked at him. "I'm not sure you'd be able to remember it."

"Ah, come on. What's your name?"

"Against my better judgment, I will tell you. It's Mia."

"Mia?"

"Right."

"Like M-I-A?"

"That's how it's spelled, yes."

"Mamma mia," the guy said, laughing. "That's just perfect. Because that's what guys probably say when they meet you. Mamma mia! And who can blame them?" Then he actually sang the line from the ABBA song. "Mamma mia! Mamma mia!"

I was tempted to gently encourage the guy to stop being an idiot, but I felt certain Mia would handle it better than I ever could. I was sure she had plenty of experience dealing with men like him.

"I've never heard that before," she said.

"Seriously?" Jack asked, apparently too drunk to recognize sarcasm. "Never."

"But it's so obvious!" Jack said. "Your name's Mia!"

"True, but you've somehow blazed new territory with your fresh and witty approach. I mean, I'm no pushover, but you're sweeping me off my feet with your charm."

I let out a snort. Couldn't help it. Jack glanced my way quickly, now realizing he was the butt of the joke. I shook my head at him.

"I was just saying you're hot, that's all. Why you gotta get all uptight about it?"

"Right," Mia said. "I should be thrilled to receive clumsy compliments from every random drunk guy I encounter."

"I'm not drunk. Besides, I didn't say nothing wrong."

"Then go home and tell your wife what you said and see if she agrees."

He sputtered for a second, then said, "Well, fuck this." He rose from his stool a little unsteadily and wandered off with his drink into a back corner of the tavern.

"Now *that* was entertaining," I said.

"Was it?" Mia asked.

"Oh, it was awesome."

"I didn't overreact?"

"Not even a little."

"Good to know. I was warned about guys like him, but there's no way I'm putting up with that. I'll quit the job first."

"How long have you been tending bar?"

"I literally started fifteen minutes ago."

"Well, you handled it like you've been doing it for years."

"Thanks. You need another one?"

My beer glass was nearly empty.

"Please," I said.

As she put a new glass under the tap, she said, "Do guys really think that kind of approach works? Well, obviously some think that, but why?"

"Got me. It's crass. Rude. Outdated."

"I agree."

"Besides, there are ways to let a woman know you're attracted to her without being a buffoon."

She looked at me for a moment, her eyes narrowing, obviously a bit apprehensive that I was going to turn out to be just another jerk on a bar stool. "Really?" she said. "Such as?"

"Hey, I didn't say I *know* any. I'm just saying they exist."

She gave me a laugh, and then got called away by another customer before I could extend the conversation.

The damage had already been done. I was smitten.

35

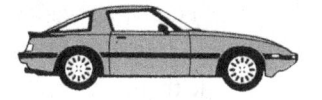

SHE DIDN'T TEXT ME BACK when she landed in Bend, or anytime that night, or by the next morning, and I can't say I blamed her. She'd wanted to make sure I was okay after the shooting, but there was no more to it than that.

Focus.

The Conlee case was essentially over, at least for me, but I had two tasks I needed to take care of: remove the cameras from outside the house and remove the GPS tracker from Franco's Porsche. Neither was urgent, but there wasn't any reason to dawdle, either, especially with the tracker, since I'd placed it on the vehicle illegally. That put it at the top of the list. If the cops impounded or searched his car for any reason and found that tracker, it would be easy to deduce who'd put it there.

I opened the GPS app and saw that Franco's car hadn't moved in two days. It was parked in the gated community of garden homes where he lived in Westlake Hills. He'd been laying low, probably on the advice of an attorney. I was hoping Ruelas had gotten Franco's cell phone records by now, including texts and other data, but I knew that Franco probably had not used his personal phone to send any incriminating information. Too risky to retrieve the tracker where it was, so it would have to wait.

I called Evelyn Conlee, but she didn't answer, so I left a voicemail, explaining about the cameras.

Then, out of curiosity, I googled her condition: corticobasal degeneration. I learned that it's a rare disease that causes areas of your brain to shrink and nerve cells to degenerate and die. It's a Parkinson-plus syndrome, meaning it features the classical symptoms of Parkinson's disease, plus other symptoms on top of that. Usually afflicts people between the ages of 50 and 70. Characterized by problems with motor skills and cognition. Rigid muscles. Tremor. Spasms and contractions. There is no viable treatment; the symptoms are resistant to therapy. The prognosis for most individuals is death within eight years.

I was beginning to suspect why Evelyn Conlee didn't answer calls, but would return them later, and why she wasn't available to be seen if I dropped in. She wanted to wait until she was having a good moment before she interacted with people.

Right then, she called me back, saying I was welcome to come over now to get the cameras.

I arrived less than an hour later. Carmen greeted me at the door and said, "She's on the patio again." As she led me through the house, she said, "I'm glad you're okay. That must have been terrifying."

"The drive over?" I said.

"No, I mean—" Then she realized I was kidding. "The detective said the man who shot at you is a friend of Franco's. We were all very surprised by that—and the implications."

"Which detective?" I asked.

"Lynann. I still can't pronounce her last name."

"Chukwueze."

"Right."

"How about a guy named Ruelas?"

"He called and asked us both some questions."

At least he was actually working the case. "That go okay?"

"It went fine, but I'm afraid we weren't much help, since we didn't know the man who tried to shoot you."

"Do you know if Lynann or Ruelas have talked to Franco and Olivia?"

"Sorry, I don't know. We haven't seen either of them since Sunday night. Olivia hasn't returned our calls. We think she's with Franco. It's been hard on Evelyn to think Franco might've been involved with everything that took place around here. We can only hope Olivia knew nothing about it."

We'd reached the back door, and Carmen paused for a moment. "Do you think Brett Murtaugh shot Norman?"

"Honestly, I don't even want to hazard a guess. If he did, Lynann and Ruelas will figure it out."

"I hope so."

We exited through the door and walked onto the patio by the pool. Evelyn Conlee had her wheelchair parked in the same spot at the table.

"Good morning, Mr. Ballard," she said.

"Please call me Roy," I said. "Good to see you again."

"Have a seat. Would you like something to drink?"

"No, I'm fine."

"Just let me know if you need anything," Carmen said, and she went back inside.

I took a seat.

Evelyn said, "I like to spend time outdoors this time of year, while it's still bearable. In another month, it will be ninety degrees, and one hundred shortly after that. Then I can sit out in the early morning, but that's about it. The afternoons are just too hot and humid, even in the shade."

"It *is* nice right now," I said.

"I heard a pair of ravens a moment ago," Evelyn said. "They fly some distance apart, but call back and forth. You know they mate for life?"

"I don't think I knew that."

At the bottom of the sloped yard, the lake looked like dark-green glass. At the moment, I couldn't hear any boats.

"I wanted to say thank you for attempting to untangle all of the chaos around here," Evelyn said quietly.

"I appreciate that. I'm sorry I didn't figure out who shot your husband."

"I'm still hoping the police will solve it. Is that naïve at this point?"

"Not at all. I hope they will, too. I bet they will."

I noticed that the bruising on her arm was fading. For some reason, that lifted my mood a bit.

"Do you think Franco was involved somehow?" Evelyn asked.

"Carmen asked me that, too. Honestly, I just don't know."

"Why else would he have sent that man after you?"

"He might not have wanted me to find out what Olivia did in California—being an escort."

"Oh, that's true," she said. "That hadn't occurred to me. On the other hand, she really doesn't have a reason to be ashamed of that. I mean, it's not something she should put on her résumé, but it was a harmless lark."

That was the same phrase she'd used last time: a harmless lark. Of course, she didn't know that Olivia was more than an escort, or that she and Franco had concocted a blackmail scheme. I saw no reason to mention any of this to her. What purpose could it serve except to agitate her? Why would I do that to a woman in her condition?

We sat quietly for a moment, and then I heard a low croaking sound far in the distance.

"There it is," Evelyn said, holding a finger up. "One of the ravens."

I smiled at her. I found myself reluctant to leave, with the murder of her husband still unresolved. I wanted to bring her some closure, but I had to let it go, even though I knew the case would eat at me until I had something else to distract me. Fortunately, after I told Evelyn goodbye, gathered my cameras, and went home, a client emailed me with a new case that very afternoon.

36

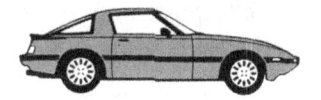

A MAN NAMED CLINTON DUBOIS claimed that his deceased wife's fur coat had been stolen. He said he'd put it in his car to take it in for an appraisal and then a cleaning prior to selling it, but he forgot about it and left it in the back seat of his vehicle for a few nights. Then he discovered one morning that somebody had broken a window and stolen several items, including the coat. He filed a police report and an insurance claim for the amount of $15,000, which was high for a fur coat nowadays, based on what I saw online, but it was hard to argue with a recent appraisal.

DuBois was sixty-six years old. Worked at the butcher counter inside a local grocery store. He had not remarried. Lived in the same home he had occupied with his wife, Lois, who had been dead for six years.

Was the claim legit? In general, it was a credible story. The adjuster had reviewed the police report and was preparing to pay the claim when she received an anonymous email.

Clinton DuBois didn't get that fur coat stolen. He gave it to his girlfriend. No lie. Clinton is always screwing around and its time he pays for one of his dumb ideas.

That's all it said. There was no supporting evidence. It did not include the girlfriend's name.

The adjuster dug deeper and learned that DuBois had filed a claim for a stolen truck five years earlier—a truck that was later found submerged in a creek two miles from his house. Before that, when his wife was still alive, they'd reported a burglary in which he'd had $10,000 in firearms stolen. Based on this pattern, my client, the insurance company, decided it was time to play hardball.

They knew that an agency as large and busy as the Austin Police Department wouldn't be able to put much time or resources into this case, so they contacted me. My job was to get video evidence proving that the coat had not been stolen.

Late that afternoon, I jumped online to see what I could dig up. Took me less than a minute to learn that the girlfriend was a petite redhead named Patricia Blevins. That's because Clinton DuBois had proudly posted quite a few photos of Blevins on his Facebook page. Judging by those photos, Blevins was much younger than DuBois—probably around forty years old. She appeared to be a fun-loving, extroverted type.

I clicked over to her Facebook page, and right then I received an alert that Franco's Porsche was on the move. I turned my attention to that for a moment. Maybe I'd get a chance to retrieve the tracker.

The Porsche took Bee Caves Road to the HEB grocery store at the Loop 360 intersection. That was a ten-minute drive from my location, so I grabbed the keys for the van and headed out. But just as I neared the store, the Porsche was on the move again, back the way it had come. I pulled into a strip center and watched for a few minutes. Franco went back home, into his gated community. So I gave up and also went back home.

By now it was nearly six o'clock, so I put a frozen pizza into the oven and returned to my computer. Patricia Blevins's Facebook profile was locked down tight, unfortunately. Perhaps there was a photo, visible to friends only, showing her wearing the fur coat.

Which made me wonder what Clinton DuBois had told her when—or if—he'd given her the coat. Did he admit it had been his dead wife's coat? Did he mention that he was claiming it had been stolen? Or had he even pondered these issues? Maybe he thought insurance companies didn't bother checking smaller claims like this one.

I checked other social media, including Instagram, but Patricia

Blevins valued her privacy and none of her accounts were visible to the public. I considered sending her a Facebook friend request from one of my fake profiles—a middle-aged woman named Harriet Jones—but I didn't want to risk tipping my hand just yet.

The timer dinged for my pizza, so I took it out of the oven and cracked open a cold bottle of Lone Star. I sat in front of the TV tuned to a UT baseball game.

Would a woman wear a fur coat in April, when the temperature was in the sixties and seventies? Was that too warm? I had no idea.

Did women even wear fur anymore? I texted Scarlett.

Does anybody wear fur nowadays?

She didn't text back right away.

I ate more pizza and settled in for the seventh-inning stretch. The Longhorns were currently giving the Aggies a thorough beating.

I wasn't thrilled about the idea of simply placing Patricia Blevins under surveillance and hoping she might wear the coat, because that could mean a whole lot of man-hours that might never pay off. If the claim was for, say, $150,000, that kind of time and effort would be justified, but the actual claim was small potatoes.

A few minutes later, Scarlett texted back. *Can't remember the last time I saw anyone in a fur. What's up? Buying yourself a special present? :)*

New case, I said. *Involves a fur allegedly stolen from a vehicle.*

Was the victim an older woman who bought the fur a long time ago?

Surprisingly, no.

Was it a vintage fur? Some people are okay with wearing an old one.

I checked the case file and saw that Clinton DuBois stated he had originally inherited the fur from his mother, who'd bought it sometime in the fifties, well before the anti-fur movement gained steam.

You nailed it, I said.

She sent a thumbs-up, then said, *How are you supposed to track down a stolen fur?*

So I told her about the anonymous tip.

She said, *How old is the girlfriend?*

Appears to be about forty. He's sixty-six.

She sent a vomiting emoji. Then she said, *I wouldn't count on her ever wearing that coat. But you never know. What style of fur is it?*

Right then I got another alert that Franco's Porsche was on the move again. I would monitor it for a few minutes and see where it went.

Lynx, I said.

I mean what is the cut? Formal or more casual? She might be more likely to wear it if it's casual.

A waist-length jacket, I said. *Doesn't look fancy to me.*

Then I realized I could just send her a photo, so I did.

She might wear that. She might even tell people it's a faux fur. That way she can make her codger boyfriend happy and also avoid any drama.

I sent her a thumbs-up. *Thanks for your help.*

Going into the ninth inning, the Longhorns were up by seven.

Franco's Porsche stopped at a place called the Grove Wine Bar & Kitchen on Bee Caves Road, just a few hundred yards away from the HEB grocery store he'd visited earlier in the day. It was now 7:17 and the place was open until ten o'clock.

I didn't really want to go out right then, but it sure would be nice to grab the GPS tracker and be done with the case completely.

Franco would recognize the RX-7, so I took the van north on Cuernavaca. When I hit the light at Bee Caves Road, the Porsche hadn't moved. After I turned left, I realized that my gas gauge was below E. A stupid slip-up on my part. I whipped it into a Shell station on my right and bought three gallons. No sense in spending the additional time to fill the entire tank. I was back on the road in less than ninety seconds, and the Porsche still hadn't moved.

A few minutes later, I took a right into the parking lot for the strip center that included the wine bar. It was surprisingly crowded this late in the evening, but the place hosted a busy happy hour for people who were mostly in their forties and fifties.

I spotted Franco's Porsche sandwiched between a BMW and a Mercedes. I parked in an empty space five slots away. From here, I had a decent view of the front door to the bar, but three small trees planted in a neat row in front of the place obscured all the windows.

No sense in waiting. I stepped from the van and began walking toward the Porsche, keeping the row of vehicles between me and the building. I was pretty sure the Porsche would be visible from inside the bar, meaning I could be spotted. Not much I could do about that. If some random guest saw me kneel beside Franco's car, that person would assume I was the owner, or they'd think maybe I was looking for something I'd dropped.

I passed the rear bumper of a Lexus, then a Lincoln SUV, and the Mercedes, and now I was standing behind the Porsche. From here, I could see one of the windows into the bar, but a big group of customers was clustered on the sidewalk in front of it.

I moved along the passenger side of the Porsche and took a knee behind the front tire. I knelt lower and reached into the wheel well for the tracker, but I didn't immediately find it. I felt left, I felt right, but no luck. I knew the magnet was too strong for the tracker to have slid around. And I knew the tracker was still on the vehicle, or I wouldn't have been able to follow it to this location.

Oh, good lord. I was slipping. Normally I like to put a tracker on the passenger side of any target vehicle, but when the Porsche had been parked at Ski Shores, I'd had more discreet access to the driver's side, so that's where I'd placed it.

I got to my feet and walked to the rear of the car, and as I came around to the driver's side, the cluster of customers in front of the bar moved toward the front door.

Now I could see inside the bar, and seated at a table right beside one of the windows were two people having an intense conversation. Two women.

Took me a moment to realize it was Olivia and Carmen.

37

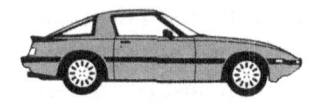

OLIVIA AND CARMEN. HAVING DRINKS together.

That didn't make a lot of sense, no matter how I looked at it. Not if there was an innocent explanation. I'd seen no indication at any point that Carmen and Olivia were friends or had ever socialized. In fact, Carmen had made it clear she wasn't particularly fond of Olivia. She'd called her a narcissist.

First things first. I quickly removed the tracker from the Porsche and slipped it into my pocket.

Then I focused on the women again. They were both leaning forward over the table, which would allow them to keep their conversation low and private.

Honestly, I had no idea what I should do, if anything. The case was over, right? For me it was. I could simply tell Lynann Chukwueze what I'd seen tonight and be done with it. Maybe it meant nothing.

Or I could go a different route. Go inside and see how they reacted. Why the hell not?

I walked across the parking lot, into the bar, and approached their table. They were so focused on their conversation, neither of them noticed me coming. I stopped at the end of the table.

"Hello, ladies," I said, because I'm suave that way.

They both looked up, but I was paying special attention to Carmen. The moment she recognized me—and realized I wasn't a host or a manager stopping to see how they liked their meal—her eyes widened. Her lips parted slightly. Her face blanched a bit. In short, it was the reaction of a guilty person who'd been caught totally unprepared.

"Saw you through the window and thought I'd say hi," I said.

"What?" Olivia said.

"I didn't know the two of you were friends," I said.

"We don't need any company right now," Olivia said. She was doing a much better job of masking her surprise.

"I'm sure you don't. Looked like you were discussing something important. What's the topic on this fine evening?"

"That's none of your business," Olivia said.

I continued to focus on Carmen. "How are you doing tonight? You look surprised to see me."

"Don't answer him," Olivia said.

"I'm just being friendly," I said.

"I'm leaving," Olivia said.

I looked at her.

"I'm curious—do you know Brett Murtaugh?"

"I don't have to answer your questions," Olivia said.

"He's one of Franco's pals."

"I know who he is. So what?"

"He tried to shoot me on Sunday night. Actually, it was early Monday morning. I'm sure you've heard about it. Before that, he came to my house and made some vague threats."

"I have no idea what that's all about," she said. "You must've done something to him first."

I was keeping my voice low, so nearby customers wouldn't hear, but nobody was paying any attention to us anyway.

"At first I thought Franco might've sent him to protect your little blackmail operation."

Finally, Olivia appeared somewhat flustered.

"What on earth are you talking about?" she said.

"I know all about it," I said. "But there are other things I didn't know, and after I shot Brett, while we were waiting for the ambulance, he spilled the beans. Told me everything he knew."

It was a calculated risk. How much did Brett really know?

Olivia didn't reply. Carmen was staring down at the table, her face as white as the napkin in her lap.

"It was an interesting story," I said.

"Brett's a liar," Olivia said.

"Well, sure, I considered the possibility that a guy like Brett, with his sterling reputation and impeccable record, might not be telling the truth. So I didn't tell the sheriff's investigator what Brett told me. I wanted to take a step back and look at all the evidence—all the statements, the timeline—and see if any of it made sense. I've done that, and frankly, it all seems legit. And now that I've found you two having a little powwow, well, that's just the cherry on top. Now I know it's all true."

"You don't know what the fuck you're talking about," Olivia said, picking up her phone and rising from her seat. She looked at Carmen, expecting Carmen to also stand, but she didn't. "I'm leaving," Olivia repeated, pulling her purse off the back of the chair.

"Now's the time for both of you to tell your side of it," I said. "Before Brett's account goes on the record. As soon as he gets out of the hospital and ends up in jail, I think he'll talk. He'll want out, so he'll strike a deal."

Olivia gave Carmen a sharp look. "Don't talk to him," she said. "He's making stuff up. He doesn't know anything, because there's nothing to know. You don't have to answer his questions."

Carmen didn't reply. Olivia took two twenties out of her purse and tossed them on the table. She looked at me again. "You can get bent."

"I'm already bent," I said. "Wanna see?"

She marched out of the bar with her head held as high as possible, to show me that she wasn't rattled at all, and she had nothing to hide, and she certainly wasn't going to listen to any more of my nonsense.

I watched out the window as Olivia crossed to the Porsche and got inside. But she didn't drive away. Instead, she made a phone call. Pretty easy to guess who was on the other end. A few seconds later, she began making a lot of heated, animated gestures.

I turned toward Carmen again. "I'm going to sit down, okay?"

She nodded. Good sign.

I took Olivia's chair, still warm.

"They have decent food here," I said. "Good service."

"How did you find us?" she asked quietly. "Did you follow one of us?"

"I followed you," I said.

At this point I saw total resignation on her face.

"I thought you weren't working on this case anymore."

"That's what I wanted you to think."

The waiter came—appeared confused for a moment that I had replaced Olivia—then asked me if I wanted anything. I declined, and he left us alone again. I glanced outside and saw that Olivia was still sitting in the Porsche, and still on the phone. I knew my time was going to be limited. Olivia had driven Franco's car, but he had a motorcycle. He could hop on that and be here in minutes.

I said, "You said you saw Olivia coming out of her bedroom ten seconds after Norman was shot, and she said she saw you, so you provided mutual alibis for each other. It all hinged on that. But Brett told me what really happened."

I waited for Carmen to reply, but she said nothing.

I said, "If you think Olivia won't throw you under the bus, you are very much mistaken. She'll blame everything on you. That's why you need to be the first to talk. The person who flips first will get a better deal. You'll have leverage. Assuming you didn't pull the trigger yourself. Just tell the truth, hire a good lawyer, and get the best plea deal you possibly can."

I tipped my head toward the parking lot. "Olivia's out there talking to Franco right now, and they're trying to work out a story. It will be two against one. That means you need to—"

"Norman was a terrible man," Carmen said.

I kept quiet. She was about to say more, and I didn't want to derail that.

"I'm ready to tell the truth and put this all behind me," Carmen said.

"I think that's a good idea," I said.

"You saw how Norman was," Carmen said. "I knew he had some anger issues when I worked for him at his office, but once I came to work at the house, I saw how hostile he could be. He was ugly to everybody, but especially to Evelyn. Abusive. Mostly verbally, but occasionally physically. I only suspected that at first, because he never did it in front of me, but as Evelyn and I became closer, she finally admitted it all to me. She had a busted lip one morning, and when I asked her about it, she began to cry. This was three years ago. She said Norman had slapped her—and it wasn't the first time. I pleaded for her to call the police, but she wouldn't. There were other injuries after that, including a broken arm about six months ago. She went to the emergency room for that, so there will be a record."

"But she still didn't call the cops?"

"No, and she told the doctor at the ER that she fell down some steps. She told her personal physician the same thing. She blamed it on the progression of her disease."

I was worried that Franco might show up at the bar at any minute. What would he do? Come inside and try to stop this conversation? Wait outside and try to fight me? I didn't want to rush Carmen, but I also wanted to hear the full story before we were interrupted.

"What led up to the shooting?" I asked.

"Let me see your phone," she said.

Smart. Checking to see if I was recording. I pulled it from my pocket and showed it to her. Then I placed it flat on the table.

She leaned in closer and began to talk again.

38

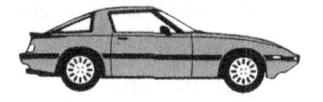

"ABOUT A MONTH AGO, OLIVIA and I saw Norman grab Evelyn by the arm again—the same arm he'd broken before—and yell at her. He was always grabbing her by the arm."

"I saw the bruises," I said. "I thought maybe her condition had made her fall."

"Hell, no. It was Norman. He and Evelyn were out by the pool and he didn't know we were watching. And he grabbed her and shook her and yelled at her. That was the first time Olivia and I talked about it, because we were both there, and we saw it, so we had to talk about it. We both got angry, and Olivia said, 'I could kill the son of a bitch.' Then she gave me a look that said she wasn't kidding. She really meant it."

Carmen took a deep breath.

Please hurry, I thought, but I said nothing.

"I didn't respond at the time, but I began to wonder if she might do something rash and get herself in trouble. I contemplated calling the sheriff then and reporting the abuse myself, but how would I prove it? Would my word be enough? Plus, Norman would've fired me, and I wouldn't have been able to help Evelyn if I weren't in the house with her. Then Ed Gray's truck got burglarized, followed by the vandalism at our house. At first, I thought it was just some teenagers, or maybe it was Jeremy Olson. But then late one night I couldn't sleep and I noticed that the motion-activated lights aimed at the driveway had turned on. I looked out my window and saw Olivia walking away from Norman's Jaguar, heading toward the front door. I didn't think much of it, but the next morning, Norman announced that his tires had been slashed."

"Did you ask Olivia about it?"

"No, I just figured her anger got the best of her, so she just had to do something to make herself feel better. I assumed she was the vandal all along, and I admit I took some pleasure in that, because it made Norman so mad. I never imagined it would end the way it did."

"You never talked to Olivia about the vandalism?"

"Yes, we talked about it in general, but I never revealed that I'd seen her, and she never confessed to me."

I needed to move on, because Franco was surely on his way over here by now.

"Tell me what happened the night of the shooting," I said.

"The sound of the shot woke me. At first I was confused, wondering what the sound was, or whether I'd dreamt it. Then I heard a man yelling—or I guess it was more of a loud moaning. I didn't know who it was or what was happening, so I opened my door and stepped into the hall. Olivia's room is off that same hallway, but at the rear side of the house. I could see from my room that her door was open, and she usually keeps it closed when she's in there, especially if she's sleeping."

The waiter approached again, but I waved him off before he could reach the table.

Carmen said, "As soon as I started down the hallway toward the front door, I heard somebody coming, so I stopped where I was. A few seconds later, Olivia stepped into the hallway and she froze when she saw me. She had a gun in her hand. Her right hand. A silver gun."

"Did either of you say anything?"

"I asked what happened, and Olivia told me to hang on for a second, and she went into her bedroom. She looked really upset, and I could hear her in there calling 911, so I stood in her doorway and listened. She said somebody had just shot Norman in the driveway and he needed an ambulance."

"So Norman was outside by himself at that point?"

"Yes. Then I heard Olivia say she couldn't stay on the phone because she needed to go help Norman, and when she came out of the bedroom, she told me I shouldn't tell the police that I saw her with a gun. I should tell them we came out of our bedrooms at the same time."

"She wanted you to give her an alibi," I said.

"Right."

"Did you take that to mean she shot Norman?"

"I wasn't sure, but there wasn't enough time for her to have heard the shot, gone outside to see what happened, found Norman, and then come back inside."

"How much time elapsed between the shot and when you first saw Olivia?"

"I'd say twenty seconds, or maybe thirty at the most."

"Did you know before then that Olivia owned a gun?"

"I had no idea. But I own one, too, and nobody knows that."

"Obviously, you agreed to cover for her."

"By the time I was interviewed, yes. I'd decided that even if Olivia shot Norman, I was okay with it. I know that sounds horrible, but it's true. I wanted Evelyn's remaining time to be as happy as possible, instead of living under the thumb of an abuser."

"So you both said you came out of your bedrooms at about the same time."

"Right. We said we went outside together and found Norman, and Olivia called 911 while I tried to stop the bleeding. That last part was true. We went outside and I tried to help him."

"Was he conscious?"

"By then, no."

"Did Olivia ever actually admit she shot him?"

"No. I didn't ask."

"Do you think she did it?"

"I don't know what else could explain it, and who can blame her? She wanted to protect her aunt."

Carmen was overlooking the profit motive—a massive inheritance—but there was no reason to bring that up right now.

I said, "Are you willing to tell Lynann exactly what happened?"

"Yes. I'll hire an attorney, and then—"

She stopped talking, because something through the window had caught her attention. I looked outside, and instead of seeing Franco, I saw that a Travis County deputy had just pulled into the lot in a marked

SUV.

Uh-oh. Obviously, she hadn't called Franco. Just as I had done a few minutes earlier, she'd gone a different route.

Olivia got out of the Porsche and began to wave the deputy down, and it was clear from her body language that she was pretending to be distraught. Putting on a big show, in fact. Frantic. Emotional. Bordering on hysterical.

What exactly had she reported? I would find out very soon, obviously.

"What's happening?" Carmen asked.

I decided it would be better to exit the bar, rather than waiting for the deputy to enter and find me.

"Olivia is siccing the dogs on me," I said as I rose from the table. "You stay here, okay? We can finish talking later. For now, everything you just told me is confidential, okay? I won't tell anyone, including the deputy."

She said, "I'll wait. I'm ready to be done with all this."

Just then, a second deputy in a marked SUV pulled into the lot. Now I was getting concerned. A back-up deputy indicated that Olivia had reported something serious, and she'd said she was currently still in danger.

So imagine how I felt when a third deputy squealed into the lot.

Nobody else inside the bar had even noticed yet. I weaved my way through the crowd and exited the bar, my hands empty, and began to walk toward the first deputy, who'd stepped from his SUV and was talking to Olivia.

I was twenty yards away.

Olivia saw me coming and pointed. Her face contorted. She began to scream.

The deputy drew his service weapon, smoothly and quickly, but before he even aimed it at me, I placed my hands over my head, turned around, and dropped to my knees.

"All the way down!"

I lay flat on the pavement, arms outstretched.

"Do not move!"

Within a few seconds, I had a knee on my back and the deputy cuffed me. Then he frisked me, telling me I wasn't being arrested, I was merely being detained. When he got to my right front pocket, he said, "What's this?"

"GPS tracker," I said.

"What do you use it for?"

"Tracking things with GPS," I said.

He pulled my phone from my front pocket, and then my wallet from my back pocket. He looked at my ID. He didn't seem to recognize my name.

He lifted me to my feet and walked me toward his SUV. Now I was able to get a good look at him, but I didn't recognize him. His nametag said DOYLE. I did recognize one of the other two deputies, a young woman named Shandra Lewis. When she saw me from ten yards away, she shook her head, like, *Oh, God, not you again.* I smiled at her. She did not smile back.

"What did Olivia Reed tell the 911 operator?" I asked Doyle.

The sun was dipping below the tree line now and it would be dark soon.

"In a minute," Doyle said, steering me into the rear of the SUV.

"Based on this response, she's jerking your chain," I said. "Ask the woman inside who was with her. Her name is Carmen Romero. I was just talking to her."

"What happened in there tonight?"

"I saw Olivia Reed and Carmen Romero having dinner, so I went inside to say hello. I met them both recently while I was working a case."

"What kind of case?"

"I'm a videographer and I was trying to catch a repeat vandal at a home over by City Park. But then the homeowner got shot. Guy named Norman Conlee."

Doyle said he was familiar with the case.

I said, "Olivia is the Conlees' niece. She has a boyfriend named Franco who got upset with me poking around over there, and a couple of days ago, it got physical. He lost. I think Olivia is holding a grudge and is using you fine folks to get back at me. I have no idea what she told you, but again, just ask Carmen. She'll back me up."

"Hang tight," Doyle said and he closed the door.

I sat quietly for a long time. Doyle and one of the other deputies went inside the bar. Shandra Lewis was talking to a cluster of patrons who had exited the bar, apparently asking if anybody had seen or heard anything. I had no idea where Olivia was at this point. I couldn't see the Porsche from here. Maybe she was waiting in one of the other SUVs.

Ten minutes passed. I guess Doyle was interviewing Carmen and getting the full story. Probably asking a lot of questions, just to make sure he knew what really happened.

Shandra Lewis walked over and opened the SUV door.

"Hey, Shandra," I said.

"Last time I saw you, a man had accused you of punching him in the face," she said.

"The captain of the party barge on Lake Travis," I said. "Remember what happened with that one?"

"No charges."

"Because he made it all up," I said.

"This seems to be a pattern with you," she said.

"My foes cannot vanquish me with the truth, so they resort to chicanery."

"Uh-huh."

"You mind telling me what she called in?"

"She said you showed her a gun and told her you'd be waiting outside for her. She said you assaulted her boyfriend a few days ago."

"But I stayed inside the bar and she's the one who came outside," I said. "How does that story make any sense?"

"That's what we're trying to find out."

"After she came outside, she could've simply driven away," I said.

"She said she thought you'd lost sight of her, so she was afraid to do anything, because she didn't want you to see her and follow her."

"And my van's gonna keep up with a Porsche?"

"What happened with the boyfriend?"

I told her the same brief version I'd told Doyle.

Shandra Lewis said, "You sure do get yourself caught up in a lot of tough situations."

"I realize it's hard to believe that none of them are my fault, but none of them are my fault."

"Right."

"Is Doyle talking to Carmen Romero or what?" I asked. "She'll back me up."

"Lemme check," she said, and closed the door.

After another three minutes, Doyle returned to the SUV.
"No Carmen Romero," he said.
"I'm sorry, what?"
"The waiter says she hauled ass."

39

THEY COULDN'T ARREST ME, OF course.

There was no evidence whatsoever to support Olivia's claim. No gun was found inside the restaurant. They wanted to search my van—which made no sense, because I'd supposedly been carrying a gun inside the bar and had not gone back outside before the deputies arrived—but I let them search it anyway. They didn't find one there, either.

Nobody inside the bar could confirm anything Olivia had said. And when they pressed her on it again, she said if they weren't going to believe her, then she wasn't going to answer any more questions. They let us both go. They warned her that she might get charged later for filing a false report.

Now I had a decision to make.

What should I do with the account Carmen Romero had given me? Was it even accurate? It *sounded* right, but that didn't mean it *was* right. There was still so much I didn't know.

Had Olivia really shot Norman?

Had she committed all the acts of vandalism, or had someone helped? Had she used the vandalism to set the stage for the shooting, or had Norman caught her doing something else, and she shot him in response?

How did the burglary of Ed Gray's truck figure in, if at all? And why had Jacob Buckley been killed?

What was the story behind the gun Jeremy Olson found under his hedge? Where had it come from? Was it Olivia's gun?

When I got back into my car, I called Carmen, hoping she had merely been spooked by the incident at the bar and had fled to buy some time. Maybe she could answer all of these questions. The call went to voicemail, so I asked her to call me back. I wanted to assure her that everything she'd told me was still between us, but it was possible the cops could be hearing the recording sometime soon, via a search warrant, so I didn't get into that.

I waited a moment, just in case she called back immediately, but she didn't.

The moment was strangely anticlimactic. One minute I was being cuffed, frisked, and questioned, and the next I was sitting quietly in the van, wondering whether or not I finally knew the truth.

I went home, and by now, it had been dark for an hour.

I grabbed a beer out of the fridge and sat on the couch. Still no word from Carmen, so I texted her again.

Can you call me back, please?

I watched my phone, hoping to see that little bubble with three dots in it, but I got nothing.

By the way, I'm not in jail, I added.

I waited again, but nothing.

Despite my promise to Carmen, if she didn't get back to me, I would need to tell Lynann Chukwueze the full story. Then she could sort through it and figure out if it was true. But it would be nice if Carmen would talk to me first and fill in the details, just to satisfy my own curiosity.

Why did you take off? I asked. *You left me in a tight spot. Fortunately, I used my wit and charm to wiggle my way out. Now I'm hoping we can continue our conversation.*

No response. No bubble.

You need to give me a call within 15 minutes or I'll have to break my promise.

Fifteen minutes passed with no response. Okay, I'd had enough.

I sent a text to Lynann.

Tonight Carmen Romero gave me new information about the shooting. If you are awake and want to hear it, give me a call.

My phone rang less than thirty seconds later.

I answered with, "What are you wearing?"

"Not much right now, but I can get dressed and come over there and kick your ass, if you want."

"I'll pass."

"Let's hear what you got."

I spent a few minutes recounting my conversations with Carmen and Evelyn earlier in the day, and then I said, "I'd basically given up on the case, but about three hours ago, I decided to pop over to the Grove Wine Bar at Bee Caves and 360, and when I pulled into the lot, I saw Franco's Porsche. So then—"

"Wait a sec. You just happened to be there at the same time?"

"Yes."

"Just a coincidence?" she asked.

"Completely," I said. "Austin is a big city, but Westlake Hills is a small town. You run into a lot of people you know."

"Uh-huh. Proceed."

"Of course, if you end up reading the deputy's report about the incident, it'll say I had a GPS tracker in my pocket."

"Roy," she said.

"We shouldn't get distracted by minor details, should we?"

"Keep going."

I told her everything that had taken place after that, starting with surprising Olivia and Carmen and ending with my eventual release.

When I was done, Lynann didn't reply right away.

I said, "Amazing work on my part, huh?"

"Well, yeah, if you mean you have a skill for stumbling into the middle of things."

"It's like they say…better to be lucky than good."

"Who says that?"

"They do. Them. Those people who say things."

"Problem is, Carmen's word isn't enough to prove Olivia Reed did anything at all."

"I know."

"Especially if Carmen isn't willing to tell me the same story on the record."

"The important thing is that I've dumped this into your lap, and now I can continue on my merry way, with nary another thought about it."

"Let me know immediately if you hear from Carmen," she said.

"I will."

"I'm not bullshitting, Roy."

"I really will. This case is a merry-go-round and I'm ready to hop off."

"I'll be calling her myself, and probably interviewing Olivia again tomorrow, if she'll talk. And Franco."

"Good luck," I said. "You get out there and show 'em why you're the best in the business."

"For that, Mr. Smart Aleck, you won't be getting any updates from me."

"Promise?"

She snorted and disconnected the call.

So now—finally, at long last—the Conlee case was completely out of my hands, without question, and that was a good reason to celebrate. I poured myself a bit of Irish whiskey over ice and got settled on the couch again.

At 10:15, Scarlett sent a text: *Hey, how about dinner at my place tmw night?*

Sounds great. Who is this?

Funny. Be here at 7:00 or I'll call the other guy I'm seeing.

I sent her a wow-face emoji.

We went back and forth for another ten or fifteen minutes, but I didn't say anything about the incident at the Grove Wine Bar or the confession from Carmen. I'd save that for tomorrow night. I didn't have the patience to get into it tonight.

I wasn't feeling particularly tired, so I opened my laptop and returned to my investigation of Clinton DuBois, Patricia Blevins, and the allegedly purloined fur coat. I'd gotten lucky with the Conlee case—stumbling upon Carmen and Olivia having drinks together—so

I decided to see if my luck would hold with this case.

I used my fake Harriet Jones account to send Patricia a friend request. Unlike most spammers and scammers out there, Harriet appeared perfectly real, because I'd taken the time to cultivate her legitimacy over an extended period. She had plenty of publicly visible posts that would make most people think she was nothing more than an active, extroverted, single, friendly woman about town. She had more than two hundred friends, many of whom probably still wondered how they knew her. I posted for Harriet once or twice a week, just to keep things real, so to speak.

I knew from experience that women were much less likely than men to accept a friend request from a stranger—even another woman—so I'd just have to wait and see if Patricia Blevins took the bait. If she did take it, the odds were slim that she would've posted a photo of herself in the fur coat, unless she didn't know Clinton DuBois had reported it stolen.

I was hoping she would accept the request by tomorrow morning, so I could sort through her photos before deciding on other measures.

40

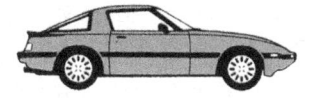

NOPE.

The next morning, I saw that Patricia Blevins had not accepted my friend request—but after some more thought, I came up with another idea.

Let's say you're Clinton DuBois and you decide to give your dead wife's fur coat to your new girlfriend. Wouldn't you actually get it cleaned, just as he'd claimed he'd been planning to do, before it was stolen from inside his vehicle? Almost certainly yes, because it would've been musty after being in storage for six years. He wouldn't give it to the new girl all smelly and dusty.

However, even if he hadn't had the social graces to get it cleaned, Patricia would've had it done, right? I mean, it was a vintage coat, not new, so she would've insisted on a cleaning. Right? I thought so.

Okay, where would she have taken it? A regular dry cleaners that handles shirts, blouses, and blue jeans? Or a store that claims to have special skills in the cleaning of furs? My money was on the latter.

Some quick googling revealed that there were only a handful of higher-end cleaners like that in Austin, so I began to email them, one by one. I included a photo of the missing fur and said there would be a $250 reward if they'd seen this coat and could provide evidence it had been in the store. Video of the person dropping the fur off would be ideal. I mentioned that the fur had been reported stolen, so anyone who was in possession of it, or who had possessed it previously, had technically committed a crime, so the best course of action, now that they had been informed, was to come forward and report what they knew.

When I finished sending the emails, I decided that was enough work for the day. After all, it had taken a full twenty minutes.

I cleaned my house. After that, I changed the oil in the van, which was long overdue. I showered, ate a ham sandwich for lunch, and took a nap. When I woke, three of the fur shops had replied to my email, all of them saying they'd never seen that coat before. One of them attached a coupon good for ten percent off any alteration over $100. A hundred bucks for an alteration? I owned very few items of clothing that cost that much brand new.

I considered texting Lynann to see if she'd spoken with Carmen, but honestly, I was enjoying the fact that it wasn't my problem anymore. Carmen still hadn't responded to my texts, so I was pretty sure at this point she'd changed her mind and was going to keep her mouth shut, or she was busy finding a lawyer to represent her. Or maybe everything she'd told me was a lie. Lynann would figure it out.

I called Ruelas to see if he could give me an update on Brett Murtaugh's condition. No answer, of course, so I left a voicemail.

"Hey, it's Roy Ballard. Since Brett Murtaugh is the suspect in two murders and is an all-around scalawag, can you do me a favor and give me a heads-up if he gets out on bail after he gets out of the hospital? That would be peachy. Also, if he does get out and something happens to me, I hope you'll set aside your unwarranted dislike for me and prosecute the guy to the fullest extent of your service revolver. You'd be doing the world a favor. That's all for now. I miss you. Mean it."

An hour later, he still had not replied, but I received a call from one of the fur shops.

"People are crazy," the man said. He was the owner and his name was Bill Emerson.

"That's true. Others are just stupid."

"I have that coat in my shop right now," he said.

He had an East Coast accent and sounded to be in his fifties or sixties.

"Any chance it's a lookalike?" I asked.

"I haven't seen many coats like this one before, but I guess it's possible."

"Who brought it in?" I said.

"A young woman named Patricia Blevins," he said.

"Then I can confirm that's the coat I'm looking for," I said.

"Gotta be honest—she didn't seem like a thief or a burglar."

"Technically, now I know that the coat hasn't been stolen, it's simply been *reported* as stolen," I said. "And she may or may not have any idea what's happening."

"Oh, I get it. Somebody's committing fraud and they gave the coat to her."

"That's what it looks like."

"Boyfriend?"

"Something like that."

"So what do I do now? Call the police?"

"Yes, and feel free to give them my number." I gave him the detective's name and the case number. "Do you have security cameras at your place?"

"I do, yes."

"Can you send me a clip of Patricia Blevins dropping the coat off?"

"I'll have my son do it. He takes care of all that stuff."

"Perfect. I appreciate it. How would you like me to send the reward money?"

"I don't want it. I don't need my shop being associated with stolen goods. Thanks anyway."

Fine by me, because that reward would've come out of my cut.

One hour later, I had the video clip, which I forwarded to my client. Even better, Emerson sent another clip from an exterior camera, clearly showing Clinton DuBois parking outside, with Patricia Blevins in the passenger seat. That put a tidy bow on the case.

If I could solve them all this easily, I'd be known far and wide as a fraud-busting genius. Or farther and wider.

I sent my client an update, then took a shower.

I rang the bell at Scarlett's place a few minutes after seven, and when she answered, before I could greet her, she said, "Ssshhh. Don't say anything yet."

"Uh..."

"Nope. Quiet."

She pulled me inside and closed the door behind me. "You have a decision to make. I need to share some news with you, and you can hear it now or later."

I looked at her. She looked at me.

"Can I talk?"

"Just to give me your answer. Do you want to hear it now or later?"

"Depends on what might happen now," I said.

"Well, I was thinking we could fool around," she said.

Of course, I had an idea what the news would be. The job in San Francisco. She'd made a decision, and now she was offering me one more intimate night before we acknowledged that this relationship—whatever it was—was going to be killed by sheer distance.

"Later," I said.

She nodded and reached out with one hand to cup my cheek. "Good choice," she said softly.

Then she took me by the hand and we went into the bedroom.

Afterward, we sat on her back patio, drinks in hand, and ate dinner delivered by a Chinese restaurant on Far West Boulevard. Hank the cat watched us from a windowsill.

Then Scarlett said, "Okay, well, I guess we'd better get this over with."

"I'm glad you didn't say that before we went to bed."

She smiled. "I guess you know what the topic is."

"Pretty sure you're taking the job in San Francisco."

She nodded. "I have to. I'd be an idiot if I didn't. It's literally a once-in-a-lifetime opportunity."

"I understand," I said. "I'm sure you'll be great. Your talent is obvious."

"Thank you. I'm nervous as hell, to be honest. Not just the job, but the move and all that."

"That's understandable," I said. "At least you have some time to prepare."

"Well, there's something else."

"Uh-oh."

The sun had set twenty minutes earlier, but there was still enough light that I could see her face.

She said, "The creative director—the one who's retiring—he had some chest pain two days ago and went to the doctor. He needs a quadruple bypass."

"Jeez."

"He decided that it's—he's not returning to work. He's done."

Easy to see where this was going. "So instead of needing you in three months…"

"They want me out there as soon as possible. They added a big hiring bonus to make it happen. I mean *big*."

"Big is good."

"Indeed."

I took a sip of whiskey. "I'm afraid to ask how soon," I said.

"One month," she said. "I promised one month. Any sooner than that would be crazy. Thirty days is crazy enough, considering all I have to do before then. All the packing, and then I have to decide if I'm going to sell this place or lease it out. Then I have to find a place to stay in San Francisco. They're putting me up in an executive suite until I can find a place, which brings up Hank, and how he's going to handle it. Do I want to move him twice? Just when he gets settled into the suite, we'll have to move again. I'm stressed to the max, if you can't tell."

I reached for the bottle of whiskey and poured another ounce into her glass. "Are you? It's not noticeable at all," I said.

She laughed. "Your job is to take my mind off it all for a few minutes."

"I thought I just did."

"Well, yeah, but earlier you said you had an update on all the Conlee stuff."

So I brought her up to speed, which took nearly twenty minutes, ending with the incident at the Grove Bar the night before.

"So Olivia shot Norman?" Scarlett said.

"Maybe, but keep in mind that she hasn't confessed to anything. Maybe Carmen isn't remembering everything accurately. Maybe Olivia heard the shot, then went outside and found Norman. Then she came back inside, ran into Carmen, and they decided to say they came out of their bedrooms at the same time."

"You think that's what happened?" Scarlett asked.

"I have no idea."

"But Carmen said Olivia slashed Norman's tires. Why would she do that if she didn't shoot him?"

"Maybe just to feel good. She was angry, and she didn't like him."

"Not many people did," Scarlett said. "It's kind of sad, when you think about it."

By eight o'clock the next morning, I'd decided that this would be the last time I'd see Scarlett. I'd grown attached to her in a short time, but why build on that? Why set myself up for more heartache? Better to end it now.

So, as we stood in the kitchen drinking coffee, I said, "I think maybe this is it."

She wasn't surprised. She didn't object or try to change my mind. She'd probably reached the same conclusion.

She moved closer and leaned against the counter near me. "Can I stay in touch?"

"Of course."

"You won't mind a text or a call now and then?"

"Not at all."

"Can I tell you how much fun I've had since we met?" Scarlett asked.

"Who am I to stop you?"

"I want you to be careful, okay? In your job."

"You can count on it. I want you to go out to California and enjoy every minute."

"I will."

We made some more small talk, finished our coffee, and then I gave her one last kiss. That new chapter had already ended. I tried to look on the bright side. There'd be more.

41

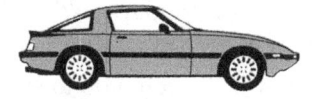

Five minutes later, I was driving slowly along Mañana Street in the RX-7. I had the windows down and the sunroof open. The weather was crisp and cool. There was no indication that this morning was about to go off the rails.

I passed the Conlee house and saw a white minivan out front. There was a logo on the side, but I couldn't make it out. So I stopped for a moment and grabbed some binoculars from the glove compartment. The van was from a home health agency. Maybe Evelyn had taken a turn for the worse and Carmen didn't have the skills to provide proper care. Sad to think about, but it was inevitable. I put the binoculars away, and continued down the street.

I'd gone no more than fifty yards when I saw Franco's Porsche coming toward me, but sunlight reflecting on the windshield prevented me from seeing who was in the car. The Porsche suddenly veered into my lane and blocked the road diagonally. The door popped open quickly and Franco stepped out. I could tell in an instant from his body language that he was boiling mad. He marched toward my car.

There wasn't enough room on either side for me to go around him. I could either put it in reverse and back up, or lock my doors and stay put, or get out of the car.

I got out.

"You need to work on your parking," I said.

"The fuck did you do?" he asked, pointing a finger at me, but he stopped ten feet away.

"You'll have to be more specific," I said to Franco.

Now Olivia got out of the passenger side and began to walk toward the Conlee house.

"You screwed everything up," Franco said.

"Well, I'm sure that's possible, but I'll still need more than that."

"We just came back from APD. Why do the cops think Olivia shot her uncle?"

"Did you?" I asked Olivia as she passed me. She just kept walking. "Did she?" I asked Franco.

"Of course not!"

"How about you?"

He made a frustrated gesture and let out a guttural groan, as if it was all he could do to stop himself from attacking me.

"I wasn't anywhere near here!" he said.

His emotion seemed so genuine; was it possible he really didn't know who shot Norman?

"You could've had somebody do it," I said.

"You're nuts, man. If you think I did it, why did you tell the cops Olivia did it?"

"I didn't tell them that. I told them that Carmen told me that Olivia did it."

"Well, if that was true, why did she disappear?"

"Who? Carmen?"

He laughed. "Oh, man, you didn't know, did you? She's gone, genius. Cops can't find her since she left the Grove Bar the other night."

Yet another development I had not seen coming.

"That doesn't mean her statement was false," I said, although I sounded weak, even to myself.

"Bullshit. She ran because she's guilty, and Olivia had nothing to do with it."

"Then why did you send your pal Brett after me? He tried to scare me off the case."

It was a test. Franco didn't know I knew Olivia was a call girl, and that they were blackmailing Albert Strauss and possibly several other johns. I simply wanted to see and hear Franco's reaction, because it would tell me the real reason for sending Murtaugh.

"Yeah, right," Franco said. "Like I'm gonna answer that."

He was dumb, but not dumb enough to confess.

I said, "If you didn't send him because of the vandalism and the shooting, there had to be some other reason."

"You're not very good at minding your own business," Franco said, grinning, because he was enjoying playing coy.

And that was probably all the acknowledgment I was going to get.

I said, "I already know the reason, and I'm curious about something. Are you Olivia's husband or her pimp or both?"

His grin morphed into a tight grimace, but he didn't say anything. He just glared at me.

I said, "By the way, congrats on getting married. I'm sure you'll have a long and loving marriage, considering that your wife is a hooker."

He made that growling noise again, and he rushed me. It was almost comical.

Right before he reached me, I stepped to my left and stuck my right foot out, tripping him. This was the type of maneuver that generally only works on *The Three Stooges*, but it worked on Franco. He sprawled headlong onto the pavement.

"Franco," I said. "You are really bad at this. Anyone ever tell you that?"

He lumbered to his feet, wiping his hands off.

I turned my left side toward him. Spread my feet a bit for stability. Bent my knees slightly. Raised my fists. And waited.

He took a deep breath. Then another. And he charged me again.

If anyone had been able to watch the subsequent few seconds in slow motion on video, they would've seen me twist to my left and dip my shoulder, in preparation for throwing a left hook. I'd always been fond of the left hook. It's not unlike a golf swing, in that you coil your body like a spring, and then explode back the other way, channeling all that kinetic energy into your punch.

Fortunately, my timing was perfect. Just as Franco rushed into range, with both hands raised, planning to tackle me, I came around with my fist and caught him square on the jaw. Hard. One of the hardest punches I'd ever landed. He staggered to my right, his legs wobbling as he gamely attempted to remain standing, but a second later his knees buckled and he collapsed to the ground.

He wailed and moaned and muttered something with his teeth clenched, but I couldn't make it out. Then I realized he'd said, "You broke my fuckin' jaw."

I almost asked if he needed a ride to the hospital, but at this point I was sick of Franco, and I was sick of his car, and I was sick of the people he ran with, and mostly I never wanted to see him again.

I spoke calmly. "Leave Albert Strauss alone. He's a good man and he doesn't deserve your crap. If you contact him again, you won't see me coming until it's too late, and it will be brutal. You're in over your head. You hear me?"

He nodded and said something, but I couldn't make it out, and it didn't really matter, did it?

I got into his Porsche and pulled it onto the right side of the road.

Then I got into the RX-7 and drove around it, while Franco was still seated on the pavement, cradling his jaw.

I parked in the lot at Ski Shores and simply sat for a moment, breathing deeply to get my adrenaline in check. My left hand ached a little, but I hadn't broken anything, which is a real risk when you punch somebody in the head.

After I'd lowered my heart rate, I texted Lynann Chukwueze.

Carmen took off?

She called me immediately. "Hey, you made me promise not to give you any updates."

"I'm fickle that way, but I'd like to know."

"Nobody's seen Carmen since the Grove Bar. We're assuming she left town, but we have to consider the possibility that something happened to her."

"Like, say, Franco or Olivia trying to keep her from telling her story to you?"

"That crossed my mind, but I don't see any indication that happened. She filled up with gas one hour after she left the Grove Bar, and then she went to an ATM and got more than a thousand dollars from several different accounts. That was the last activity on her bank cards, and her cell phone has been dead. I mean, she's gotten some incoming calls, including from you, but she didn't answer any of them, and she hasn't placed any calls."

"She ran."

"I'd say so. We know she has a passport, because she's traveled out of the country several times with the Conlees. I was able to get a warrant to search her emails, hoping maybe I'd get a clue where she went. I didn't, but I learned she was the beneficiary on several of Norman's money-market accounts—to the tune of one-point-six million dollars. Carmen did some of the bookkeeping for the Conlees, so she had access to those accounts online, and that beneficiary was changed the day *after* Norman was shot. Evelyn was the beneficiary before that."

I remembered now that Carmen had told me one of her responsibilities was paying the Conlees' bills. Apparently Norman had given her greater access than he should have.

"Was Carmen authorized to make that change?" I asked.

"Nope. Just Norman. Or Evelyn, but I called her and she said she didn't do it. I pointed out that Carmen had basically embezzled from her, and she said that was ridiculous, and it didn't really matter, because Carmen deserved that money. Then she said she might've instructed Carmen to make that change, but then forgot about it."

Memory issues were one symptom of corticobasal degeneration—but I was inclined to believe that Evelyn had simply chosen to cover for Carmen.

"Is that money still in those accounts?" I asked.

"I have no idea. I doubt I could get a warrant to check, because I have no evidence that Carmen committed any kind of crime, especially with Evelyn saying she might've okayed the whole thing."

"But you were able to get warrants for her bank cards and that other stuff," I said.

"Yeah, because of the possibility she might be in danger, but checking those account balances wouldn't tell me anything about her welfare. A judge would never okay it, especially now that everything points to her taking off voluntarily."

I quietly digested this information for a moment, then I said, "Is the implication here that Carmen's story was a lie, and maybe she was the shooter?"

"Maybe, but I don't think she acted alone. When I talked to Olivia an hour ago, she was willing to give her version of events, and you know what she told me?"

"I can't even imagine."

"She told the same story Carmen told you, but in reverse. In other words, she said she came out of her room and saw Carmen come back into the house carrying a gun. I mean it was identical down to the last detail—almost like they'd agreed to point the finger at each other."

"Meaning you think that's what they did?"

"I do."

"To intentionally muddy the water."

"Sure looks that way. I think they agreed to create confusion, hoping we wouldn't be able to charge either of them. How could we charge either of them if the other might've done it? Olivia gave her statement—sounding pretty rehearsed, if you ask me—and then she said she wasn't willing to talk anymore. No questions, so I couldn't pick it apart. I had no choice but to let her leave."

"What's your next step?"

"I'm gonna keep hassling Olivia and see if I can get a warrant for all her cell phone data—both phones. I'm hoping to see some texts between her and Carmen, but she probably uses an app that erases them after they're read."

"Wouldn't surprise me."

"And I'm going to interview Evelyn Conlee again. Honestly, I haven't pushed her too hard so far, because I don't think she was involved, but if she's covering for Carmen or Olivia or both of them, I'm going to badger it out of her."

I didn't envy her having to put the pressure on a woman in Evelyn Conlee's condition.

"Okay, well, like last time, I don't want any updates. No updates at all."

"Meaning you want updates," she said.

"You know me so well."

42

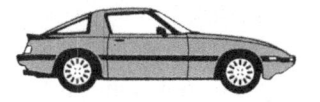

Everything was quiet for three days—no important phone calls, texts, or emails, and no new cases. I enjoyed every minute.

The day I'd met Scarlett at Ski Shores, she'd said she needed to get a flask for herself. It had been an offhand remark and she probably didn't mean it, but I bought one for her anyway, and I had a message engraved on the side.

Scarlett,
Best of luck in San Francisco.
Cheers,
Roy

I put it in a nice gift box and sent it by mail. I doubted she would ever use it, but it would sit on her office shelf and remind her of our time together, and I figured that was good enough.

That afternoon, Lynann Chukwueze called.

"Here's an update for you—one that might help you sleep better. Late yesterday, I got a call from Paul Murtaugh, and it seems his conscience got the best of him. He said he wanted to come in and talk to me, so we sat down an hour ago. He brought a hammer with him, in a paper bag."

"I like where this is headed," I said.

"On the night Manuel Solis was killed, Paul woke up and realized Brett had gone somewhere in his truck. The next day, Paul noticed some blood on the hammer in his toolbox. Just a small smear on the handle, but when he heard Manuel had been killed, it wasn't hard to piece it together. In a perfect world, we'll get both Brett's and Solis's DNA off the hammer, but even if we only get Solis's, that and Paul's statement will be enough to bust Brett for that murder."

Obviously I felt a sense of relief. It would be nice to have one less violent lunatic free on the streets, fantasizing about revenge. He would've gone back to prison for trying to shoot me, but a murder charge would almost certainly put him away until he was old and gray, or dead.

"Outstanding," I said. "How quickly will you get those results?"

"I'm hoping no more than two or three weeks, but you know how that goes."

"I'll be patient. This is great stuff."

"I'm not done. Remember when I told you we'd tracked Jacob Buckley's cell phone, and that's how we knew you'd met him in that parking lot? We also knew he'd gone over to Paul Murtaugh's house right after that. Paul said he heard Brett yelling at Jacob about something that night. Then Brett and Jacob left together, and Jacob was never seen alive again. That was new information, because the first time we talked to Paul, he said Jacob left on his own and Brett stayed at home."

"But we don't know what Brett was yelling about," I said.

"Nope."

"Not much to build that case on."

"Nope. By the way, Brett Murtaugh is scheduled to get out of the hospital tomorrow, at which point your pal Ruelas will arrest him for trying to put a hole in you. I don't know if he'll get bond or not, but you might want to stay on top of that."

"Thanks, Lynann," I said. "You're the best."

"Then how come I haven't solved this Conlee case yet?"

"What's the latest?"

"Olivia's phones were a dead end. Nothing useful at all, unless I want a bunch of phone numbers for her johns, which I don't. I'm still trying to meet with Evelyn, but she keeps putting me off, which is making me wonder."

Did Evelyn know who shot Norman? Was she protecting the killer? It wasn't inconceivable, but my conversations with her gave me no indication of that. Sure, she might have suspicions, but we all did.

Yet again, I wished Lynann luck, and we disconnected.

That conversation reminded me that I should check in with Albert Strauss and make sure Franco was leaving him alone. I called Strauss's number and was routed to voicemail.

"Hey, it's Roy Ballard," I said. "I realize we haven't spoken in several days, but I had a conversation with that guy we talked about last time, and I think everything should be fine now. You shouldn't hear from him again. But if you have—or if you do—feel free to give me a call. Talk to you later. Thanks again for your help."

I set my phone down—and then something amazing happened.

Two minutes later, my phone rang. The screen said UNKNOWN, which made me grin. Perhaps Strauss was taking security measures a bit too seriously now.

"This is Roy," I said.

"Hello, Mr. Ballard," Carmen Romero replied.

I sat up a little straighter. "Well, this is a surprise," I said.

"I'm sure it is, but I think we need to have a conversation."

"Are you in town?" I asked. "We should sit down and talk."

"I'm not even in the country," she said. "But I think you knew that."

"Where are you?"

"The truth is, I could tell you and it wouldn't be a concern, but I think I'll keep that to myself."

Which meant she was someplace that wouldn't extradite, assuming that someday there might be a warrant for her arrest. Right now, there wasn't one. Even if the cops knew exactly where she was, they couldn't do anything. She was as free as every other citizen. Right now, anyway.

"I understand," I said. "So you want to talk?"

"I do."

"What's the topic today?"

I was using speakerphone now, and simultaneously opening an app that would record our conversation.

Carmen said, "I was hoping I would never have to make this call, but I understand the detective is still trying to question Evelyn. I tried to call her—Lynann—but she didn't answer, so you're next."

"Fine by me."

"I don't know why she's bothering Evelyn."

That told me Carmen was in contact with someone who was providing information. Olivia? Evelyn?

"What's the problem?" I said. "Why won't she agree to an interview?"

"She doesn't know anything. There's no reason to question her."

"Then there's also no reason she should avoid it," I said.

"Quality of life," Carmen said. "She doesn't need the stress. The aggravation. I know you don't know her well, but she's a wonderful woman. She deserves nothing but the best in her remaining time. That could be a year, or two years, or six months. It's impossible to know."

I started to push back, but I changed my mind. "I get that," I said. "You're a good friend to look out for her."

"Olivia and I had an agreement, but…I don't want Evelyn under suspicion, because she didn't do anything wrong. That's why I'm calling."

"I understand."

There was silence on the line for a full ten seconds.

"Carmen?" I said.

"I'm going to tell you everything. The full story. Are you ready?"

"I'm ready," I said.

Much of the account she'd given me at the Grove Bar was accurate—assuming she was being truthful this time around.

Norman was abusive, and Evelyn's doctors would confirm the resulting injuries, if Evelyn would allow them to discuss her medical records. Carmen said Evelyn may or may not allow that. She valued her privacy, and her dignity, and she didn't want anyone to feel sorry for her, or to question why she hadn't simply left Norman and gotten a divorce.

"Norman would've fought like hell and dragged it out as long as possible," Carmen said. "Evelyn's remaining time would've been miserable. It was easier for her just to stay. It was the better of two bad choices, unfortunately."

Just as Carmen had said last time, she and Olivia had seen Norman grab Evelyn roughly by the arm, and it had started a conversation. They discovered that they both despised Norman. They wanted a better situation for Evelyn, but the options were limited. Call the cops? Move Evelyn out of the house? She wouldn't have cooperated with either of those scenarios.

"Wouldn't it be great if Norman would just drop dead?" Olivia asked at the time.

"Or if somebody shot him," Carmen replied without much thought.

"That would solve everything."

They looked at each other, both thinking, *Are you serious?*

It grew from there. How would they do it? Poison him? Run him over? Just shoot him? Pay someone to do it? Maybe they should make it look like an intruder or a burglar caught in the act. Wouldn't it be better if it were random violence?

"Olivia came up with the idea," Carmen said. "I was out of town with Norman and Evelyn—a business conference in Atlanta—so Olivia had the house to herself. One night Franco came over, and he brought Brett Murtaugh and Jacob Buckley. I'm sure you know who that is."

"I do."

"Olivia said they were all drinking and smoking pot and Brett started giving Franco a hard time. Apparently the two of them used to do some crazy stuff in high school—breaking into houses and cars, mostly—and Brett was saying Franco didn't have the balls to do that anymore."

Franco, of course, insisted that wasn't true. So Brett dared him to break into a car that very night. Franco said he would, if Brett would do it with him. Olivia said it was the kind of stupid stunt that could wind up with someone getting shot.

And that put an idea in her head. A way to take care of Norman. Dumb kids out getting into mischief. Maybe some vandalism. What if things went badly? What if one of them was carrying a gun? Things could get out of hand quickly.

"The Grays are out of town," Olivia said at the time. "Clancy told me."

"Who's Clancy?" Franco asked.

"Their yard guy. I saw him the other day and he said the Grays were going to Cancun."

"What, was he flirting with you?"

"No, he's just friendly."

"Pretty stupid of him to be sharing that kind of info," Franco said.

"Let's fuckin' do it," Brett said.

"Right here on the same street?" Franco asked.

"I knew you didn't have the balls," Brett said.

"Hell if I don't."

They left five minutes later, just Franco and Brett. No reason to take Jake along. He stayed with Olivia.

By that point, Olivia was fascinated by this turn of events. She could picture Franco and Brett sneaking up the driveway, slowly approaching Ed Gray's truck, which he always parked in front of his house. The vehicle was far enough from the street, and this was such a quiet neighborhood, that the truck might very well be unlocked.

Turned out it was. Franco and Brett were back in less than ten minutes, pumped with adrenaline, laughing, and carrying a canvas bag filled with various hunting-related items. Olivia remembered that the bag had a deer emblem on it.

At this point, I couldn't resist interrupting Carmen to ask a question.

"What happened to all that stuff?"

"They gave it to Jake and told him to get rid of it."

It was easy to guess what happened next. Jacob Buckley priced the items in the bag and couldn't resist selling the scope. Easy money, right? A couple thousand dollars at a minimum. But then I confronted him. Forced him to talk. He remembered the name of the yard guy, Clancy, so he spat that out, because it was better than telling the truth. But then he was stupid enough to tell Brett what had happened. Who knows why? Maybe, in his version of it, he outsmarted me, so he bragged about it, trying to impress Brett, just as Barry had said.

But Brett knew that the cops would soon have Jake's name, and they could connect Jake to Brett. That pissed Brett off, because another burglary charge could mean serious prison time. So Brett took Jake to the creek and shot him. All conjecture, of course. We might never know.

"What happened after that?" I asked.

43

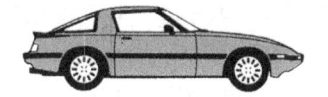

THE NIGHT AFTER FRANCO AND Brett burglarized Ed Gray's truck, while Carmen and the Conlees were still out of town, Olivia strung a rope from the rear axle of her car to the ridiculously expensive fountain and toppled it. It was a smart choice, because nobody could be sure what had happened. Was it vandalism, or had it simply shifted for some reason and fallen over? That meant Norman wouldn't necessarily be on alert afterward. Olivia called Evelyn in Atlanta and told her what happened. Norman said he'd deal with it when he got home. He did, by hiring someone to haul the pieces off—after filing an insurance claim, of course.

Five days after the fountain incident, at three in the morning, Olivia punctured all four tires on the Jaguar and poured brake fluid all over the car, which damaged the paint. Norman was livid when he found it the next day, and he began to suspect that the fountain had not fallen innocently. Now he reported both incidents to the police. Evelyn suggested getting security cameras, but Norman nixed that idea. Carmen figured Norman was worried he might get caught abusing Evelyn on video. He began to get bids to fence the property instead.

He also began staying awake later, and occasionally stepping outside with his handgun to check the property. And he was increasingly short-tempered with everyone inside the house.

"Then you came out and installed cameras," Carmen said. "We thought at first we should give the whole thing up, but Olivia told Franco she didn't like having all the cameras around—she felt like her privacy was being invaded—so he took your hotspot and threw it into the lake."

"He had no idea of the real reason?"

"None at all."

Carmen and Olivia decided they would make their final move that very night.

"We realized we'd never discussed how we were going to do it. Or who was going to do it. We ended up flipping a coin. I lost. Or maybe I won, depending on how you look at it. The plan wasn't complicated. I waited until Evelyn had gone to bed. Olivia was in her room. Norman was watching TV in the great room. Drinking scotch. His gun was right there on the table."

Carmen was speaking slowly and deliberately.

"It seemed kind of surreal, to be honest. Was I really going to do this? I was a lot calmer than I expected to be. I kept telling myself it was the best thing for Evelyn. Norman was a monster. I knew—I *knew*—that Evelyn would be relieved he was gone. She would be upset at first, because of the turmoil, but then she would be relieved."

She stopped for a moment. I didn't say anything.

"I went to bed, too. Then, at around midnight, I went to the great room and told Norman I thought I'd heard something outside. I wasn't sure. It was just a noise—like somebody hitting something with a stick. He jumped right up and went outside. I waited for a moment, then I followed him, as if I were curious. He said, 'Get your ass back inside.' You know, if it weren't for that, I might've changed my mind. I might've backed out."

Right then, I heard a sea gull. That's something I'll always remember about the call. Doesn't seem like much, but it showed how lucky she was to have gotten away with it. It was an amateur mistake—leaving a window open or standing outside during the call, so that I could hear a sea gull and narrow down her possible location. Granted, there were thousands of locations where she might be, but think of all the places I could rule out. Ultimately, though, it didn't matter. All I wanted was the truth.

She said, "I walked down the steps and approached him. He was beside the Jaguar with his back toward me. I had my gun in the pocket of my robe and now I pulled it out. He heard me behind him and turned around and said, 'I told you to get inside.' I just raised the gun and shot him. I remember the look of surprise on his face. He dropped his gun, and he just stood there for about ten seconds, and then he fell. I turned and went inside. It never occurred to me that he wouldn't die right away, although, to be honest, I don't know whether I would've been able to shoot him again there on the ground. You know how it went after that."

She stopped there and a moment passed.

I had questions, of course. Lots of questions.

Why should I believe you this time?

How did I know you weren't still covering for Olivia?

Was it your gun Jeremy Olson had found under his hedge? I assumed it was, and that she had planted it there days later to throw off the cops, but I wanted to know for sure. If that was the case, it was another amateur move. Better to throw it into the lake with the hotspot.

Did Evelyn ever suspect that you had done it? Or maybe I wouldn't ask that one. If Evelyn ever suspected, it was only afterward, and could I blame her for keeping her suspicions to herself?

But I never got the chance to ask any of these questions. When I said that something amazing happened, I wasn't talking about the call. Sure, the call was enlightening and intriguing and it provided some closure, but it wasn't amazing. Not compared to this.

From where I was seated on my living room couch, I heard an engine. A deep rumble. A familiar sound. Then a car passed the front of the house slowly and it took my breath away.

A red 1968 Mustang fastback. Mia's car. There wasn't another one like it in town.

Now I stood up to move to the window, where I could see my driveway—and there it was, pulling in. I could see Mia through the windshield. She killed the engine and sat for a moment.

Carmen was saying something, but I didn't hear it.

"I have to go," I said.

"Pardon?"

"I have to go."

I hung up and reached the front door just as Mia was ringing the bell.

44

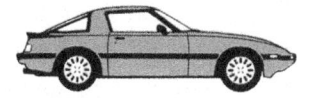

SEVENTEEN DAYS LATER, I WAS well into the newest chapter in my life.

It was now mid-May and I was sitting in my van, which was parked outside a bland office complex in northeast Austin. A super-zoom camera was resting on my dashboard, already aimed at a particular spot and recording video. It could store several hours of footage on the SD card.

Mia was waiting in her Camry—her "work" car—which was parked closer to the building, not far from the main walkway to the front door. Off to the right was a crushed-gravel path that led to a small park next to the office complex. The park had several picnic tables and people would walk over there to have lunch, especially on a day as gorgeous as today.

I waited patiently. It was 11:32.

A lot had changed in seventeen days.

The DNA test on Paul Murtaugh's hammer had come back just the way we wanted, and it would likely put Brett Murtaugh away for the rest of his life. He was in jail right now with no bond, and he wouldn't get out before his trial.

I had sent the recording of Carmen Romero's confession to both

Lynann Chukwueze and Ruelas. The bottom line was, I believed her. She killed Norman and Olivia helped. Carmen didn't have any reason to implicate Olivia in a conspiracy, and Carmen didn't seem the type to do that out of spite. Also, the fact that the two of them had met at the Grove Bar to have an intense conversation seemed to support her account. Maybe Carmen had been giving Olivia a heads-up that she was about to leave the country. Maybe she'd been assuring Olivia that even if Carmen told the truth, there was too much confusion and doubt—and lack of physical evidence—for Olivia to be charged. Which was true so far.

Olivia had hired an attorney and was sticking to her most recent account—that she'd seen Carmen come back inside with a gun. She said the idea that she and Carmen had schemed together to kill Norman was outrageous. Maybe that story would hold, or maybe it wouldn't. For instance, if Franco were to come forward and verify that he and Brett Murtaugh had burglarized Ed Gray's truck, that would be a big step toward legitimizing Carmen's account. How else would Carmen have known the details of the burglary if Olivia hadn't told her? Maybe Olivia would eventually realize that she should strike a deal and tell the truth. She hadn't pulled the trigger, so she could probably get out in six or seven years. But so far, Franco was keeping quiet. I still wondered whether Olivia had taken part in the murder because of the money, or because she genuinely cared about Evelyn. I'd probably never know the answer to that question.

Evelyn seemed to be doing well, according to Scarlett, who had texted me a week ago, saying she had gone over to the Conlee house to see if Evelyn needed anything. Evelyn had around-the-clock home health care now, and her spirits were good. She seemed happy. That was the last time I'd heard from Scarlett.

Of course, Lynann and Ruelas were both plenty irritated that I had hung up on Carmen Romero without asking any questions, but I didn't care. Just as I was ending the call, Mia was ringing my doorbell. I guess it was good that she'd shown up unexpectedly, because I didn't have time to get nervous or let my mind wander in a dozen different directions.

I simply opened the door. Oh, good lord. There she was. I hadn't seen her in three months and I thought my heart might explode. She was wearing jeans, tennis shoes, and a loose blouse covered by a light jacket. Her hair was pulled into a ponytail, which always made her appear about twenty years old.

"Hey," I said. "I thought you were in Bend."

"I was," she said. "But I kept thinking about you. I had to see that you were okay. I had to see you in person."

I raised both arms, like *Take a look. You can see that I'm fine.*

She stepped forward and wrapped her arms around me in a tight hug. I hugged her right back, of course. Amazing how quickly a lump formed in my throat. We stayed like that in the doorway for a full thirty seconds.

What was happening?

When she let me go and stepped back, a tear was streaming down her left cheek. She wiped it away.

"Sorry," she said.

"You okay?"

She nodded. "I'm fine. It's just—it was hard to come here. I did want to make sure you're okay, but there's more to it than that. Can I come inside? I want to talk to you about something."

We had a long conversation, and what I saw, once she'd gathered herself, was the old Mia. She'd made incredible progress with Beth. She felt like she'd regained control of her life. It was like something had lifted. That's the way she phrased it. Lately, each day seemed to be better than the one before it. She had even gotten her PI license and had opened an agency of her own. Things were going well.

I was happy for her, and proud of her, and I told her so.

Then she dropped it on me. An idea. She was hesitant to even ask.

What if we worked together again? She really thought she could handle it. And if she could—

"Are you saying we could try again?" I asked. "You and me?"

"Unless you—"

"I don't mean as partners," I said.

"Right. Me neither. Maybe it's a bad idea. I wouldn't want you to—"

"No," I said. "I'm in."

"Are you sure?"

"I'm completely in."

"It might not work, Roy," she said. "We have to be honest about that."

"I know. I don't care. Let's try it."

She was beaming now, and I'm sure I was, too.

"Well," she said. "Where do we go from here?"

We were waiting for a man named Donald Hanover. He worked at a firm that created network hardware, but that part was irrelevant. Five weeks earlier, he claimed to have slipped in a grocery store bathroom and injured his right shoulder, to the point that he might not ever regain full functionality. Of course, there were no cameras in the bathroom, so it was hard to refute the claim. He went to a doctor who backed him up, but this particular doctor had been censured several times by the medical board for questionable practices, including writing indiscriminate prescriptions for opioids.

It was now 11:55.

Mia sent me a text. *I'm pretty nervous.*

I know you are, but you're gonna nail it.

This would be a nice, easy case to start with. We'd see where it goes from here.

Hanover exited the building two minutes later, and Mia got out of her Camry immediately. She was carrying a paper bag and she proceeded toward the office complex. She was dressed for office work in a skirt that hugged her hips perfectly, and she was wearing four-inch heels. She looked fantastic.

Hanover could see her coming, and she had his attention.

As they got closer, Mia stopped and opened the bag. She pulled out a jar of almond butter. She said something to Hanover, and he stopped beside her.

She was recording the conversation, but I couldn't hear it, so I could only imagine.

Excuse me. Would you mind opening this for me? I'm going to the park for lunch, but I can't get it open. It's really stuck.

This wasn't a normal jar of almond butter. We had already removed the lid and glued it back on. It would take significant force with both hands.

The moment of truth. Would Hanover try to open the jar? I mean, there was always the chance that he really was injured and couldn't do it.

Sure thing. That's what I imagined he said as he put his hand out and Mia passed him the jar.

He grabbed the jar with his left hand and the lid with his right and gave it a twist. No luck. He tried again. It still wouldn't budge. He tried a third time, really bearing down, and his face contorted and turned red with the effort.

Pop!

The lid came off.

Wow, that was a tough one, he probably said.

Mia thanked him, put the jar back in the sack, and proceeded toward the path that led to the park. Hanover watched her for a few seconds, then turned around with a grin on his face.

I was grinning, too.

We were back.

EMAIL ALERTS

Want to know when Ben Rehder's
next novel will be released?

Subscribe to his email list at www.benrehder.com.

Have you discovered Ben Rehder's
Blanco County Mysteries?

Turn the page for an excerpt from

BUCK FEVER

the first novel in that series.

BUCK FEVER

Chapter 1

BY THE TIME RED O'BRIEN finished his thirteenth beer, he could hardly see through his rifle scope. Worse yet, his partner, Billy Don Craddock, was doing a lousy job with the spotlight.

"Dammit, Billy Don, we ain't hunting raccoons," Red barked. "Get that light out of the trees and shine it out in the pastures where it will do me some good."

Billy Don mumbled something unintelligible, kicked some empty beer cans around on the floorboard of Red's old Ford truck, and then belched loudly from way down deep in his three-hundred-pound frame. That was his standard rebuttal anytime Red got a little short with him. The spotlight, meanwhile, continued to illuminate the canopy of a forty-foot Spanish oak.

Red cussed him again and pulled the rifle back in the window. Every time they went on one of these poaching excursions, Red had no idea how he managed to get a clean shot. After all, poaching white-tailed deer was serious business. It called for stealth and grace, wits and guile. It had been apparent to Red for years that Billy Don came up short in all of these departments.

"Turn that friggin' light off and hand me a beer," Red said.

"Don't know what we're doing out here on a night like this anyhow," Billy Don replied as he dug into the ice chest for two fresh Keystones. "Moon ain't up yet. All the big ones will be bedded down till it rises. Any moron knows that."

Red started to say that Billy Don was an excellent reference for gauging what a moron may or may not know. But he thought better of it, being that Billy Don weighed roughly twice what Red did. Not to mention that Billy Don had quite a quick temper after his first twelve-pack.

"Billy Don, let me ask you something. Someone walked into your bedroom shining a light as bright as the sun in your face, what's the first thing you'd do?"

"Guess I'd wag my pecker at 'em," Billy Don said, smiling. He considered himself quite glib.

"Okay," Red said patiently, "then what's the second thing you'd do?"

"I'd get up and see what the hell's going on."

"Damn right!" Red said triumphantly. "Don't matter if the bucks are bedded down or not. Just roust 'em with that light and we'll get a shot. But remember, we won't find any deer up in the treetops."

Billy Don gave a short snort in reply.

Red popped the top on his new beer, revved the Ford, and started on a slow crawl down the quiet county road. Billy Don grabbed the spotlight and leaned out the window, putting some serious strain on the buttons of his overalls, as he shined the light back over the hood of the Ford to Red's left. They had gone about half a mile when Billy Don stirred.

"Over there!"

Red stomped the brakes, causing his Keystone to spill and run down into his crotch. He didn't even notice. Billy Don was spotlighting an oat field a hundred yards away, where two dozen deer grazed. Among them, one of the largest white-tailed bucks either of them had ever seen. "Fuck me nekkid," Red whispered.

"Jesus, Red! Look at that monster."

Red clumsily stuck the .270 Winchester out the window, banging the door frame and the rearview mirror in the process. The deer didn't even look their way. Red raised the rifle and tried to sight in on the trophy buck, but the deer had other things in mind.

While all the other deer were grazing in place, the buck was loping around the oat field in fits and starts, running in circles. He bounced, he jumped, he spun. Red and Billy Don had never seen such peculiar behavior.

"Somethin's wrong with that deer," Billy Don said, using his keen knowledge of animal behavioral patterns.

"Bastard won't hold still! Keep the light on him!" Red said.

"I've got him. Just shoot. Shoot!"

Red was about to risk a wild shot when the buck finally seemed to calm down. Rather than skipping around, it was now walking fast, with its nose low to the ground. The buck approached a large doe partially obscured behind a small cedar tree and, with little ceremony, began to mount her.

Billy Don giggled, the kind of laugh you'd expect from a schoolgirl, not a flannel-clad six-foot-six cedar-chopper. "Why, I do believe it's true love."

Red sensed his chance, took a deep breath, and squeezed the trigger. The rifle bellowed as orange flame leapt out of the muzzle and licked the night, and then all was quiet.

The buck, and the doe of his affections, crumpled to the ground while the other deer scattered into the brush. Seconds passed. And then, to the chagrin of the drunken poachers, the huge buck climbed to his hooves, snorted twice, and took off. The doe remained on the ground.

"Dammit, Red! You missed."

"No way! It was a lung shot. I bet it went all the way through. Grab your wirecutters."

Knowing that a wounded deer can run several hundred yards or more, both men staggered out of the truck, cut their way through the eight-foot deerproof fence, and proceeded over to the oat field.

Each man had a flashlight and was looking feverishly for traces of blood, when they heard a noise.

"What the hell was that?" Billy Don asked.

"Shhh."

Then another sound. A moaning, from the wounded doe lying on the ground.

Billy Don was spooked. "That's weird, Red. Let's get outta here."

Red shined his light on the wounded animal twenty yards away. "Hold on a second. What the hell's wrong with its hide? It looks all loose and..." He was about to approach the deer when they both heard something they'd never forget.

The doe clearly said, "Help me."

Without saying a word, both men scrambled back toward the fence. For the first time in his life, Billy Don Craddock actually outran somebody.

Seconds later, the man in the crudely tailored deer costume could hear the tires squealing as the truck sped away.

Just as Red and Billy Don were sprinting like boot-clad track stars, a powerful man was in the middle of a phone call. Unfortunately for the man, Roy Swank, it was hard to judge his importance by looking at him. In fact, he looked a lot like your average pond frog. Round, squat body. Large, glassy eyes. Bulbous lips in front of a thick tongue. And, of course, the neck—or rather, the lack of one. It was as if his head sat directly on his sloping shoulders. His voice was his best feature, deep and charismatic.

Roy Swank had relocated to a large ranch southwest of Johnson City, Texas, five years ago, after a successful (although intentionally anonymous) career lobbying legislators in Austin. The locals who knew or cared what a lobbyist was never really figured out what Swank lobbied for. Few people ever had, because Swank was the type of lobbyist who always conducted business in the shadows of a back room, rarely putting anything down on paper. But he and the entities he represented had the kind of resources and resourcefulness that could sway votes or help introduce new legislation. So when the rumors spread about Swank's retirement, the entire state political system took notice—although there were as many people relieved as disappointed.

After lengthy consideration (his past had to be weighed carefully—life in a county full of political enemies might be rather difficult), Swank purchased a ten-thousand-acre ranch one hour west of Austin. Swank was actually planning on semi-retirement; the ranch was a successful cattle operation and he intended to maintain its sizable herd of Red Brangus. He had even kept the former owner on as foreman for a time.

But without the busy schedule of his previous career, Swank became restless. That is, until he rediscovered one of the great passions he enjoyed as a young adult: deer hunting. The hunting bug bit, and it bit hard. He spent the first summer on his new ranch building deer blinds, clearing brush in prime hunting areas, distributing automatic corn and protein feeders, and planting food plots such as oats and rye. It paid off the following season, as Swank harvested a beautiful twelve-point buck with a twenty-two-inch spread that tallied 133 Boone & Crockett points, the scoring standard for judging trophy bucks. Not nearly as large as the world-renowned bucks in South Texas, but a very respectable deer for the Hill Country. Several of his closest associates joined him on the ranch and had comparable success.

Swank, never one to do anything in moderation, decided that his ranch could become one of the most successful hunting operations in Texas. By importing some key breeding stock from South Texas and Mexico, and then following proper game-management techniques, Swank set out to develop a herd of whitetails as large and robust—and with the same jaw-dropping trophy antlers—as their southern brethren.

He had phenomenal success. After all, money was no object, and the laws and restrictions that regulated game importation and relocation melted away under Swank's political clout. After four seasons, not only was his ranch (the Circle S) known throughout the state for trophy deer, he had actually started a lucrative business exporting deer to other ranches around the nation.

Swank was tucked away obliviously in his four-thousand-square-foot ranch house, on the phone to one of his most valued customers, at the same moment Red O'Brien blasted unsuccessfully at a large buck in Swank's remote southern pasture.

"They went out on the trailer today," Swank said in his rich timbre. He was sitting at a large mahogany desk in an immense den. A fire burned in the huge limestone fireplace, despite the warm weather. He cradled the phone with his shoulder as he reached across the desk, grabbed a bottle of expensive scotch and poured himself another glass. "Four of them. But the one you'll be especially interested in is the ten-pointer," Swank said as he went on to describe the "magnificent beast."

Swank grunted a few times, nodding. "Good. Yes, good." Then he hung up. Swank had a habit of never saying good-bye.

By the time he finished his conversation, a man who sounded just like Red O'Brien had already made an anonymous call to 911.

ABOUT THE AUTHOR

Ben Rehder lives with his wife near Austin, Texas, where he was born and raised. His novels have made best-of-the-year lists in *Publishers Weekly, Library Journal, Kirkus Reviews*, and *Field & Stream*. *Buck Fever* was a finalist for the Edgar Award, and *Get Busy Dying* was a finalist for the Shamus Award. For more information, visit www.benrehder.com.

Made in the USA
Coppell, TX
24 April 2024